FAMILY
ABOVE
ALL

LIAM STONE

Printed in the United States of America

Paperback ISBN: 9798651562541

First Trade paperback edition in 2020.

Author Consultant and Editing: Company 614 Enterprises, LLC.
Additional Editing: Liz Badovinac
Additional Editing and Proofing: Michelle Beal
Proofreading: Angela Walker
Cover Design: Tawni Franzen at ayaristudio.com
Text Design and Composition: Rick Soldin

To my children: I love each of you so very much. Though I've missed a great deal of your lives, I've tried justifying that absence by telling myself it was for God and country. I can only hope you will read this book and understand the life I led, the real reasons for my deficiencies. And if I am blessed to have that occur, I beg for your forgiveness. It's the only thing I feel I can ask from you now.

—Liam

Contents

Prologue

I drove down the winding dirt road, a swirling dust cloud following my truck. Mötley Crüe's "Kickstart My Heart" blasted out through the speakers. The music motivated me, jacked me up, made my heart race. It helped me get into character.

After a very long approach, I turned into an open area and saw six motorcycles lined up with perfect spacing between them. This told me the six bikers that owned them believed in teamwork and leadership. Only a good leader could make order out of criminals.

For a brief second or two, I studied their spotless chassis. The sun reflected off each one, making their chrome dazzle. Then the dust cloud I carried settled over the bikes, ruining their appearance. It shouldn't matter much. In one hour, they'd all be seized and stored in a government warehouse.

I came to a stop, putting the black and gold Ford King Ranch in park and shutting off the engine. This gave me a moment to collect my thoughts and focus on what we were about to do.

I looked at the wooden structure through the windshield, knowing six nasty bikers were inside. I was pretty sure they were armed to the teeth. With just me and my partner, this was an excellent place to get killed. Agents like us had been whacked before they even exited their vehicle.

I was parked ten feet away from the bikes, which gave us a clear line of fire at anyone unexpectedly approaching our truck. Criminals could pop up out of nowhere. Believe me, it had happened before.

I glanced at my partner as he scanned the area for problems. Dan Collins was solid, a reliable guy in all situations. We'd been working together for five years and he never let me down.

One time, during a firefight, he'd dragged me to safety after I'd been wounded. "Never leave your partner behind," the Bureau drilled into us. And we didn't.

I took in a deep breath and let it out slowly. As the lead agent, this bust would hopefully be a career-maker—a major case, one that would move us up the Bureau's ladder.

I hoped this was my career-maker, giving me a chance to supervise my own squad. Or maybe a job in D.C. That meant regular hours and office work—the easy life. My wife was desperately waiting for that. And with my three college degrees, nothing was holding me back... except a career-maker.

The game plan was to meet the leaders of the Centenarios at a remote location east of Scottsdale. It was just past a tribal casino. The gang had selected this location because it essentially trapped us there with them.

To get to this place, we had to turn south off Highway 87 and snake our way for a half-mile through a forest of scrub trees and ground cover, all nourished by the Verde River. There was one way in and one way out. *Clever.*

During our operation planning meeting, we reviewed images of the area. The Bureau had sent an aircraft up to get some hi-res photos. Now, we could see the building for the meet-and-greet. It was vacant, its owners having been busted on drug charges a year earlier. They were still in jail awaiting trial while the State of Arizona tried to take the property in a forfeiture suit.

From the paperwork we'd examined, the building had recently served two purposes. First, it had taken in stolen vehicles and chopped them up for valuable parts. The second purpose had been to remove drugs from hidden panels in the cars and replace them with cash for delivery to the Mexican cartels.

The wood-frame structure had initially been built as a getaway place for some wealthy man back in Phoenix, a place he could go and fish in the river or drink some scotch. But that was forty years ago. The city had expanded, putting it just on the outskirts yet not within the jurisdiction of any police department. With only the Maricopa County Sheriff's Department to worry about, it was a criminal's paradise.

Our SWAT units were staged back down Highway 87, waiting for a signal. The bag we carried, the one with $200,000 in cash, had tiny cameras and microphones cleverly concealed in its sides. Placed on a table, it would pick up the faces of all the players—the soon-to-be federal inmates.

Once they agreed to a sale and provided us with the meth, the units would move in. Worst-case scenario, our guys lost transmission, and we'd tell them from the truck to pick up the gang members as they reached the highway. It was as close to a perfect plan as we could get in the undercover business.

As with most operations, my truck was outfitted with cameras and microphones. The tech guys rigged it up so the SWAT team could see and hear everything live inside and outside the vehicle. All I had to do was hit a tiny button on my armrest above the window switches.

"You ready?" I asked.

"Let's do it," Dan replied, his freckled face gleaming in the sunshine.

I pressed the button to start transmitting. "Six bikes here, so likely six tangos. We're going in. It's showtime!"

The SWAT team could not talk back to us. That was for our safety. We didn't need a bad guy hearing a strange voice coming from our truck.

Dan grabbed the bag from the floor between his legs, and we exited the vehicle. I glanced at the bikes, now dusty. They would clean up nicely for the forfeiture sale.

Making our way to the main entrance, I took the lead with Dan directly behind me. By not walking side by side, we made it harder for someone in the building to kill both of us. It was little details like that that kept us alive, or at least minimized the risk.

The door opened before we reached it. Fuse, the biker who had been our first connection, nodded and let us in. I scanned the interior quickly. Our intelligence matched up. The place was a warehouse with junk scattered everywhere. Up against the back wall were large tanks for emptying the gas, oil, and antifreeze from vehicles before they were chopped up. A half dozen acetylene and oxygen tanks stood next to them. A sheet of plywood sat on some barrels filled with fluid. This was my life: attending criminals' boardrooms.

The door closed behind Dan, and we made our way to the table. A leader emerged from the group of six and identified himself as Stallion. "You got the cash?" he asked.

Dan dropped the bag onto the plywood.

"Yes," I replied. "You got my fuel?"

Stallion turned to two of his men. "Fuse, you and Rattler go outside and keep an eye out." Fuse nodded and left with his buddy.

The story we'd pitched to Fuse was one of expansion. We'd told him we were based out of Henderson, Nevada, 300 miles northwest of Phoenix. We wanted to expand into Las Vegas, where new opportunities were emerging. Our current supplier couldn't even meet our demands for Henderson. How could they possibly provide a product to our Las Vegas customers? Fuse had assured us his gang could.

Fuse wasn't a confidential informant. A CI we'd busted six months earlier had introduced us to Fuse. If this all went down right, that CI's case would be dismissed.

Because Fuse was being tricked, he thought we were the real deal, not a bunch of liars from the FBI. Like all our past busts, he'd be surprised when he learned the truth. Surprise would quickly turn to anger. For my safety, I hoped steel bars and concrete would be between us when he learned the truth.

"I need to count it," Stallion said.

"Be my guest," I replied.

Dan pushed the bag toward him. It was a clever move, one that altered the angle of the different cameras. This would pick up the rest of the room as well as the faces of all the targets— *tangos*, to us.

Stallion unzipped the bag. "Zeke, start counting this stack. I'll take these two."

The two men hunched over the plywood and removed the rubber band from each roll of cash. While they counted and stacked the bills, I looked around the place and studied it even harder. No telling when my observations would come in handy.

In every drug or weapons deal, there are two dangerous moments: the initial meet, and the flash—when cash makes an appearance. During the initial meet, a criminal will worry that the guy he's meeting is an undercover agent. That can result in a killing. Many criminals were whacked because they were suspected of being someone like me. It's a job hazard that criminals and undercover agents shared.

When cash makes an appearance, problems can happen. Adrenaline mixes with greed and paranoia. Add some drugs to the criminal's veins and a deal can go off the rails fast. That's when guns are pulled. And people die.

Dan and I faced these precarious conditions more than either of us liked. Because of that, I eased a hand to my hip, getting it closer to the holster stuck in my rear waistband. Any moment now, everyone in this room would learn their fate.

Stallion conferred with Zeke and acknowledged the money was all there. He put the rolls back into the bag, zipping it shut and handing it to Zeke. Suddenly, gunshots rang out. They came from outside.

Did our SWAT team leader jump the gun?

The four bikers in front of us jerked their heads up. All six of us pulled a weapon, pointing it at someone on the opposite side, waiting for the lead to start flying.

Dan and I were easy shots. There was no way they could miss. My only hope was to kill one guy with a chest shot and wound another before I was hit. If Dan did the same, we might be alive when our backup arrived.

Before any of us could move, the front door opened and Fuse staggered in. He fell to his knees and grunted out a warning. "The Hammerheads. A bunch of them. They're coming."

He fell flat on his face as a pool of bright red blood oozed from underneath his chest.

"Close the door!" Stallion yelled to one of his bodyguards. "You two take those windows. Me and Zeke will handle this side." Stallion pointed a finger at us. "And you two take those windows. Shoot anything that moves, since they probably killed Rattler already."

Before Dan and I could move, glass from a window sprayed our feet. Two dark green projectiles streaked into the warehouse between the burglar bars. One hit the wall near the two bodyguards and bounced around. It was a grenade.

The other caromed off the plywood table, landing between two large tanks, one labeled *Oxygen*. This was going to be bad.

I crouched closer to the concrete slab and ran. If I could just make it to the rear wall, then all the piled-up junk between me and the grenade might block the shrapnel.

Vrroooomm!

An enormous orange-black fireball filled the interior. I found myself flat on my stomach, the smell of napalm all around me. My backside stung. The heat singed my beard and long hair. All sounds disappeared.

When the world felt like it had ended, I opened my eyes and tried to collect myself.

Am I dead? Where am I?

I laid facedown as a dark black cloud of smoke sat on top of me. Coughing several times, I looked around but saw nothing. A slight breeze stirred, removing some of the smoke. That's when I spotted my partner a few feet away, buried under sheetrock, siding, and two-by-fours.

Crawling over to him, I noticed a dangerous piece of lumber sticking out of his left shoulder. I tried to lift off some siding and two-by-fours but couldn't. Looking down his body, his right leg was bent at an awkward angle.

"Dan, are you alive?" I yelled, shaking him.

He gave no reply.

I looked for signs of breathing but saw none. A dire still-
ness enveloped him. My partner was gone.

A piece of wood exploded in front of me. I glanced up to
see the flash of a biker's gun. He was firing at me. With my
weapon missing, I saw Dan's Sig Sauer and snatched it up.

I took aim at the Hammerhead and dropped him with one
shot. A second biker took the place of the first and died right
next to him. This gave me a chance to get to my knees and see
if I was injured. I wasn't.

More wood exploded around me. And a new enemy
emerged, crouching behind our truck. I fired at him. The windshield fractured, sending glass into the cab.

His muzzle flashed, and I fired back. As he ducked, I
popped off several more rounds, using the cover fire to run
toward the river. Dodging bullets, I slid down its bank, relieved
as I hit the muddy water.

I heard a loud splash a few feet to my right. I grimaced at
the green oxygen tank stuck in the mud, smoke leaking out the
top. Those tanks still had gas in them, making them dangerous
missiles. With the place behind me on fire, there was no telling
when the next launch would occur.

A small splash to my left caused me to spin and fire.
Instinctively, I knew I probably had only two or three rounds
left. Since I carried magazines for my Browning, but not the
Sig, I'd be out. If the bikers kept coming, I'd need a place
where I could fire with a steady hand. If not, I would die.

Looking down the river with its vegetation dotting the
banks, a different scenario came to mind: escape.

As a large biker slipped coming down the bank, I plunged
into the moving river. I leaned back and let the current take me
southward, away from Highway 87 and my backup team.

The Hammerhead regained his footing and fired at me. I held my gun above the water and ducked. Where his bullets went, I had no idea. I welcomed the company of the snakes and gators in the water. I just needed to put some distance between me and my assassin.

Seconds later, through a smoky haze, I saw a man standing on the bank. His muzzle flashed in my direction.

Startled, I ditched the gun and started swimming with all I had. If they were able to chase me down this river—well, good for them. They could have me.

My last memory was lying on my stinging back and staring at the orange-pink clouds of the Arizona sky. It felt good to float towards an unknown destiny.

I wondered if I'd make it out alive.

Chapter One

One month later

"How are you sleeping?" Dr. Afton Clark asked. "Have the pills helped?"

Will shifted his six-foot frame around, hoping to find a comfortable spot. "Yeah, somewhat. I still have nightmares."

"Afghanistan?"

"Yes."

"We've gone over this before," she said. "You did all you could to save them."

"But that doesn't stop the screams, does it? Should I double up on pills?"

"No! Please follow the directions on the label." She tapped her silver iPad with a pen. "You pulled your gunnery sergeant from the helicopter. The Marines gave you a medal for your actions. There's nothing more you could've done... unless you're leaving something out. Are you?"

Will coughed. "Maybe."

Dr. Clark said nothing.

"I keep thinking I could've picked a better landing spot. I had a few seconds to decide. I was too close to a boulder that cracked the fuel tanks. I feel like I could've dragged Carson out."

"Who's Carson?"

Will rubbed his hands. "My copilot. Instead, I crawled out my window and grabbed Gunny from the ramp. When I went back to get the rest of the men, we started taking fire. I tried to free the gunner from the twisted metal, but I wasn't strong enough."

"And you blame yourself for that?"

"I pulled on that iron bar hard. It was red hot. It fuckin' burned right through my gloves. Hernandez, his face... his face. He just looked at me and said, 'Tell my fiancé I love her. Promise me? Tell her I love her.' He needed to come home with us. He *was* coming home, but those flames pushed me back. I reached in and pulled on his arm, but it was charred. Flesh, it drops off like candle wax. Like fuckin' candle wax." Will squeezed his right forearm compulsively. He had faded as his thoughts came back to him.

Dr. Clark brushed back her straight black hair. "These screams. Are they blaming you?"

"No. But they still wake me up."

"I see." The doctor typed in some notes. "How do you feel about this last assignment, leaving your partner behind?"

"Terrible. You never leave your partner behind. But he was dead. I thought he was dead. That's the only reason I left him. I had to get out of there, or it was going to be two of us."

"How's he doing now?"

"Okay. Turned out it was just a piece of wood in his shoulder. It messed up his muscles, but they reattached them. He was lucky. No organs were hit."

"That's good news. Sounds like he'll be up and around soon."

"Uh, not necessarily," Will said, as he leaned forward in the overstuffed chair. "His leg was a mess. They had to surgically repair his right knee. He's in a cast now. I'll be seeing him at the office today for the first time in about three weeks."

"Is he back on duty?"

"We both are, starting today. Bullshit work."

"What's that?"

"Guardian leads," Will replied, gaining more confidence. "That's what we call reports from the public. You know, 'If you see something, say something.' Well, guess what? Lots of people see something. We check out addresses and locate witnesses. Most of the reports are a complete waste of our time. But sometimes we hit the jackpot. You never know."

"Do you think you're ready?"

This was the question Will had been waiting for. He needed her approval to go back on duty. "Sure. I spent the last month with Jennifer and the kids. It was nice."

"And your marital troubles?"

"Better, I think. It's tough on her. She's a pharmaceutical rep. You know, those girls visiting the doctors' offices, pulling the rolling bags behind them? I'm gone all the time, and she has to take care of our twins. Her hours are long. She doesn't get much time off. Now I have six months of busywork, just decompressing from this last assignment. I'll wait until they insert me into another operation. I can spend time with my boys, give Jennifer a much-needed break."

Dr. Clark typed in more notes. "How do you feel about the biker gangs you took down? You spent a lot of time with them."

Will chuckled. "You mean, am I dealing with Stockholm syndrome?"

Dr. Clark remained silent.

"I'm glad they've been taken down. I don't identify with them at all. In fact, I can't see ever identifying with a target. They're all criminals. I'm not."

Dr. Clark removed her glasses. "Well, you act like it isn't possible to get in so deep that you lose your real identity. Do you think it's possible?"

"For other folks, maybe." Will shook his head. "For me? No way. I know who my wife and children are. I understand my duty to God, country, and the Bureau. I didn't go to Afghanistan and join the Taliban."

Dr. Clark showed no emotion as she typed away.

"Are you going to approve me for duty?"

"Let's go over a few more things."

•••

The blue-white light bounced off Will's folder as he waited in a large conference room. He checked his cell phone for the fifth time, making sure he wasn't late.

He wasn't.

Will thought back to his escape from the biker gang. After the SWAT team had located Will, he was taken to the hospital. The doctors had removed shrapnel from his back and treated him for second- and third-degree burns. Three days later, he was released. Dan wasn't so lucky.

He had spent eleven days in the hospital, with Will by his side the final eight days. Then Dan had been released to his family. Now, they were about to be reunited.

As Will typed out a text, the door swung open and his partner, Dan Collins, maneuvered in, careful not to catch his one crutch on a chair.

"There you are!" Will said. "Great to see you." He moved around the table and hugged his partner in a lasting embrace. The bond of brothers was strong. They'd been through a lot in the past five years.

"Great to be back," Dan said. "And alive. How are you feeling?"

"Wonderful. The doc approved me, so I'm ready to roll. How's the shoulder and collarbone healing?"

Dan carefully maneuvered his chair until he could sit down. "The shoulder is better, but the Tommy John surgery on the elbow still hurts. The doctors let me get rid of the sling yesterday. I'm good so long as I don't get into a brawl."

Will stared at the cast that reached up to Dan's mid-thigh. "When does the cast come off?"

"Another two weeks, *hopefully*. How did your debriefing go?" Dan said, steering them back to work.

"Good," Will replied. "They matched the two slugs in the Hammerheads to your gun, so that checked out. Kept me clean."

"You know if those Hammerheads had not been wiped out, I'd be dead. They would've found me in that pile of debris and double-tapped my head just to make sure."

"I know. The two wounded turds who were trying to get back into their van collapsed before they could get away. Man, those Centenarios could really shoot. They took down six Hammerheads before another grenade passed judgment."

With his good hand, Dan smoothed back a lock of red hair. "Schneider couldn't believe it. Two gangs toppled, and it looks like we won't even have to testify. Those two Hammerheads are still in the hospital, and one is on life support. Low-level guys, you know. If they live, the taxpayers will be paying for their public defenders who will help them cop a plea. We won't even have to blow our cover."

"Did they show you that photo of the biker crumpled over the bag?" Will asked. "Did you see that tattoo burned right off his back? The money bag was completely fine. Hell, it's so clean we can use it in another operation. We got some great videos from it too."

"We didn't lose one dollar, or you know they'd be checking us for missing money."

Will nodded, remembering a time he'd worked undercover and the local cops had kept some money for themselves. Sadly, it had turned into a bigger arrest pool. He learned that you don't ever cross that line. You don't take a taste no matter how hungry you are.

"Right," Will said, "but Schneider gave me all kinds of hell for shooting up the truck." He lowered his voice an octave, imitating his boss. "'That's government property, mister. There's $50,000 in cameras and recording equipment in there.' So ridiculous. I was only trying to survive."

"Forget that blue flamer," Dan said, pointing at Will. "We've got these Guardian leads for six months."

"I need it," Will said, pushing around some files. "I have to spend some serious time with Jennifer, or we aren't going to make it."

"I saw the leads they want us to work. I'll sit at the desk, make calls, and pull the reports. You do the fieldwork. Which case do you want to start with?"

Will opened the first file. "Let's see, two young Middle Eastern men fishing on a bridge in a restricted area. Park ranger thinks they may be scouting the area to blow up the dam. You can start calling on that one."

"Gee, thanks."

"Next one. A Muslim woman spotted dragging extension cords and a ladder into her garage. May be planning something sinister, according to her neighbor. You can call on that one too."

Dan looked up from his notepad. "Are you doing any work today?"

"This one right here," Will said, tapping a blue file. "A young Caucasian male making anti-government threats. Spends a lot of time at the Boardroom. I know a chick who works there. She was a credible and reliable CI for me for several years when I worked for Dallas PD. What a small world."

Dan coughed. "So, you get to visit a strip club while I make calls on two fishermen. Something is definitely wrong with this picture. Alright, but if you get finished first, you go check out the Muslim woman."

"Okay," Will said. "But not before I beat you to the fridge. I saw that lunch Diane packed for you. You're a lucky man to have an Italian wife."

"I guess you ought to have a chance at it since your wife is refusing to make your lunch. It's your lucky day with me on this crutch. You *might* actually have a chance."

"You got that right," Will responded, taking the good-natured blow from his partner.

•••

Will guided his black Chevy Silverado, west on Northwest Highway, through light traffic. The new truck had been forfeited after a big drug bust and now served in the FBI's stable of undercover vehicles. It was that or the government-standard white Chevy Impala with black tires, a car that screamed federal agent. He chose the truck.

Arriving at his destination, Will pulled into a potholed parking lot and found his favorite spot. At two in the afternoon, it was usually available.

He turned off the engine and sat in the truck for a few minutes, taking in the scene: an isolated one-story retail building in a seedy area. The exterior sported worn dark-brown metal panels attempting to simulate wood. At least, that's how they used to look when they were new. But that was more than twenty years ago. Now, the panels had faded, much like the area around it.

A large sign stood tall over the roof, with a massive Styrofoam bra loosely draped over the last "O" in Boardroom. Below it in smaller letters was "A Gentleman's Club." Will shook his head. *Some things never change.*

Back when he was a cop, he came here all the time. The vice squad he'd been assigned to was poorly structured. Strip clubs weren't a priority. Will handled other crimes, using his ability to bust strippers to get information. It was a great strategy.

All he had to do was get a stripper to grab his crotch during a table dance, and he could arrest them for public lewdness. If they didn't take his bait, he'd meet with each stripper in the dressing room and have them remove the latex covering up their nipples. This was required because Texas law stated a woman must have her nipple and areola covered.

Crafty strip club owners had discovered latex. It was cheap and easy to apply. Done correctly, the customers had no idea the nipples were covered. It was a creative solution.

As an undercover cop, Will would make each stripper remove the latex and lay it over a newspaper. If it were transparent enough that he could read the print, she'd be busted. But the real intention of this crude exercise was to get information, and the girls were more than willing to play ball. The last thing they wanted was to visit the local jail and lose a night's income.

One of Will's favorite girls was Sandera. During her early years, the club put her on stage from nine to midnight. That was prime time—the haul, they called it. After midnight, the dregs came on the stage. These were girls way past their prime. They'd do anything for the drunk patrons who didn't care how they looked.

Will knew Sandera had two children. Like most women, her body had most certainly changed. By the usual standards, that meant late-night shifts. But when Will called the club to inquire about Sandera's shift, he learned she worked as a MILF. MILFs—Mothers I'd Like to Fuck—worked the noon-to-four shift. Businessmen could enjoy a late lunch and toss back a few martinis while watching a hot soccer mom shake it for some extra money. By four, the moms would be off the stage, dressed, and ready to pick up their kids from school. Many married women made serious money on the MILF shift while their husbands were none the wiser.

Will pulled the heavy door open and walked inside. His nose instantly recognized the distinct booze-sex smell that all these clubs gave off. However, his older eyes needed time to adjust to the dark interior.

A bouncer at the entrance checked him, grunting out something about a five-dollar cover charge. Will flashed his badge and the bouncer stepped aside.

Will surveyed the scene and found what he was looking for. Seated at a corner table was Sandera. Will noticed she was still smoking, probably the same Marlboro lights she was addicted to. Sandera spotted Will and waved at him to come over.

"When I heard you were coming in, I could hardly believe it. You're coming to rescue me."

"Do you need rescuing?" Will asked, pulling up a chair.

"I do. I picked up a case of indecent exposure. I was in my car, minding my own business, visiting with a lil' friend. I can't help it if it takes me a bit longer to get dressed these days. Then the po-po rolled up on us. One had a body cam on, so I was being real considerate. I made an extra effort to give him a little show—free entertainment to download to his friends." Sandera smiled amusingly. "But I still got busted. Can you believe that shit?"

Will chuckled. "Just give me the info and I'll take care of it."

"Done. In the meantime, how can Sandera please you? Your wish is my command."

Will pulled out a photo. "What can you tell me about this guy?"

Sandera studied it. "Comes here regularly. I've danced for him several times. Average tipper. Seems like a loner, never with anyone."

Will put the photo away. "Does he seem violent?"

"No."

"Mentally disturbed?"

"Maybe." Sandera sucked on her cigarette, blowing the smoke to the ceiling. "He seems like a kid who was always picked on and left out of everything. What has he done?"

"This and that," Will said, deflecting her question. "Does he have a favorite dancer?"

"No, not that I know of. Here, honey," she said, standing up and placing her foot on the table. "Fix my strap. I have to go on stage in a few minutes."

Will grabbed the high heel and threaded the strap through the buckle. As he finished, someone slapped him hard on the wrist. Startled, Will turned around.

"What are you doing to *my* girl?" a woman said, looking directly at Sandera. "I want a lap dance right now!"

"What?" Will said, confused.

The woman tried to scoot his chair over. "You're hoggin' up my time."

Will grabbed the table so his chair stayed put. "She's on my nickel right now. We're talking. You'll have to wait your turn."

"Who is this guy?" she asked Sandera.

"He's a really good friend of mine," she replied, putting her hand on Will's red wrist. "We're great buddies. I haven't seen him in a long time."

The woman reached into her Louis Vuitton purse, tilted it to Will, and exposed rolls of cash—hundreds, fifties, and twenties. It looked to be at least $2,000.

The woman peeled off $500 and slammed it on the table. "I'm ready for my lap dances!"

Will pushed the money aside. "Like I said, you'll have to wait your turn."

"Then I'll have to leave," the woman said, frowning. "I can't stay that long."

He couldn't believe the boldness of this strange woman. "Sorry, but you're just gonna have to wait." Will knew this kind of woman, one who liked the pushback.

With a grin, she said, "You don't know who I am, do you?"

"I don't really care who you are," Will said, with an unbendable dead stare.

"People know me around here."

"I don't know you," he replied.

"You're not from around here, are you?"

"No, I'm not."

The woman pointed around the dark room. "People know me. Everybody in this club knows me. I don't even have to pay a cover charge."

Will curtly responded, "I didn't pay a cover charge to come in here either, so I guess they know me too, right?"

"I'm Sadie," the agitated woman said, folding her arms. "What kind of work do you do?"

"It's really none of your business what I do."

"Let me guess. You're a cop."

"Do I look like a cop?" Will asked, stunned it was that obvious.

"No," she replied.

Relieved, he kept going. "What do you think I do?"

"You're a truck driver."

"No, I'm not a truck driver."

"So, what do you do?"

Sandera blurted out, "Will is one of us."

With a smirk, Sadie nodded. "Oh."

"I'll tell you more about him later," Sandera said.

Sadie impatiently unfolded her arms. "I can't wait until your puny nickel is done. I've got to go. My kids will be waiting."

"So, you have kids?" Will asked.

"I have two girls."

"What are their names?"

"Kodi and Brooke. They're twins."

"I have twins too," Will said, hoping to make a connection. "Eight-year-old boys."

"Mine are four. And let me tell you, they're a handful."

Sadie relaxed and sat down. The conversation gravitated around buying two of everything and confusing one for the other. Sandera, her shift starting, quietly slipped away.

"Why are you in town?" Sadie asked Will.

"I'm looking for work."

She reached into her purse, found an old receipt, and wrote on the back. "Here," she said, handing it to Will. "This is my number. Call me. I think I can find something for you."

"Okay, I'll do that."

"Give this cash to Sandera." Sadie pushed over $500. "Tell her I'll collect tomorrow at two." With that, she got up, turned around, and walked away.

As she did, Will's eyes followed her. Smooth tan legs climbed up to a cutoff denim miniskirt that revealed the honest curves a man wants to see. Her sheer blouse rested against a naturally full chest and was held up by the thinnest of spaghetti straps. Will let his imagination spin out of control. *For someone with two kids, she has a rocking body.*

Sandera finished her dances and came straight to Will, ignoring a businessman waving a twenty-dollar bill in her face.

"Here's your money," Will said, sliding the cash over. "She said she'll collect tomorrow at two."

Sandera pulled out a chair. "That's so like her."

"Who is she?"

"She's part of the Sterling family. Do you know them?"

"No. Should I?"

"I would think so," Sandera replied, fastening on her top. "They have tons of money from legit businesses. But I think they dabble in the other side too. I had a customer tell me they're into all sorts of illegal stuff."

The bartender set two drinks down. "Thanks, Tommy," she said, clinking glasses with Will. "They might be a—what's that term I heard you use—a whale?"

"It's 'career-maker.' A 'whale' is a rich person who's getting ripped off." Will took a sip of his highball. "What does she get from you, a lap dance?"

"Usually four. That's her minimum. If she has time, she pays for a private room where she loves to lick my boobs and suck on my nipples if I take the latex off. She demands that I return the favor. She's always in and out in an hour unless I have to go on stage. Then she'll wait for me and finish up her dances."

"Does she always come in alone?"

"No. Sometimes she comes with a guy, acting intimate-like. I've seen her brother-in-law, Brace Sterling, peek in like he's checking on her. Next thing I know, whoever she's with is gone. Like gone from everywhere." She leaned forward and whispered in a low voice, "I know these guys who were regular customers at Rick's. They were known around town, but after Brace sees them in here with her, they evaporate. I've heard that he's a psychopath, or sociopath—you know, whichever one can kill people and it's no big deal."

Will stored this information in his mind as he looked around the club. "Have you ever witnessed anyone being harmed?"

"No. But you know me. Sandera hears all. Something's going on with that family. You need to call her because she changes phone numbers every two weeks."

Will shook the cubes in his glass. "That's interesting."

"Are you going to take care of my case?" Sandera asked, caressing his hand.

"Yes. You know how I work. I'll peer into the fog and figure it out." He tossed the remainder of the drink down and stood up. "I'll also check her out."

"Hey," Sandera said, standing up with him, "if that wife of yours isn't handling her share of the workload, you come and see Sandera. Believe me, your fog will lift."

Will grinned. "I have a formula I live by—UC plus CI equals UE."

Sandera furrowed her brow. "Let's see, UC means undercover plus confidential informant. What's UE stand for?"

"Unemployed," Will said with a straight face.

"Don't worry. Sandera will give you a *good* job. And I have all the benefits you'll ever need."

"I'll keep that in mind," Will said as he turned and left.

Chapter Two

Will leaned back in his chair, staring at the ceiling. He had a lot to consider.

After returning to the office, he had performed the usual background work on an unknown. First, he ran Sadie's name through a Texas driver's license check. That gave him an address, date of birth, and her photo.

Next, he plugged that information through the primary criminal record databases—NCIC and TCIC—National Crime Information Center and the Texas version. Then he'd checked her through Lexis/Nexis, utilities, and social media. With all the information he'd compiled, Will felt he had a good handle on what he was dealing with. Now, it was time for the crucial decision.

If he contacted Sadie, it might lead to a career-maker. He needed it. Maybe he could escape the undercover rat race. But then he'd be off chasing the dream. That meant less time with Jennifer and the boys. Family vs. work. The eternal conflict.

He wrung his hands, weighing both sides. Just as he straightened, Dan hobbled in, sliding gently into his chair opposite of Will.

"So, give it to me," his partner said. "What did you find out on this hottie?"

Will grabbed his pad. "A lot. Her full name is Sadie Jina Sterling."

"Jina?! Are you serious?"

"I just report the facts. Probably a misspelling on the birth certificate like that girl we busted named Temptress when it was meant to be Tempestt."

"Yeah, that was crazy. A prostitute with a real name like that. Such a self-fulfilling destiny."

Will continued. "Her father-in-law is Grayson Sterling, the big shot of the family. Lots of money. His wife is dead, but they had four children—Brace, Victoria, and Cole. Cole is Sadie's husband."

"Nothing sinister so far," Dan said.

"Nope, other than she uses a burner phone. Oh, there's another kid—Declan Sterling. He's a country-western singer."

"Declan. Is that the name he uses?"

"No. Let me see, it's Dallas Dillon."

"No shit?" Dan said, trying to get out of his chair.

"You've actually heard of him?" Will asked, surprised at his partner's reaction.

"Yeah, too bad you hate that kind of music. He has a bunch of hits. 'You're Gonna Shoot Me for This' is on the chart now. 'Farming for Beer' was his first one. He's not a Garth Brooks or even a Dierks Bentley, but he's moving up. And he's still in his late twenties, I think. Are you going to call this chick? I'd like to get his autograph."

"Sandera said she's heard they're into all sorts of stuff, and she's been very credible and reliable in the past. How can a call hurt me?" Will said with a shrug, ignoring that nagging feeling of family.

"That's what you said when you called those bikers. And you saw how that ended up." Dan rubbed his shoulder.

"I'm pretty sure the Sterling clan doesn't deal in hand grenades."

"Let's hope not. Because I'm not taking any more for the team."

Will got up and closed the office door. "I'll call her now." He picked up his burner phone and dialed the number Sadie had given him. The phone rang four times before she answered.

"What do you want?" she said brusquely.

"Hey, it's Will. I met you at the club with Sandera."

"Oh yeah, you stole my girl from me today."

"Well, I had business to do. I hadn't seen her in a while."

"I'm going to be at this Italian restaurant over in North Irving. Lamberti's. Meet me there at seven. Ask for Maria."

"Okay. I'll see you there."

Will set the phone down, making sure it had hung up. "It's on for seven."

"Do you want me to go with you?" Dan asked. "I can get a driver. Park nearby."

"No. It's a public place. Besides, I don't know what I've got. Maybe nothing."

"Are you doing it off the books?"

"Of course, I am. No need to make a report." Will handed him a Post-It. "Here's her number. If I don't check in with you by midnight, something's gone wrong. Send out the cavalry."

"Let's hope nothing goes wrong. I hate breaking in new partners."

• • •

Will held his jacket over his head to avoid the rain. The deluge had started around five, refusing to let up. The drops hitting his skin were cold, but always welcome in June.

Stepping inside the restaurant, he shook himself off. At the front desk, he asked for Maria.

"I'm Maria. Come with me."

The aroma of fresh bread and garlic invaded Will's nostrils as he followed the hostess. She led him past the bar to a small back room. Five small tables provided intimacy for perhaps ten people. Sadie, the only person in the room, sat at a table farthest from the entrance.

"I'll leave you two alone," Maria said, closing a curtain on the way out.

"Please have a seat," Sadie said, motioning to Will. He pulled back a chair and sat down. "I guess it's still raining."

"Yes," he said. "I tried to stay dry."

"Would you like some wine?" she asked, grabbing a full bottle.

"I'd love some."

"Do you like Chianti?"

"Well, it's not my favorite, but yes, it's raining outside. I'll drink anything."

"Have some appetizers." She pushed over a large plate of zucchini fritti, calamari, and breadsticks with marinara sauce. Will took a breadstick and dipped it in the sauce.

"So, what do you do?" Sadie asked.

"Anything that makes money."

"Do you have a record? Are you on paper?"

"Yeah, I got a record. But I'm not on paper. I finished my parole three years ago."

"What's your history?"

Will hesitated, looking around the vacant dining room.

"You want to work?" she added.

"Yes," he replied, swallowing some bread. "I've got two homicide cases. Both were dismissed."

Sadie smirked. "Let me guess, the witnesses decided not to testify?"

"Something like that."

"If you were on parole, you've been to prison. Right?"

"Yeah," Will said, remembering the two-week incarceration that was part of his undercover training. Even the guards hadn't known who they were.

To give them some protection, one trainee was put in a cell with Will, while the other two were one cell over. It wasn't perfect, but they could try to help each other if trouble started.

Will remembered the instructor had given them two goals: learn everything they could about being incarcerated and take care of each other. And learn they did.

Will couldn't believe how loud it was in prison. Every noise bounced off the walls, keeping him awake. At times it was deafening.

He'd adjusted quickly, though. Up at four to have breakfast. At work by five. Lunch at eleven. Back at the crib by two. Dinner at five and lights out by nine. He would have just shut his eyes when the lights popped on and the new day started. It didn't take long to understand how this routine hammered the time out of a person.

When Will had completed his two weeks and left, the noise of the last gate slamming shut stayed with him for years. After a few months of being free, he couldn't decide if the prison training was meant to help them be better undercover agents or keep them from going rogue. Either way, it worked. At least it quelled a few myths. He certainly never saw some big Black guy banging a weak white guy. Although his cellmate did turn in a guard who'd smuggled cell phones to the inmates. The lesson he carried away was to continually remind himself never to cross that line.

"Any child molestation or pornography?" Sadie asked, snapping Will back to the present.

He blinked a few times. "Uh, no. That's sick. I've got mostly assault, evading arrest, drugs."

"Are you past all that?" she asked, lifting her chin and eyes to focus on him.

Will ran his fingers through his dark brown hair and sighed. "I just turned forty. I need a good job. My ex is threatening to have me arrested for not paying child support."

"You got any tattoos?"

"I can't. I had malaria."

"Malaria! How'd you get that around here?"

"Not here," he said, lowering his voice. "Some Central America work I did."

"I see." She slid over a piece of paper and a pen. "Fill out your name, date of birth, social security number, and driver's license. Put your record on there too—everything."

Will filled out the paper while Sadie sipped on her wine. She seemed to enjoy staring at him, like he was a new catch.

Will handed it back to her.

"Now, let's have some wine and get to know each other," she said, refilling his glass. "But first, I need to know what's going on with Sandera."

"She picked up a case. She's having problems with a bondsman. I'm going to try to help her."

Sadie opened her purse and started digging. "If it's a money problem, I'll pay it."

"It's a money problem, but I got a solution. Let me run with it and see what happens."

She stared at Will. "Okay. In that case, I'll buy dinner."

"You were going to buy dinner anyway," he said, grinning.

She tried her best not to smile, but her eyes gave her away. "There's something about you that I can't figure out. I don't know why, but I trust you." She flipped her brunette hair back. "Do you trust me?"

"No. I just met you. I've trusted too many people in my past who've screwed me."

"I get you on that," she said with a serious look. "But really, you can trust me. Though I can't promise I won't screw you."

Will's eyes opened wide. When Sadie began laughing, he joined her.

"Are you married?" he asked.

"To Cole Sterling. I'm part of the Sterling family. Have you heard of them?"

"No," Will said, lying.

"If I get you a job, you will."

He poured more wine into both their glasses. "Then let's hope you're successful. I could sure use one."

They made small talk about their twins and munched on the appetizers before ordering dinner.

"Do you find me attractive?" Sadie blurted out. "If I was single, would you go for me?"

"No," Will replied bluntly.

She furrowed her brow. "Why not?"

"First, you're out of my league. I couldn't afford to buy one percent of the bubble you live in."

"I'm not that expensive," she protested.

"You keep telling yourself that. Your tab with Sandera alone would be enough to break me."

"Okay, what else?"

"I go for blondes."

"I could color my hair."

Will shook his head.

"No? I could find you a girl. You're not gay, are you?"

"No, but I need a job before I'm back in jail for not paying child support. That's my first priority. After all, I can't take my girl out to dinner or drinks if I'm in jail."

Sadie licked her lips. "What are you doing for the rest of the evening?"

"I've got to be at an AA meeting at ten. I'm supporting a friend."

She leaned back from the table, scrunching up her face. "With Chianti on your breath?"

"Mouthwash followed by mints will cover it up. We learn that in AA. Besides, I got a free dinner with a beautiful brunette out of the deal."

She showed her dimples. "If you're not careful, you're going to get on my good side."

"Right or left?"

"Front," she replied, lifting her breasts with both hands. "Where all the goodies are."

Will swallowed hard and coughed. "More wine?"

"Definitely. I'll order another bottle and hope you try to take advantage of me."

You don't know how right you are.

Chapter Three

Will sat at his desk, studying a photo of his wife and kids. They looked so happy in their wet swimsuits, the vivid colors of the fabric and the sun glimmering off the water.

Cedar Creek Lake had provided a lot of cheap entertainment—water skiing, fishing, and swimming off the dock. It'd only been two summers ago, but it seemed like another lifetime.

Right next to that happy scene was a black and white photo of Will's mentor, Dr. Z. He recalled how the man had towered over him, an imposing figure when he first leaned over Will's desk and announced, "I sometimes select a student from my class for additional training. I've decided that you have the raw talent to warrant that time and labor."

Dr. Z was in his mid-fifties, with gray and black hair resting just above round glasses that obscured his piercing black eyes. He had a shadowy reputation around the Bureau, seemingly floating between the CIA, FBI, and NSA. Some agents had reported seeing him on an aircraft carrier in the Gulf during hostilities in the Middle East. Another guy had said his brother met him at a black ops site in Burkina Faso. Who and what his background entailed remained a mystery to all.

"But I don't have the best grades," Will had pointed out. "Why me?"

"True, but you have a quick mind. You have the *it* factor." Dr. Z said as he chewed on a green plant stem the exact size of a cigarette. It was probably something he'd brought back from

South America. Will assumed it was a tactic to break the habit of smoking. "Good grades won't be necessary where you'll be going. The targets won't be interested."

Dr. Z, chewing on the plant stem again, stood a little taller. "It's your wit and composure that will keep you safe, get you deep into the heart of the organization. You'll be learning different material than the rest of your class. Are you up for that?"

"Absolutely," Will said, never knowing that a class in tradecraft would lead to the most physically and mentally specialized training he could ever imagine. How he'd survived, he had no idea.

"So, big guy," Dan said. "How'd your date go?"

Will spun his worn vinyl chair around to face his partner. "I might be on to something. Still don't know what, but it's like I hooked something big. I have to reel it in to see what it is."

"I can't hold a rod yet, but I can at least turn the reel."

"I might need help with Jennifer. She wasn't happy I came in late with wine on my breath. I don't think she believed I was working."

Dan clicked his tongue. "85-3. Remember the training?"

"No. What was that?"

"In undercover work, eighty-five percent are divorced in three years."

"Oh, I remember now. But if I could just snag a career-maker, I could get that supervisor job and be home by six each night. Then it'd be some other gumshoe out there doing this shit."

Dan moved closer to Will. "Face it, Rockton—you're addicted to this life. Though I have to admit, I thought our last gig would make our careers. But hearing Schneider in the breakroom, he acts like it was no big deal."

"We produce," Will said. "That makes him look good. If he makes *us* look good, we'll be promoted away from him. Then he won't look so good."

"You're right. If the folks in Washington think it's a good op, Schneider will probably take all the credit. If it goes to shit, it sticks to us. He's got the good life."

"The one I want," Will said.

There was a knock on the open door. "Hey, Rockton," another special agent said. "You got your alias ran. Some cop in Granbury checked your record."

Will thought of the small careful details the Bureau had taken to plant records on his criminal and credit history. It was for moments like this.

He wondered how the cop in Granbury would feel when they busted him. They'd wait six months to do it to make sure it didn't come back on Will.

"Well," Dan said, slapping Will with his good hand. "It's definitely game-on."

"I guess it is."

• • •

A cargo plane gunned its engines, screaming for oxygen as it climbed to the skies. Will leaned against the grill of his Chevy Silverado, watching the trail of exhaust fumes. After it disappeared, he checked his watch for the umpteenth time. He studied the address Sadie had given him. Everything appeared to be in order.

Will had arrived at the international shipping complex early—a quarter before ten. It was now after eleven. The coffee he'd inhaled pushed hard against his bladder, searching for a way out. To take his mind off that, he pulled out a Cuban cigar and lit it up. The smoke relaxed him.

Halfway through the cigar, he couldn't sit still any longer. He started walking to a nearby office, hoping to use their restroom. Between rows of cars, a black Range Rover swerved to cut him off. He reached for his weapon, ready for whatever was going down.

"You Will?" a voice said from inside the SUV.

"Yes," he replied, easing his hand away from his hip.

"I'm Green. Get in."

Will studied a man in his mid-thirties. He wore a green John Deere ballcap over a military-style haircut. Clean-shaven, his face was dotted with acne scars. From the way he carried himself, he was definitely ex-military.

Green drove to an empty industrial area near DFW airport and told Will to get out.

This is a great place to be shot, Will thought.

At the back of the Range Rover, Green spread out a towel and opened an ink pad.

"I need your fingerprints," Green said, grabbing Will's left hand and pressing each finger onto a form. Will cooperated, confident his prints would match his undercover name and backstory.

As Will wiped the ink from his fingers, another black Range Rover came to a stop. Without saying a word, Green handed the forms to the driver.

"I have to take a leak," Will told Green as the other SUV sped off. "Unless you need a UA."

"Go behind the vehicle. I need to keep you in my sight."

Will stood there peeing, grinning. He'd just hit the jackpot.

Keeping a prospective associate around while the credentials were verified was the standard operating procedure for criminals. If things didn't check out, they could chop off fingers until they learned the truth—who the stranger really was. Will was safe, unless they had someone inside the FBI. If that were the case... well, his family problems would disappear, along with his body.

Green stayed inside the SUV while Will leaned against the driver's side. Ten minutes later, the second Range Rover returned. This time, a man with a shaved head and horn-rimmed sunglasses was driving.

"I'm Anders," he said gruffly, exiting the SUV. "Are you carrying?"

"I'm a felon," Will said, dodging the question.

"I already know that," Anders said, his voice rising. "Are you carrying?"

"I am."

"Let me see it."

Will hesitated. Giving up your gun was the first and most crucial step to being killed. His training had drilled that into him. Yet Dr. Z had given him wiggle room. "Never be afraid to go with your instinct, Will. You're the reason why we don't have robots flying planes. We need a live person—*you*—to make on-the-spot decisions, because a computer can't decide when to pull the trigger or when to do nothing."

Growing impatient, Anders pulled out his gun and handed it to Will. "Here, you hold this while I check out your gun."

Will grabbed Ander's Glock and gave him his Browning high-powered nine-millimeter. This was another critical detail. "Never carry a cop gun like a Glock," Dr. Z had told him. "It smells like undercover."

Will watched as Anders inspected his Browning. "Did you file off these numbers?"

"If I say yes, I'll be admitting to a felony."

"You're a felon in possession of a firearm," Anders said, ripping off his glasses. "You're already good for that."

Will stared at the pavement. "I guess someone filed them off."

"Sure, they did," Anders grunted, handing the Browning to Will and taking back his Glock. "So, you want a job?"

"Of course, I do," Will replied, holstering his weapon.

"I'm going to start you at the bottom. You can work your way up."

"Bottom of what?"

"Bottom of a pyramid filled with gold and riches. If you want to climb up, I'll take care of you."

Will nodded. "Okay, let's do it."

"Not with that outfit." Anders passed him a card. "Go to this business and tell Mr. Chu you met me. Tell him I want you to have five suits with all the works. He'll take good care of you. When you get them, call me at this number." He handed Will a piece of scrap paper.

"Got it," Will said, pocketing both. "Thanks."

Anders ignored him as he sped away. Green drove Will to his truck and dropped him off.

Once Green was out of sight, Will dialed Sadie's number. "I got the job!" he said excitedly.

"Great!" she replied. "Come meet my kiddos. We're at Hurricane Harbor. Find the ticket manager. He knows me. Tell him you're here to see me. He'll take you to us."

Three hours later, Will found Sadie lounging in a sexy one-piece bathing suit. Next to her, a small boombox played Jason Aldean singing, "Don't You Wanna Stay."

"This is Kodi and Brooke," she said, holding a child with each hand.

"Are you the cutest girls that ever existed?" Will asked as the girls smiled. He kneeled down. "I brought you some fruit roll-ups."

"How thoughtful," Sadie said, beaming. "You're so good with kids."

Once the twins were settled and munching on their treats, Sadie turned the boombox down. "What took you so long?"

"I had to meet with Mr. Chu and get fitted for some suits."

"Oh. We have standards to keep." She handed him a piece of paper. "Here's my new number. They'll take this phone and crush it up somewhere. Brace makes us switch phones every two weeks. 'Can't be too careful,'" Sadie said, mimicking a male voice.

Will studied the paper and put it in his front pocket.

"You sure get along with children."

"I have to since I can't see my boys much."

Sadie placed the long nail of her index finger on Will's thigh, drawing an imaginary picture. "With some finagling, maybe you'll be seeing these two more."

Will nodded, staring at her finger. Then he thought about his marriage. It was hanging by a thread. Jennifer constantly berated him for never being home. He began to wonder about this investigation, if it would lead to anything that Schneider and the front office would fund.

"Everything's on a tight budget," his boss constantly blared. "I have to see some real promise before I let you go and have fun."

Sadie leaned forward. "Here, honey, rub some lotion on my back. And don't be shy about it."

She removed the swimsuit's straps from her shoulders and buried her face in a towel. Will took the sunscreen bottle and squirted white lotion into his hand. Warming it up, he gently massaged it into her soft skin.

When Clay Walker's "She Won't Be Lonely Long" came on the radio, Will glanced around the lounge area for anyone who might know him.

Thank God Jennifer is working right now. This wouldn't look so good.

Chapter Four

"How it fit?" asked a woman with a thick Asian accent.

"Great," Will said, adjusting the slacks. "Do I get to keep the belt?"

"Yes. And brown one too."

"What about the shoes?"

"Yes. You keep all."

Will couldn't believe it. Five custom-made first-class suits, ten shirts, two pairs of Italian shoes, two belts, and twelve pairs of socks. The shoes had rubber soles, just like what the Secret Service wore. The only thing he'd have to provide was underwear.

"You take off. I wrap for you," the woman said.

Will stepped out of the dressing room and handed her his slacks and shirt. "How much does all this stuff cost?'

She lowered her tone to a whisper. "It cost $15,000. But you work for Anders, right?"

"Yes," Will whispered back.

"Don't worry. They pay. They pay everything."

"I'm just curious. That's all."

She came closer. "You not ask questions like that. We don't."

Will nodded. He quickly gathered up his clothes and left the store.

• • •

One of the tedious aspects of any law enforcement job was filling out reports. Everything had to be documented. Everything! The devil was in the details.

Will spent several hours making sure his report read like a novel. He wanted a guaranteed greenlight. To accomplish that, he'd learned to make his reports not just easy to read, but entertaining.

Now came the hard part—the critic's review.

He sat in his boss's office, watching him read the report. Schneider's face alternated between a furrowed brow and a grimace. Will didn't think it was going well.

Just as Schneider put it down and rubbed his eyes, Will blurted out, "Did you see they ran my prints and criminal history? That tells you something right there."

"Yeah, that they know how to pay a cop to run prints."

Will ignored his remark. "I think I'm on to something here."

"Oh, I agree," Schneider said sarcastically. "It looks like you're going to get into that hottie's bathing suit right after you rub some more lotion on her. You already have the top off."

Will decided to remain silent. Nothing he said made a dent. It was so typical.

The other agents made fun of his boss. From his toupee to his designer suspenders and the fake gold Rolex supposedly purchased for almost nothing from a forfeiture sale. Schneider was a blue flamer—a supervisory special agent on fire for the Bureau, someone who breathed the fumes he created. Still, Will had to admit this turd knew how to play the Washington game. Schneider enjoyed it.

Schneider also liked everything gold, which included the Cross pen he picked up to sign a form. "I know we usually give you three months to get started, but I'm only giving you a few more days of this. If you don't show me some results, I'm shutting you down. Remember the war on terrorism? I need to get some productivity out of you. You UC agents don't seem to understand the nature of a budget. This isn't like the movies where the cops have an endless supply of money and bullets. We don't have George Lucas here, funding the next *Star Wars*."

"But I may need more than a few days to get to some of the big players identified. There's something there. I can feel it."

"What you're feeling is that chick's body. Too bad for you that my touch is more experienced than yours. And right now, I'm not feeling it. Besides, I've checked with my sources, and no one knows of anything there. If these folks are into something illegal, it's for collecting too many awards because they give away too much money. And if doing that's a crime, I'm not going to be the guy who slaps cuffs on it."

Will shook his head. "I'll see if I can find out something."

Schneider pointed to the door. "And make sure you turn in those suits. We might be able to use them for some other investigations."

Stunned, Will stopped at the door. "But I have to wear them for my job."

"Not much longer. You work *here*, not for the Starlings."

"Sterlings."

"Sterlings. Starlings. Whatever."

Disgusted, Will walked back to his office.

"How did it go?" Dan asked.

"Not good," Will grunted as he slumped into his chair. "I have a few more days before he shuts it down. And he told me to turn in those suits. I'll remember I heard that when the investigation shuts down."

"Great," Dan said with a lopsided grin. "Just tell him those suits were the *fabric* of the investigation."

"Man, you just keep me in *stitches*," Will said with irritation. He glanced at his watch. "Shit! I've got to get moving. I'm supposed to be at a Waffle House in Weatherford."

"Okay. Don't go dying on me."

"Not planning on it. I have to get back here so I can listen to your smart-ass comments. Besides, someone has to babysit you."

•••

Weatherford was an hour's drive from the Dallas office, giving Will plenty of time to think about his life. As he drove, he thought about where his life should be versus where it actually was.

Jennifer made good money as a pharmaceutical rep. It easily exceeded his government salary. That didn't bother him as much as it bothered his wife. Sometimes, he wondered if she felt like she'd married too low. He was out there risking his life while she supported the family and raised the twins. He had to find a way to get a career-maker and that promotion he desired. That would be his ticket out. Then he'd be making more than his wife, with less travel and more time to be with his family. This Sterling clan had to be the home run he'd been waiting for. If it wasn't, he had no fallback plan. That was dangerous for anyone in law enforcement. It encouraged agents to fudge evidence or to take shortcuts. He knew it'd happened with others before. He was determined not to be one of those guys.

Will arrived at the Waffle House and scanned the parking lot looking for problems. It appeared to be just a bunch of farmers and ranchers, all clinging to the last place on the planet where you could have a meal *and* smoke.

Pushing open the second door, Will glanced around the restaurant. He spotted Sadie and the others. They were in a booth, so he moved quickly toward them.

"Mr. Chu does good work," Green said, getting to his feet. "You almost look like a model. Slide in."

Will slid across the red crackled vinyl seat and faced Sadie. Green removed his John Deere ballcap and eased in next to him. Across from Green was Anders.

"Man, I don't know how to thank you," Will offered.

"You've never had quality clothes before," Sadie said, her eyes filled with concern. "Have you?"

"No. I did wear some nice slacks for my wedding. But I had to give them back to my cousin."

Sadie bit her lip and gently covered his hand with hers.

"Here's how you can thank me," Anders said, interrupting the pity party. "You're starting the day after tomorrow at 6 a.m. Meet me over at Meacham Airport in Fort Worth. Pack your suits. Get your toiletries. You'll be gone for about a week. Where do you live?"

"An apartment in the mid-cities," Will replied.

"How much are your rent and utilities?"

"Rent is $1,400. I haven't gotten my utility bills yet."

Anders peeled off $2,000. "Go ahead and pay your rent and utilities in advance, because you may not be back for a while."

"Okay," Will said. As he held the cash, he thought about how Schneider was going to love the money but blow a gasket when he learned about the new development.

Out of nowhere, a serious-looking man—probably a military lifer—pulled up a chair and placed it at the end of the booth. He pushed his dark pilot sunglasses to the top of his black hair and checked out the new man. Will was surprised, but no one else was.

"Listen up," the man said, staring directly at Will. "We don't fuck around in this outfit. People follow orders and focus on their job. Understand?"

"Yes," Will replied.

"Good. If you don't understand something, say something."

"Most definitely," Will said.

Anders tapped the table. "Brace, tell him about the hours."

"The hours are simple. We work all the time, but I'm not stupid. I know you can't concentrate if you're exhausted. You'll have plenty of rack time, and I expect you to be sleeping or working out, not playing video games or playing grab-ass with a maid. Got that?"

"I got that." Will studied Brace, committing to memory his stout body and black hair, trimmed close on the sides in military fashion. His right hand continually twisted a skull ring on his left hand. He was obviously the head honcho.

"Good," Brace said, picking up a menu. "Now, let's order. I don't often get a chance to eat this kind of high-quality food."

•••

Dan laughed. "No way you're getting a full week with these guys. I need you to help me with this new lead we got in."

"What is that?" Will asked.

"Some guys painting the outside of a house. One of them wrapped a painter's cloth around his head—I'm thinking to avoid the spray. So, a neighbor called and said they had to be Muslim, and it's obvious these guys are planning something big."

"Crap. It never stops. What a waste of resources."

"But really, do you mind helping me with this stuff today?"

"Sure," Will replied. "I got nothing else to do until tomorrow."

Twenty minutes later, he heard the boss storming down the hall.

"What the hell is this?" Schneider bellowed into their small office. "One week? Maybe more? I'm pulling the plug on this. You get back on Guardian leads until I insert you in the next op."

Will stood up, facing his supervisor. "This could be huge. Come on. I've been busting my ass for you and the Bureau. Give me this one."

"You need to spend time with your family. Remember them? Leave the other family for someone else."

An administrative assistant tapped Schneider on the shoulder. "Coleman and Ashcroft are on the phone."

Schneider's eyes widened. "Uh, okay," he said, collecting himself. "What do they want? Did they say?"

"No. They just want you and Rockton."

Schneider spun to Will, seething. "Did you send Washington something behind my back?"

"Of course not," Will assured him. "I type the reports in. That's it. You're the only one reading them, right?"

"Yeah, but they can access anything." Schneider swallowed hard and tapped Will's chest. "You let me do the talking, Rockton. Understand?"

"Okay," Will replied, wondering where this was headed.

They sat in Schneider's office as his boss hit the speaker button. "We're here. How can I help you?"

"A report by one of your agents was flagged—Will Rockton. Will, can you answer some questions?"

"Of course."

"Do you think you have a chance to get inside the Sterling family?"

"I'm already in. They just made five suits for me. Over $15,000 in clothing. Ran my alias criminal record *and* finger-prints. They checked my UC gun and gave me $2,000 to pay my rent in advance. Brace Sterling told me to be at the Meacham Airport tomorrow morning and be ready to leave. I'll be gone for one week or more."

"Fantastic! That's wonderful news. I haven't read the entire report. We just got a hit when Brace Sterling's name popped up."

Schneider spoke. "I've been working with Rockton to get close to Brace. He's our main tango."

"Excellent work. This guy has been on our radar for quite some time. We think he might be racking up the body count, but we can't find any remains. It's like they just vanish into thin air."

"I didn't know all that," Schneider said, "but I had a hunch this Brace Sterling was big game."

"Your hunch is right on the money. Rockton, are you good with this? The records say you need some family time."

Will was certain they had read the psychiatrist's notes on his recent visit. "I'm good. I'll talk with my wife and explain it's for God and Country and Bureau."

"God and Country. For sure," the speaker crackled. "We'll monitor this operation through your reports. Good luck. And again, excellent work, Schneider."

"Thank you," Schneider said. "I'm on top of it!"

Schneider ended the call and pressed a button. "Send in Rodgers."

A pudgy-faced man entered the office. "You called?"

"Yeah, I want you to be Rockton's handler. Washington is watching this one, so I want first-class reports. Understand?"

Rodgers nodded, eager to please his boss.

"This might be a career-maker. Let's win this one for once, Rockton. And no fuckups, you hear me?"

Will rolled his eyes as he walked out, thinking of all the assholes he had to work for.

Maybe one day, I'll be that asshole.

Chapter Five

The winglets of the Gulfstream sent wisps of condensation trailing behind as it landed in the early morning fog. It was rare for the dew point to be so close to the temperature, but this morning—a Thursday—was one of those days.

Will had fought through the fog to get to the Meacham Airport on time. With each turn he'd made, he prayed he wouldn't be blocked by traffic. Not making it to the airport on time would have been bad on so many levels. But he was here now, and so was the aircraft.

The Gulfstream G550 pulled up in front of the hangar. On its tail, there was a large "F" sitting above a horizontal line. Below the line, a mirroring "A."

F Bar A.

That was the message. But what did it mean?

Will checked his watch as the door popped open and a stairway folded down. A cute blonde in her early forties emerged. She stepped off the stairs and came toward him.

"I'm Hannah," she said, smiling and shaking his hand. "I'm your flight attendant." Two men emerged behind her. "This is Captain J.D. and First Officer, Nate."

Will shook both their hands.

"We're headed to the pilot's lounge," J.D. said. "Give the line boy your luggage. He'll put it in the cargo hold."

A teenager appeared and took Will's black duffel bag—the scroungiest he could find at a Goodwill thrift store. He stacked it on top of a loaded pushcart.

"I'm carrying the hanging bag," Will stated, not fully trusting this kid with his expensive new suits.

The two walked to the aircraft, where the line boy pulled on a lever that opened a cargo hatch. Will gazed at all the Louis Vuitton luggage as it was loaded. He crammed his crappy duffel bag next to a silver suitcase. Then he laid his hanging bag over the top, hoping to save it from wrinkles. His cheap bags helped maintain his cover. That was their purpose.

Will stood at the base of the stairs, uncomfortable in boarding without permission. Soon, Hannah emerged from the hangar.

"You can get on the plane and make yourself comfortable," she said. "I'll join you shortly."

Will stepped up into the cabin and checked out the space, feeling overwhelmed.

There were six first-class-sized seats, each one covered with expensive leather. A couch along the right side had four sets of seat belts. If they put a butt in every seat, they could haul ten passengers. He wondered how many passengers were going on this trip.

Will studied the layout, searching for the best seat. Nearest the cockpit were two seats facing aft. Opposite those were two seats facing forward. The configuration was repeated throughout the plane, with two seats grouped together in the back. *Those are probably where the powerbrokers sit,* he thought, eyeing the rear seats.

He selected a seat among them, facing forward. This allowed him to see all the passengers as they entered—if there were any.

As he got comfortable, he played with the various buttons on his seat. One button extended his leg rest out. Another leaned his seat back. There was a button for air. One for light. A burled-wood ledge ran along the side of his armrest, with two silver-lined holes for drinks. *This is luxury living, for sure.*

Will relaxed, thinking back to his training. "We're going to put you into operations that you're somewhat familiar with," Dr. Z had told him. "While here, you will learn close quarter combat, intense shooting, and ultimate driving skills. Do you understand?"

He had. They never asked if he liked the plan or agreed with it. All they were interested in was that he understood their orders.

The acute training took several months. He learned to shoot in every condition imaginable and break down any weapon on the market. Will learned to drive through any obstacle course until he'd mastered them all with no issues. It was the same for the close combat training. Will was expected to handle each situation with surgical precision. Each course was very different, but he absorbed every detail of their mechanics and form.

One of Will's classmates came from a wealthy family in Boston. The Bureau put him in the white-collar UC training program. He had been introduced to extravagant cars and private luxury aircraft. His name was Jonathon, but the trainees nicknamed him First Class. He had been given the good life, one less likely to be dodging bullets. Although the assignments made sense to Will, it seemed unfair.

"We just expect more from you," Dr. Z told him when Will had asked if he could get some white-collar training. "You'll be dealing with the unpredictable. That's where we put our best special agents. You are one of them."

A movement caught Will's eye. It was Hannah walking with the line boy, who was pushing a cart loaded with food and drinks. She grabbed a few items off the cart and climbed up the stairs.

"Do you need my help?" Will offered, standing up.

"Thank you for asking, but we've got it. Just make yourself comfortable."

It took a few minutes until Hannah had everything put away. As the line boy pushed the empty cart back to the hangar, J.D. hopped up the stairs and pointed to Will. "Sit in this one," the captain said, pointing to a seat on the left side of the plane facing forward. Will didn't question it. He understood his place in the pecking order.

Nate came on board and pulled the stairs up, closing the door behind him. Will realized he was the only passenger on the plane.

Why can't I sit back there?

As the two pilots went through their pre-flight checklist, the noise level of the engines climbed. Hannah worked up front, checking the supplies and putting everything away. A few minutes later, the engines screamed.

The Gulfstream eased forward, rolling toward the runway. When the aircraft had moved no more than a few hundred feet, it lurched to a sudden stop, its brakes squealing, and engines shutting down.

Will frowned. Something was wrong.

Hannah moved briskly to the door and opened it, lowering the steps. A black Range Rover pulled up. Will couldn't see who the new passengers were until they climbed on board.

Green's face and John Deere ballcap were first. Behind him was Brace, smoothing back his black hair with the skull-ringed hand. Then a gorgeous woman appeared. A hint of amber in her olive skin told him she was likely Middle Eastern.

As she moved in closer, her clothing revealed a tight, muscular body. Something in her demeanor told Will she was more than capable of handling herself.

"Will, you already know Brace," Green said. "This is Sterry."

Will stood up and shook her hand, testing her firm grip. "Pleasure to meet you," he said, staring directly into her eyes.

She returned the stare with confidence. "Thank you, Will," she replied, turning his hand loose and heading to the back with Brace.

Green took a seat next to Will. "Enjoying yourself?"

"So far, I'm very impressed. This is the only way to fly."

"That's the Sterlings. Everything is first class."

Before long, the Gulfstream was above the clouds, leveling off.

Hannah rose from her jump seat and stood next to Will. "Would you like a drink? We have most anything you could possibly want."

Will instantly recalled his alcohol training with Dr. Z. They had spent a week with various drinks to determine how much they could consume before growing lazy with words. Will struggled with vodka, tequila, and rum. But scotch—with a much higher alcohol content—somehow worked for him. He could sip it very slowly, making it seem like he was always drinking. After getting dialed into scotch, Dr. Z had shown him that the higher-quality scotch made it easier for Will to stay alert and on script.

"Single malt scotch neat?" Will asked.

"You got it," Hannah replied, smiling. "I'll pour you one."

After serving everyone a drink, she carried out a tray of salami with various cheeses.

"Have some," Green said to Will.

"I don't eat pork," he replied.

Green's eyes narrowed. "Are you Jewish or Muslim?"

"No," Will replied. "I got food poisoning from pork. Can't stand it now."

Green's face relaxed. "Okay, that's fine," he said, grabbing the plate from Hannah. "More for me."

Will sipped on his scotch and gazed out the window. From the angle of the sun, he could tell they were heading west. He thought about the go-and-stop the plane had gone through.

Were they testing to see if any vehicles swarmed the plane and stopped it from taking off? Do they suspect I'm an agent?

He mulled that over during the four-hour flight. After a trip to the lavatory, he glanced out the left side of the plane and spotted the Golden Gate Bridge. They were in the bay area.

The Gulfstream landed at the San Francisco International Airport. Before the plane came to a stop, two black Lincoln Town Cars pulled up alongside it.

Hannah opened the door and let them out, giving a friendly goodbye to each. Will and Green took one Town Car. Brace and Sterry took the other.

Bypassing the hotel front desk, Will and Green were taken directly to their respective rooms. The accommodations were spacious, but not overdone. After Will inspected the entire room, he heard a knock at the door. Will assumed it was the luggage delivery. It wasn't.

"Hey, Will," Anders said, coming into the room with a backpack. "I need to outfit you."

"Okay," Will said, closing the door behind his guest.

Anders pulled a Glock 19 out of his duffel bag. "Take this and lose the Browning."

Will weighed the weapon in his hand.

"Here's a belt holster and some extra magazines." Anders tossed them on the bed. "And here's some gloves and zip ties." The rubber gloves were folded neatly around six zip ties. "We keep these on us at all times along with the Glock. Here's the itinerary for today."

"What am I doing?" Will asked.

Anders zipped up his backpack. "You and another guy are watching Sadie and the twins. You'll relieve him when his shift is done."

"Here in the hotel?"

"No. We'll be all over the place. Cole is accepting an award on behalf of the Sterling family. We're here for a week. He loves San Francisco. We are his security team. Your job is to keep track of his wife and make sure she sticks to the plan."

"Okay," Will said, studying the itinerary. "How much do I make on this job?"

"Two thousand a week. We also give bonuses depending on your performance. Does that work for you?"

"Damn, that's real good," Will replied, smiling.

"Listen, we do our best not to use curse words. It goes against the Sterlings' religious beliefs, and it makes us look uneducated. But Brace curses a lot. And sometimes, we do too, especially when we're under stress. Try to avoid it though. Understand?"

"Yeah," Will said.

"And that leads me to the next rule. Even though I know you're basically uneducated, the Sterlings like their employees to speak proper English. No yeahs, yays, uh-huhs, words like that. Say yes and no. Understand?"

"Yes, sir."

"Boy, you're ringing all the bells today. Sir is another pet peeve. Use sir when you're speaking to Grayson Sterling. But everyone else, there's no need for it."

Will nodded.

"And we don't use smartphones. Too much surfing and not enough paying attention. Here's a flip phone. This is the number." Anders pointed to a piece of athletic tape on the back of the phone. "Memorize it, then destroy the tape. We change these out every couple of weeks. It has all our numbers saved, including Brace's. You call him as a last resort. Green first, then me, then Brace. Got it?"

"Got it."

"One final thing. Hit your star button and you'll see a four-digit code. Use that code to get the elevator to the fifth floor. No one gets off on this floor while we're here. Just us. Don't let me down," Anders said. "Understand?"

"Completely," Will replied. "I'll be ready."

As Anders opened the door to leave, he found the bellhop standing there with Will's luggage. Anders gestured to the hanging bag. "And make sure to always wear one of your suits."

"I will," he said as Anders slipped around the luggage cart and left.

The bellhop placed Will's bags in the closet. Will reached into his pocket, but the bellhop stopped him.

"I've been taken care of," he said. "Enjoy your stay."

As he left, Will shook his head. *The Sterlings have every detail covered.*

Now that he was alone, it was time to inspect the room for cameras and bugs. He needed to find out how closely they were monitoring him. He hoped it wasn't that close.

•••

A rough hand gripped his neck tighter as water splashed out of the trough. Will struggled for oxygen, his hands zip-tied behind his back. He barely had time to gulp down some air before his head was pushed back underwater.

It seemed like forever.

It was only three minutes. All part of the training Dr. Z had put him through. "You must be familiar with torture. Only when you are friends with torture can you control it. And only when you can control something can you conquer it."

Will awoke from a catnap. The dream reminded him of the stamina he'd needed to get through the training. The class in torture was one of the most frightening things he'd ever endured. It stuck with him, causing an occasional nightmare.

After that class, he'd made up his mind that he wanted no part of being tortured. If he believed he was about to be made, he'd pull out his weapon and start blasting away. If it turned out he was wrong, well… the justice system could sort it out. At least he'd be alive to stand trial. Hopefully.

He sat in a comfortable chair, his hotel robe tied loosely around his thin frame. Three days of chasing Sadie and the kids all over San Francisco had worn him out. He wanted to take another nap, but he had to go back on duty in an hour, noon to midnight.

Pouring himself a Red Bull, he took a sip, trying to enjoy the remaining time before he needed to dress. He heard a sound at the door. Then a beep.

The door swung open and in stormed an enraged man.

"What did you do with my children?" he said, grabbing both sides of Will's robe. Will instinctively put his palms together and thrust them upward between the man's wrists. A quick outward motion and the man let go. Will balled up his fists and prepared for combat.

"Cole!" Anders yelled, running into Will's room. "It's not him. He wasn't on duty. Charlie was."

Cole, preparing for Will's attack, stepped back. "Who?"

"It was Charlie! Come on. Let's go talk to him."

Anders escorted Cole out of the room and closed the door. Will's heart, racing at maximum speed, began slowing down. He decided he'd better get dressed. Something was about to explode.

• • •

Will stood in a large suite next to his shift mate Charlie. Cole sat across from them, seething. The door to the room burst open.

"I want someone's ass," Brace blared, pointing at the two men. "Which one of you will be visiting the boneyard?"

Anders and Green followed behind Brace, whose expression signaled to Will the seriousness of the moment.

"You tell me your story first," Brace said, tapping Will hard on the chest with his skull ring.

Will swallowed. "I... uh... was off-duty and wanted to get some fresh air. I spotted this café across the street from the hotel, so I decided to have breakfast there."

"Wait a minute," Brace said, interrupting him. "You can have a gourmet meal delivered to your room, yet you decided to eat at a greasy spoon and pay for it out of your own pocket?"

"Well, it wasn't a greasy spoon. It's fresh and organic. But yes, I did pay for it out of my own pocket."

"Continue," Brace said, his arms folded over his massive chest.

"They have this counter facing the hotel, so I sat down to people-watch more than anything. Around nine, I saw Sadie come out with Kodi and Brooke. Charlie was helping with the luggage. I couldn't see everything, but Charlie and Sadie were talking to the valet while the twins stood still just outside of the entrance.

"Nothing much happened for a minute or so, then a yellow cab spun around to the entrance. The driver got out, looked at the twins, and loaded them into the backseat. When I saw him belt them in, it hit me that it was a yellow cab, not a Lincoln Town Car or an SUV. I'm new here, but I couldn't imagine the Sterlings taking a yellow cab anywhere."

Brace nodded, his jaw clenched tightly.

"I see the cab pull away while Charlie and Sadie are still talking with a valet. That's when I decided to act.

"I sprinted out of the restaurant and ran hard to the first light. The taxi went through it, so I kept running. At the next intersection, the traffic in the opposite direction started to slow down, so I knew the cab's light was about to turn green. I gave it an extra push and made it to the driver's window just as the light turned green. It was my lucky day. I pounded on the window and on top of the cab, distracting the driver. He could've hit the accelerator, but he didn't.

"I jerked the driver's door open and put the car in park before he knew what was going on. I grabbed the keys and put them in my pocket. The cars behind us began to honk."

Brace relaxed a bit. "Okay. Then what?"

"I just pushed the driver over and drove the cab back to the hotel. Green was there, so the twins got out. I guess he notified you and Anders. At that point, I wasn't needed, so I went back to the café to finish my breakfast. When I got there, the manager had called the police, thinking I'd skipped out on the bill. I explained to the cop what happened. It was all fine."

"So, where is this cab driver?" Brace asked, turning to Anders.

"We checked him out," Anders replied. "Some West African who wet his pants. There was another set of kids he was supposed to pick up. If he would've waited thirty seconds longer, they would've been down there."

"Did you confirm this with the parents of the other kids?" Brace asked.

Anders nodded. "We did. We also downloaded the driver's phone, ran the numbers, and sent his prints to our friends. I sent Green to the driver's dispatch to look at the records. Everything checked out. The driver begged us not to call the police. He needed the job. I think he even took a dump in his pants."

"How did the driver act when you saw him?" Brace asked Will.

"When I got to him, he didn't try to take off or act like he'd been caught. He thought I was trying to rob him. I checked him for weapons and found nothing. Oh, I forgot this part. When I got back to the hotel with the cab, I did see the kids he was supposed to pick up. I called another cab for them while Anders took the driver somewhere. That was all I saw before going back to the café."

Brace walked over to Charlie. "What do you have to say about all this?"

Charlie's voice cracked as he told his story. "Sadie came out with Kodi and Brooke but went back inside for something. The luggage we brought out busted a wheel. I was trying to fix it, and Sadie came up to give advice. Behind my back, the taxi driver came in and scooped up the kids. Really, Brace, it was all so fast, I didn't have time to react."

"Scooped up?" Brace said. "He had to strap them in. That takes a few minutes."

"He was fast. By the time I looked up, he was gone."

"You mean *they* were gone. Grayson Sterling's precious grandchildren." Brace put his arm around Charlie. "Look, everyone fucks up sometimes. Let me have your gun."

Charlie's hand trembled as he pulled out his gun and gave it to Brace.

Brace glanced at Will. "You can go back to your room. I've got this handled."

Will left quickly, walking to the end of the hall where his room was located. He'd learned the pecking order pushed the more valuable members to the center of the hotel, near the elevator. At least they had the entire floor. That made security easier.

Twenty minutes later, a grinning Anders came into Will's room. "You just moved up in the family. Unfortunately, Charlie isn't feeling well, so you'll have to handle more of his work-load. We'll work on having someone replace you at night so you can get some sleep. But from now on, you'll handle the day shift. Cole and Brace want you to handle more than twelve hours. Of course, they'll compensate you for the extra time."

"Sure, whatever you need," Will said.

Anders turned to leave, stopped, and removed his horn-rimmed glasses. "You saved our asses. Grayson loves those kids. They're his only grandchildren. If we lost them, we'd all end up at the boneyard."

"Where's that?" Will asked.

"A place where fuckups go to die. Sadie and the kids are in for the rest of the day. You relax and get plenty of sleep. You're on at 6 a.m. I'll bring you a new itinerary."

When Anders had gone, Will ordered room service. The hotel food was great, so he splurged.

An hour later, after polishing off a peppercorn-crusted filet, baked sweet potato, and a slice of chocolate cake, Will poured some wine and leaned back. He missed Jennifer and his children. They were so far away.

If Jennifer can just hang on through this investigation, the Sterlings will be my career-maker.

He could smell it coming. He just had to avoid the boneyard.

Or did he?

Chapter Six

Will rubbed his hands together, trying to stay warm. It was July. Hard to believe it was so cold. Then again, Mark Twain had commented, "The coldest winter I ever saw was the summer I spent in San Francisco." Will now understood the saying.

"C'mon, ladies," he said, sticking his head into the Lincoln Town Car. "We're not supposed to be stopped here."

The driver nodded at Will, silently thanking him. After all, it would be the driver who received the ticket from an over-zealous San Francisco police officer.

Sadie thrust her bare tanned leg out, waiting for Will to help her. He grabbed her hand, trying not to look at the skirt that had ridden up her thigh.

Eventually, the girls emerged, and the driver was set free to find a place to park until he was needed. Will ushered Sadie and the two four-year-olds to the park.

With the twins running to the playground, Sadie stopped Will and tapped his chest. "I knew you were the right man for the job. Saving my girls and all. Like I said before, you're getting on my good side."

Will scowled at her. "Look, I need this job. It pays good, and I owe child support."

"You don't worry about that," she said, tapping his chest again. "I can clear up your child support in a second."

"I prefer to work for it."

Sadie gave him a lopsided grin. "Oh, you'll work for it."

Will grabbed her by the shoulders. "Listen, Brace and Anders aren't messing around. I have a feeling that when someone gets fired, there's a muzzle flash and a spent round involved."

"You're so dramatic, Will. You should've been an actor."

You don't know how right you are.

"I'm not messing around with another man's wife. Period! That may be why Charlie's not with us anymore."

"Please," Sadie scoffed, looking away for a moment. Then her eyes locked in on Will's lips. "I don't go for just any man. He has to be strong enough to handle me."

"Cole seems very capable," he said, lightly pushing her away.

"You're wrong there. He's all about his career. I was his fixer-upper. His Project Number Two. Now that he's fixed me up, he's less interested in me. If I wasn't the mother of his children, I might be joining Charlie."

Sadie went to her girls. As she did, Will stood back, thinking about the report he would make to his handler. *This is going to be some good shit here. Schneider is going to crap his pants.*

• • •

His phone buzzed twice. Loosening his tie, Will flipped the phone open and read the text. "Damn," he said out loud to no one.

With Sadie and the twins locked safely in their suite after four hours of playing, he'd been looking forward to undressing, slipping into a fresh cotton robe, and ordering room service. Now, this.

He grabbed the phone and straightened his tie. Then, he walked to Brace's suite. The entire crew was there—eighteen men and women. The most striking of them all was Sterry. She seemed like Brace's lover, but she didn't show any signs of affection. Maybe their relationship was more brother-sister. Will made up his mind to find out.

Brace covered some specific details for the next day's events. He was wrapping up the meeting when Anders handed him a note. Brace read it and grinned.

"Okay, folks, you're dismissed," he said. "Those who are on duty, back to your posts. Those who aren't, get some rest. You'll need it."

Will secretly smiled. He'd get that robe and meal after all.

"Will, can I talk to you a moment?" Brace asked.

"Sure," he replied, his hand on the door.

When the room cleared, Will stood in front of Brace, wondering what he'd done. His pulse was racing, so he slowed his breathing, trying to reach the equilibrium Dr. Z had taught him.

"We have a situation," Brace said, twisting his skull ring.

Have I been made? Will thought, as his hand eased to the Glock.

"Charlie handled some backup for me. However, he's been dismissed." Brace picked up a toothpick and stuck it in his mouth. "My main crew is on an assignment and not available. I'm a man down. I need you to go on an op with me. Are you up for that?"

"Sure," Will said, breathing easier. "Whatever you need."

"I saw your record. You had two different homicide cases dismissed. On one of them, your attorney filed for self-defense. So that tells me you shot and killed someone for some reason."

"Yes," Will said softly.

Brace pulled out his toothpick and pointed it at Will. "This op, there might be something like a self-defense thing happening. Only there won't be any police coming to this scene. Do you understand what I'm saying?"

Will nodded. "I think so."

"Are you up for a job like that? Because I need to know I can absolutely trust you. You will literally have my back."

"I've never fired this Glock. I'm used to my Browning. Am I going to have to fire it?"

Brace sucked air between his teeth. "If you do, something's gone terribly wrong. You're a backup and a lookout. The Glock is a point and shoot. The safety is built into the trigger. If you drop it, the gun can't fire. It's a simple but effective design. That's why we use them. Can I count on you?"

Will hesitated, working up the drama, playing the part. "From the moment I took this job, you guys have been first class. The suits. The weapon. The food. You've taken great care of me. And the pay is exactly what I need for my child support. So, you can take this to the bank: I've got your back."

Brace's face brightened. "If this op goes well, you'll earn a bonus."

"Then I can absolutely promise you that it'll go well."

"Alright. That's what I want to hear. Green will get you fitted out. We'll meet downstairs in ten minutes."

"Thanks for choosing me, Brace," Will said as he left.

"It was either you or Sadie," Brace muttered loud enough for him to hear.

Will suppressed a laugh all the way back to his room.

•••

The black Range Rover cruised east over the Bay Bridge. Glenn Frey's "You Belong to the City" boomed out through the speakers. It was an appropriate song since it seemed like the Sterlings owned the San Francisco Bay Area. Since their arrival, they'd been treated like royalty.

Visits with politicians. Lunches with entertainers. Dinners with CEOs. Will marveled at the people fawning over their money. It cast doubt on if he was doing the right thing.

Maybe these people are legitimate?

But then he rolled the illegal Gen 24 silencer with his fingers. Green had given it to him. It was the first felony he'd witnessed. Hopefully, the first of many more to come.

Will sat in the very back of the SUV, his hand in his jacket pocket. The Gen 24 was cutting edge. Silent. No heat. This made it easy and safe to unscrew when the rounds were spent. The Sterlings had the best of everything. Even his Glock seemed to be specially milled.

A few days earlier, Will had taken his weapon apart and studied the components. The spring had definitely been upgraded. And the firing pin had to be a different metal—one less likely to chip or shatter. Even though the Glock was a reliable favorite of law enforcement, the Sterlings had apparently analyzed the minuscule weaknesses—a 100,000-to-one problem—and fixed the one. Nothing was left to chance.

Will studied the area they were traveling through. When Green, who was driving, turned off the highway, Will sensed they were getting close. Now, they were in a middle-class Oakland neighborhood. He noticed a mixture of Asians, Africans, and Latinos—probably immigrants and refugees. Obviously, it was an international section.

Green turned off the music and stopped the SUV at a corner house. Brace and Anders exited the vehicle, quietly signaling Will to follow them. The three began walking on the sidewalk, away from the corner house as the SUV took off.

The group covered a full block before turning north. After a half block, they turned on another street and walked back in the direction they had started. A few addresses had passed by when Anders tapped Brace's shoulder. "There's the house," he whispered, "364."

In the fading sunlight, Will analyzed the white frame structure. It was a typical middle-class home, poorly maintained, with green trim and paint chipping from age. On the dusty porch sat plastic flowers held by a dirty vase. A circular drive through the front yard had crepe myrtles hiding the house from the street. It was an excellent setup for a stealthy approach.

Or an ambush.

Just at the edge of the property, Brace turned to Will and Anders. "Glove up," he said, slipping on black rubber gloves. The two followed suit.

"Anders and I are going inside to have a chat," Brace whispered to Will. "You'll follow us in and hang by the entrance. Watch our back for anyone who might pop up. If there's trouble inside and we need help, you provide it—silently. If we have it under control, you stay by the front door and don't let anyone in. Focus on the street. Green has the back door. The car is in the alley if we need to bail. Understand?"

"I understand," Will said clearly.

As they walked on the circular drive, Will noticed the two men in front of him had their guns out and silencers on. He quietly pulled his Glock out and attached his silencer.

Brace stepped onto the concrete porch and put his ear to the door. A TV from inside boomed out. Will guessed it was a soccer match from the Spanish play-by-play announcers.

After thirty seconds or so, Brace removed a tool from his jacket pocket and kneeled to work on the lock. Will looked around. The crepe myrtles provided excellent screening. It didn't appear that the street was heavily traveled.

Brace continued working with the lock. Just when Will thought Brace had run into a roadblock, he turned the knob and stood up, a gun in his right hand.

Brace swung the door open. Three quick *pssssts* punctuated the air. Anders followed Brace in.

By the time Will reached the entrance, he saw Brace pointing a Glock at two Hispanics who were sitting in chairs watching TV. The chairs sat low in a seventies-style step-down living room. Brace signaled to Anders to check out the rest of the house.

Will peeked inside. To his left were two dead Hispanics—a male on top of a female. They had been having sex when Brace walked in. Now, they dripped blood onto an overstuffed couch.

The female's eyes were still open, her face wearing an expression of surprise. Except for the dark hole in her forehead, it appeared she was still alive.

"Turn off the TV, amigo," Brace said.

One of the men pressed a remote, and the place went quiet.

Anders reappeared from the hall. "It's clear."

Brace walked around to face the two men. "So, I hit a parlay, and you don't pay me the $300,000 you owe me."

"I-I didn't know it was you that placed that bet," the man stammered. "I'm g-getting the money together. I just need some time. The $20,000 bet surprised me."

"Your point spread surprised me. That's why I had my man place the bet with you and not some Vegas sportsbook. Then I was surprised a second time when you wouldn't take my calls. That made me very disappointed. I thought about going on Yelp to complain or maybe the Federal Trade Commission but decided to voice my objections to you personally. You don't have a problem with that, do you?"

"No, Brace," the man said, holding his hands up. "I'll get your money together. Just let me go to the bank and talk to my banker."

"Not just yet. How much money do you have in this place?"

"It's not my place. He's a client. I was coming here to collect."

Brace shook his head. "You didn't look like you were collecting. It looked like you two were watching a soccer match." He turned to Anders. "Search these guys for anything."

Anders turned their pockets out, collecting some cash and cell phones.

"I could find that much in my couch cushions," Brace said, disgusted.

Green appeared at the back door. "All clear in the alley."

Brace glanced at Will. "Post up at the front door and keep an eye out for anyone."

Will turned his back, keeping his head just inside the door so he could listen.

"So, this guy is just a client, right?" Brace asked.

"Yes, he is. I swear!"

Psssst.

"Oh no!" the bookie moaned. "Please. I'll get your money. My cousin is Carlos Santos."

"I know that," Brace said. "Is Carlos going to get you out of this jam?"

"Maybe."

"When's the last time you talked with Carlos?"

"A few months ago."

"We'll check out your cell phone," Brace said, raising his Glock. "Now it's time to cancel your friends and family plan."

"Wait! I can have the mon—"

Psssst.

"You stay by the back door," Brace said to Green. "Anders. You go through each room and collect any electronics. And look for address books, anything that has names and phone numbers. If in doubt, grab it. I'll check this room for any goodies."

Will moved away from the door to watch the street. He couldn't believe he'd just witnessed four murders. Then, it hit him.

If the Oakland PD rolled up right now, what would I say? There are four dead bodies behind me. I'm carrying an illegal silencer. Not only would my career dissolve, but I could be facing a murder rap. I'd have to rely on the Bureau to get me out of that mess. Who knows how they would fall?

Will heard Brace coming closer to the front door. He didn't dare turn around.

"Time to move," Brace said to someone else, obviously on the phone. "Two rooms, maybe some hall work... Yes. There are four buckets of paint that need to be removed. Need some plastic for that so we don't spill more paint... Park in the circular drive... All right."

Will felt Brace's hand on his shoulder. "A white box truck is going to show up in twenty minutes. The sides will say Party Central. Sterry will be in the cab with a crew. Anyone else shows up, don't let them inside. Shout so I can hear you. Understand?"

"Yes."

Sure enough, twenty minutes later, the headlights of a white box truck swung up into the driveway, pulling in far enough so its rear was right where Will stood. Sterry hopped down from the passenger's side of the cab and went to the back. Ignoring Will, she unlocked the catch and knocked on the door. It rolled up.

Out came six men, each with black hair, black eyes, and the same skin tone as Sterry. Will studied their faces and believed they were Iranians.

One of the men handed Sterry a green duffel bag. She smiled and nodded as she walked past Will. Stopping at the entrance, she pulled out a can and sprayed it around the area of the first two shootings.

Luminol. They're checking for hidden traces of blood.

Sure enough, they turned off the lights and went to work.

Will left all that and stepped around the back of the truck, catching a glimpse of the construction equipment and materials stacked neatly inside. Then he eased himself to the edge of the crepe myrtles. Someone could still show up. He had to be vigilant.

•••

Will had been standing at his post for at least thirty minutes when Green tapped him on the shoulder. "Hey, they're about to start the repairs. If you need to hit the head, now is the time. Otherwise, you'll be locked out for hours."

"Sure," Will said, desperately wanting to see how the operation worked. "I'll be right back."

Will left Green and once again walked past the rear of the truck. By now, it was half empty.

He stepped over the threshold and saw men working everywhere. Anders stood next to Brace. "The two on the couch are still stuck together," Anders said, rubbing his bald head. "Does that count as one or two?"

Brace frowned. "Well, the Bible says two will become one. So, it's one."

"We should all be so lucky to go out like that," Anders said, chuckling and rubbing his shaved head.

Plastic had been unrolled and was being tacked along the floor. One of Sterry's crew had a sheetrock saw and was busy cutting a neat square from the wall where some blood had splattered. Will walked past all of it to get to the bathroom.

Once inside, he locked the door and relieved himself. He washed his hands and made sure his DNA was flushed down the drain. Then he placed his used paper towels into a loose plastic bag on the floor.

These guys are definitely efficient.

When he exited the bathroom, he noticed the dead had been placed in black body bags. And Sterry was directing everything and everyone.

She's a cleaner. That's why she's here.

Brace appeared from the living room. "Move to the sidewalk and keep an eye out. Tell Green to go to the alley and stay in the Rover. If anyone comes, just move out of the way and reposition it when he can. Both of you have your phone out, ready to call Anders if there's a problem. Understand?"

"I understand," Will said again.

...

According to his watch, Will had been standing for almost four hours since his last bathroom break. Twice, Brace had come out with cold water bottles to check on him. Will had been alert and on duty each time.

Now, it was a few minutes past one in the morning. He wanted to get back to the hotel room.

Will had spent most of the night memorizing all the details of his time with the Sterlings. The memory techniques he'd learned from Dr. Z, and honed during his years of undercover work, would pay off... whenever he could get free to make a report.

So far, the only chance he'd seen was the morning of the twins' false abduction. Will had wanted to eat a leisurely breakfast and make sure no one was watching him. Then, he would pay the tab and slip out through the kitchen by tipping a waiter. Outside, he planned on finding a payphone and calling in. But that had been derailed when the yellow cab showed up. Now, he could only hope for some time off.

Out of nowhere, an Oakland PD SUV rolled up to the curb and stopped. Will cautiously approached it. "Can I help you, officer?"

"Yeah," the cop said, rolling down his window. "A thirteen-year-old girl ran away from home. She's Korean. Have you seen anyone walking around?"

"No, I haven't," Will replied. "But I'll keep an eye out."

"You guys having a party or something?" The cop asked, looking around Will at the truck.

"Twenty-fifth anniversary party. The crew is loading everything up since the party is over. I'm sort of the traffic director."

The cop nodded. "Okay. Call 9-1-1 if you see the girl."

"Sure will," he said, stepping back.

Slowly—too slowly for Will—the patrol SUV drove off. Will moved back to the sidewalk.

A few minutes later, Brace stood next to him. "What was that all about?"

Will told him.

"You're a damn fine man!" Brace said. "Good job. But keep an eye out. They might be back."

"I will."

"I'll man your post for a few minutes while you go to the alley and tell Green we'll be ready to leave in fifteen minutes. Then, come back here."

Will did as Brace instructed. As he walked through the house, the fresh smell of paint made him blink. Compact heaters blasted hot air at the walls. A tiny light helped him navigate his way among the layers of plastic. Except for the whir of the heaters, everything was quiet.

Will talked to Green, then made another trip through the house. Fifteen minutes after he resumed his post, Sterry's team had rolled up the plastic and loaded the heaters and leftover tools. Will was waved back to the house.

"Turn the air down to fifty-five and open up the windows," Brace said to two Iranians. "We need this hot air and paint smell out of here."

Will noticed that they all wore rubber gloves and booties. Sterry had a blacklight in her hand and snapped it off, satisfied every trace of DNA was gone. As the entire crew exited the house, they removed their shoe coverings and rubber gloves, placing them in a bag.

"Let's walk around to the side of the house," Brace said to Will and Anders. "I don't want anyone else inside since it's clean now."

When they arrived at the SUV, a voice behind Will startled him.

"Take off your gloves and put them in here," Sterry said.

Brace and Anders removed their gloves while Green and Will had stuffed them in their pockets hours earlier. Sterry held out a box for the gloves. The men dropped them into an opening.

Sterry hit a button and a red glow appeared. Thirty seconds later, liquid dribbled out into a form on the side.

They waited another thirty seconds until she poured cold water over the form. A quick tap and out popped a small horse. She handed it to Brace and he put it in his pocket.

Will shook his head before climbing into the SUV.

Man, these guys are complete professionals. Washington is never going to believe this.

Chapter Seven

Will pushed the food cart into the hall. After sleeping until three that afternoon, he'd ordered room service, enjoying a relaxing meal. With a meeting planned in Brace's suite at five, he showered, shaved, and dressed. Will had plenty of time to decompress, yet the images of dead bodies repeatedly cycled through his mind. He had to find a way to call his handler and download his memory.

There was a knock on his door. Will opened it to find Green standing there.

"I have gifts," Green said, holding a bag.

Will waved him in. "Are they good gifts?"

Green opened a bag and tossed a new pair of rubber gloves and a roll of money onto the bed.

"How much is that?" Will asked.

"A five-grand bonus. You're moving up the food chain."

I'll be a predator soon, Will thought as he started counting the money.

"You have two glasses?" Green asked, removing an expensive bottle of scotch from the bag.

"Of course," Will said, grabbing two from the lavatory.

Green poured the scotch. "Here's to your bright future. Just don't go climbing over me."

Will clinked glasses with him. "I'm not climbing over anyone. I'm just trying to take care of my responsibilities and stay in the free world."

"Deflecting those cops was smooth work," Green said, pushing his ballcap back. "And keeping the twins from being kidnapped is putting you in the Sterling's Hall of Fame. If you aren't careful, they might try to adopt you."

Will grinned. "It was a good outcome. But is there really a threat of kidnapping?"

Green swallowed. "Do some research, bro. Sinatra's son cost $240,000. Steve Wynn's daughter $1.4 million. Getty's grandson? Getty wouldn't pay, so they cut off the kid's ear. And Coors' grandson? He was killed *before* he could be returned. There's big business in kidnapping."

"Is that why Grayson has Brace?"

"Yep. Brace handles all the family's security. He's sort of a mercenary-for-hire for the super-rich. His Echo One Nine team is made up of top spec ops men. You'll rarely see them because they're usually pulling a job somewhere. If not, they stay hidden around the ranch."

"And Cole? What's his role?"

"He and his sister Victoria are the upstanding images of the family. He works for the government in intelligence. Supposedly brilliant. Gets it from Grayson, who got his start in military intelligence."

Anders opened the door.

"I need you," he said, staring at Green.

Green tossed back the last bit of scotch in his glass and handed the bottle to Will. "You keep this safe. We'll have a drink tomorrow." The two men left.

Will poured more scotch, kicking up his heels on the edge of the bed. Cradling the glass with both hands, he went over everything he needed to report. It was a lot of megabits.

"Memory is a tool that can be controlled," Dr. Z had told him, waving around a half-chewed plant stem. "We'll teach you techniques to store information in your brain for later recall."

They had.

Will learned the top-down method. The key players and the crimes they committed were at the top. Once he had that down, he tackled the next level of detail—the number of gunshots and drugs, the assistant players, the locations, and dates and times. Below that were details like clothing, cars, and conversations. Testifying to small details like the location of a potted plant in the backyard or the breed of cat sleeping on the porch allowed juries to buy the rest of the story.

Dr. Z had removed the pressure to remember everything. Instead, he gave Will the tools to store the right information and go over it during slow times until he could download it to his handler.

One of the best tools Dr. Z had given him was storing the memories in mental closets. Will could put away the details of his real family and open the door to his undercover persona. Dr. Z had said, "You can immerse yourself in a story world before you step on the set and start filming. Like a real camera, your eyes are binary. On or off. Light or dark. True or false. You choose when to hit the switch."

Will found that by reviewing his family's photo album, he could keep his wife and twins in the forefront of his mind. There were birthdays, ages, anniversaries, scars, freckles, favorite colors, and explicit detail that filled in each relation-ship. Before going undercover, Will learned that reviewing an album of his undercover persona had the same effect. It was exactly like his family album, but for his undercover family. There were fewer photos, but the level of detail was the same.

When Will had opportunities to slip away from his under-cover operations to go back home, first, he would spend time poring over his family album. After an hour or so, he was back to normal, or at least as close as possible. When it was time to transition back to undercover, he would study his criminal family's book to refresh his memory.

That process was hard on some agents, but Will found he could do it—especially when he had nightmares of a bad guy putting a round between his eyes and shutting off his camera for good.

All he had to do now was survive long enough to get to a safe phone.

•••

The men formed a semi-circle around Brace, listening to him explain various security issues. "Tonight's a big night. My father is flying in to join Cole in accepting another environmental award. The banquet will be full of high-net-worth people. You'll be running into their security teams. Unfortunately, we aren't coordinating with any of them. Too many amateurs. We run our own security ship here. Keeps the leaks down. Any questions?"

As usual, there were none.

"Good," Brace said. "For those of you on the list, get into your tux and be downstairs at six. Let's go, gentlemen. And remember, let's get them before they get us."

Will spoke up. "I don't have a tux. I only have suits."

"You sure about that?" Brace said.

"Pretty sure," Will replied.

"Check your closet and call Green if you need a tux."

Will filed out, grabbing his phone so he could call Green. Yet, when he went to his closet, there was a brand-new tux hanging on the closet rod. It had a shirt and a vest. On the floor was a new pair of shoes.

"I'll be damned," he said to himself, shaking his head. "Let's see if it fits."

It did. Perfectly.

On the closet shelf were two cufflinks and a small bottle of Burberry. Will slotted the cufflinks home before splashing on the eau de parfum. From past experience, he knew this meant a higher concentration of oils in the fragrance. Parfum lasted longer and smelled more intense. It also costed a lot more.

Would I expect anything less? he thought as he headed to the rendezvous point.

• • •

Trays of elegant hors d'oeuvres circulated through the ballroom. High heels and low-cut blouses mingled with wealthy fat cats and skinny celebrities. The who's who of San Francisco was enough to distract an undercover agent like Will. Despite this, he held firm to the last-minute orders Green had given him just as his SUV had come to a stop. "Your only job is to stay with Sadie all night. Don't let her out of your sight. Even if she goes into the women's restroom, you go in there with her. You got it?"

"Yes," Will had said, amazed at the transformation of Green from a drinking buddy to a stern boss. Gone was his perpetual John Deere ballcap. In its place was a well-manicured military cut, gelled and perfectly combed.

Will positioned himself at the hotel entrance and waited.

It was an hour later when the Sterling entourage rolled up. Sadie and Cole were the last to exit. When Sadie stepped out of the long black limousine in her strapless red velvet Oscar de la Renta dress, Will was stunned. She looked incredible.

From that moment on, he was no farther than four to five feet away. Unfortunately, the closeness gave him the full show.

It was clear she had been drinking before she arrived. Her balance was off, requiring her to cling to Will's arm. He did his best to keep her steady, but it was apparent to everyone that she was hammered.

Once in the ballroom, she switched back and forth between mimosas and Patron Tequila straight. This made her look even more ridiculous.

Will waited until they were alone in a corner before grabbing her arm. "Stop drinking so much," he ordered. "You're embarrassing yourself and the family."

"Do these p-people know about my p-past?" she slurred.

Will's eyes narrowed intently. "Stop it now. Before you pass out."

Someone grabbed Will's shoulder. He turned to find Cole.

"Will, I just wanted to say how sorry I am for what I did to you earlier. It's unlike me to act before I have the facts. You were the hero, not the goat."

"No problem," Will said. "I've already forgotten it."

Cole was about to say something else when an emcee got everyone's attention. Grayson Sterling had arrived.

"Excuse me," Cole said, abruptly leaving Will with Sadie.

The presentation of the award soon followed. Will stayed closed to Sadie as she staggered around. She tried to flirt with any man she brushed up against. It was incredibly embarrassing.

Will snuck a glance at Cole, hoping he'd come and do something. But he appeared to be in his element. He knew everyone by their first name. Cole Sterling was putting on a masterclass in social schmoozing.

Will spotted Grayson near Cole. The man looked like something out of Hollywood. He had a full head of hair, mostly gray with just a hint of black. This set off his black eyebrows, making him appear younger, more energetic, yet distinguished. His perfect nose was rounded at the tip. Below a clean-shaven and moisturized face was a tan neck surround by a button-down collar and a black bow tie. A gorgeous brunette clung to his arm. Will was sure he had seen her before, maybe as a former Miss Texas or Miss America winner. It seemed like the pair had just stepped out of a Viagra advertisement.

Grayson moved around from couple to couple, a circle of six bodyguards floating just behind him. Will had never seen these guys before. They hadn't been to Brace's meeting. But one thing was certain: They were pros.

If they have me guarding Sadie, I can see how she ranks in the family.

"I have to tee tee," Sadie said, tugging on Will's arm.

"I'm going with you," he said.

"I t-thought so," she stammered.

The pair entered the ladies' restroom, where an older woman peered into the mirror, touching up her makeup. "Excuse me!" she said, glaring at Will. "Why are you in here?"

"It's my job," he replied casually.

Sadie entered a stall as a redheaded woman walked into the restroom.

"Oh, you're one of those… *security*," said the older woman.

"Yes, ma'am," Will replied.

The redheaded woman entered a stall. The older woman, speechless, curtly closed her purse and left.

When the redheaded woman washed her hands and left, Sadie opened the stall door and grabbed Will's belt, pulling him toward her.

"Come on," she begged. "Just a quickie."

"No!" he said, jerking free. "If you're finished, wash your hands and let's get out of here before another woman comes in."

"Who are y-you? The morality police?"

"I'm *your* police. And right now, I'm getting pissed. Wash up and let's go."

Three hours later, the evening had ended. A security meeting followed. With that over, Will went to his room and climbed into the shower, a headache splitting him in two. He let the warm water and steam soothe him as he rubbed his forehead, hoping to chase away the pain.

Fearful of a camera, he removed a pill from a secret compartment in the bottom of his can of shaving cream. Then, he paused.

So far, he hadn't needed any help getting to sleep. Yet for some reason, he did tonight.

Was it Sadie's blatant proposition? Or something else?

Will tossed the pill back with a big gulp of water before reaching over and turning out the light. Then, he prayed for no nightmares.

Chapter Eight

The Gulfstream executed a smooth landing at Meacham Airport. A pack of Range Rovers raced over the tarmac to collect Brace and his team. That process took mere minutes. With the men and their gear loaded up, the SUVs set off south. Will assumed he was heading to the family's sprawling ranch.

He had been in the Range Rover forty-five minutes when civilization dropped away and the country appeared. Then, the asphalt road turned into dirt. He would have been concerned, but no one else in the SUV appeared to be.

Fifteen minutes later, the SUV slowed, turning right onto an asphalt entrance. The massive stone walls on each side displayed a large F above a horizontal line. Below the line was an equally sized A. Next to the F Bar A was the word Ranch. A small sign read, *The Sterlings Welcome You.*

The Range Rover approached a mechanical gate, causing it to slide to the side. Will's vehicle pulled in behind the leader.

A hundred yards in, they stopped at a guard booth and a lowered crossing bar. Two men operating the station checked the driver's credentials while looking inside the vehicles. They let Will's SUV pass.

Another hundred yards down were two decorative stone structures. Though they appeared to be empty, Will noticed several horizontal slots cut into the stone. Behind them, no doubt were men with machine guns. If a vehicle blew past the first checkpoint without clearance, this one would issue a .50 caliber citation.

The Range Rovers pulled into an expansive parking area near the large house, but not too near. Porters with golf carts waited on the SUVs to unload so they could take the luggage and any guests who needed help finding their quarters.

It was a smart setup. By not allowing a vehicle to get close, a surprise attack was minimized. It forced guests to walk another one hundred yards to the entrance. If someone slipped by the first few layers of security, they'd be exposed now. And a car bomb would have less effect parked so far away.

Will studied the area for details. After the asphalt parking area, an impressive circular drive came into view. Its caramel-colored concrete was stamped with a unique stone pattern. In the middle of the unused drive was a large fountain. Tropical plants ringed the base.

The ranch house had a stone exterior. Designed in a Mediterranean style, there was a second floor with a high-pitched roof. But it didn't cover the entire footprint. All around the second floor were low-pitched roofs. This created spacious verandas with clay-tiled floors and slow-turning ceiling fans. For July in Texas, it seemed like the perfect place to take a nap.

Anders motioned for Will to follow him. As they passed the edge of the house, Will noticed the windows had working metal shutters—another great defensive tool during an attack.

"How big is this place?" Will asked, pointing to the ranch house.

"Twelve thousand square feet. But you won't be staying there. You'll be in the barn."

Will nodded, hoping he was kidding.

A large staff building sat a short distance from the house. Anders showed Will his apartment on the first level. It had a kitchenette, bedroom, and bathroom. A wall separated the kitchen from the bedroom.

"Who else stays here?" Will asked.

"You have your own apartment. Your neighbors are me, Green, and Hector. Charlie's apartment is vacant since he's not with us anymore."

"It seems larger than that," Will said.

"It is. Out your back door is a hallway," Anders said, pointing. "Down there is the bunkhouse. It holds ten men who work on the property."

"Oh," Will said, happy he was considered high enough to have his own place. "Where does Sterry stay?"

"You don't worry about her," Anders said with a sly grin. "She's even more off-limits than Sadie."

Will blinked nervously. "I'm not interested in her. I just may have to protect her."

Anders continued grinning. "She can take care of herself. And she stays in the main house. There are two rooms off the kitchen. Sterry and Mrs. White stay there."

"Who's Mrs. White?"

"The head cook. If the place was on fire, Mr. Sterling would first save the twins, then go back inside to rescue Mrs. White. That says a lot." Anders hesitated. "Are those all your questions? I feel like I'm in a police interview."

Will's heart skipped a beat, but he kept a straight face. "Sorry. I've been through too many of those. That's all I have."

Anders opened Will's door. "Your luggage will be here shortly. Unpack it and use the new stuff we have in the closet. It's yours to keep." He peeled off a wad of bills. "You're staying here now. Go into town and cancel your lease, utilities, whatever. Get your gear and dispose of your furniture. Take a couple of days to get sorted out if you need to. And get rid of your Browning. You'll only be using what we give you." He reached into his back pocket. "Here's a new cell phone. Let me have your old one."

"But my truck is still at the airport," Will said, handing him the phone.

"I have a driver outside waiting to take you there."

"Okay, I'll get everything cleared away and be back."

"We're counting on it," Anders said as he left.

Will heard a strange edge to his voice, but let it go. As soon as Anders was gone, Will checked out the new luggage. It was Louis Vuitton, just like he'd seen on the plane. And it was exquisitely crafted. There appeared to be some hidden compartments behind the lining. He made a mental note to check them out later.

When his luggage arrived, he unpacked everything and put it away. Then he grabbed his Browning, car keys, and old bags and left. This would be his chance to make a report. He couldn't wait.

• • •

The Range Rover arrived at the airport at one in the afternoon. The driver hung around to make sure Will's truck started.

It did.

As Will drove away, he considered the possibility that Brace had placed a tracker on his truck. He knew there was one buried deep in the body panel. The tech guys from the Bureau had installed it. This allowed someone in the main office to keep track of him. It was likely Brace had done it, too.

Will drove east on Highway 183, thinking about his prep work. He exited early and found the large complex he had set up in his backstory. Parking in the rear of the property, he sat in his vehicle, thinking about his next move.

After fifteen minutes—long enough to ensure he hadn't been followed—he slipped out of the driver's seat and crawled underneath the truck. He inspected the undercarriage but couldn't find anything. His inspection was limited. The best way to check would be putting the truck up on a rack. But there was no way he could risk that.

A man approached him from behind, his shoes kicking some gravel. Will reached for his Browning and spun around.

"Whoa," Dan said, his hands raised. "It's the good guys."

Will relaxed. "You got your cast off. Let's find a place to talk."

They walked up to the second level, with Dan taking each step carefully. Will found a vacant laundry room and closed the door.

"We've been worried about you," Dan said.

Will spilled out a shortened version of his past week. "I need to leave this truck here. It might be tracked. Can you take me home?"

"Sure, but you need to make a report fast. That stuff's gold!"

"I will. I also need someone to backstop this apartment complex, so they'll say I had recently rented a place there and came in to close it out."

"Got it handled."

"Okay," Will said. "Let's get out of here."

Dan stopped him. "Before we leave, I've got some news for you."

Will studied his partner's face. "What kind of news?"

Dan nervously coughed. "I spotted Jennifer with some guy at a sporting goods store in Dallas. I happened to be there picking up some equipment."

"What were they doing?" Will asked quietly.

"Shopping."

"Anything else?"

"Holding hands and looking happy," Dan said reluctantly.

Will pursed his lips, pinching his chin several times. An awkward silence settled in.

Dan pulled his cell phone out of his pocket. "Look, I ran some background on him. He's a plastic surgeon. Here's his photo." He showed the screen to Will. "Jennifer services his office, or whatever you call it. He's been married two times and has a special needs child."

Will looked away from the phone and stared at the wall. "Maybe it's just a short fling."

Dan waited a beat. "I'm sorry, man, but I ran Jennifer's phone. There are texts and selfies. Lots of them. They're not good."

Will shook his head. "This can't be happening." He continued shaking his head. "Did she see you?"

"No. I'm sure of that." Dan put away his phone. "Still want to go home?"

Will took in a deep breath before exhaling. "Yeah."

"Are you going to confront her?"

"I don't know yet."

"Okay," Dan said, putting his hand on Will's shoulder. "I'm here for you."

"You're a real partner. Most guys wouldn't have said a word."

"Thanks. I know it's hard to hear. You're not going to do anything stupid, like Gates. Right?"

"Probably not," Will muttered.

"I guess I'll have to be satisfied with that. C'mon. Let's go."

The two men filed out of the laundry room, with one of them limping and the other carrying a heavy heart.

•••

Dan pulled up to Will's house and let him out. "I'll wait here for you, buddy. Just take your time."

Will nodded.

Cautiously, he turned the doorknob and entered his home. It didn't feel like his now. Instead, another man was with his wife. It felt like the other man's place.

Neither Jennifer nor the twins were home. It was probably for the best since he hated confrontations. That's why he did undercover work.

He roamed through the house, studying the mail and new photos on the refrigerator. His kids were at summer camp. He had totally forgotten. Yet another reason he should have studied his family book first.

Will wanted to linger for hours, but he couldn't. He needed to get to the offsite location to make a report.

Quickly, he stuffed more casual clothes into his duffel bag. Then, he removed some photos of his twins and carefully set them in a side pouch.

Before he left, he picked up the phone in the den and called his wife. She didn't answer. This allowed him to leave a sweet message.

Maybe there's still a chance, he thought.

After locking the front door, he rejoined Dan in his car.

"You okay?" Dan asked.

"No, but I'm dealing with it."

"Alright. Let's get you to the offsite. Maybe some work will take your mind off it."

Dan drove them to the offsite location. The place was deserted and lonely. Will sat at his desk, typing his report into the computer. It took more than two hours to get it right. He was sure this would make a big splash.

After he finished, he pulled out his sons' photos and spread them over his desk. He touched them, wishing they were real. Then, he placed them in his family book. He knew he couldn't take them with him. Instead, he studied the FBI's computer-generated photos in his inbox. The two fake twins looked like him. The resemblance was spooky. These were the photos he'd put around his apartment on the Sterling ranch.

Will glanced at his watch. "Hey, Dan, are you ready?"

"Sure," his partner said. "Let's roll."

• • •

Will shifted uncomfortably in the chair. He was growing tired of this place. And he was frustrated that the questions never changed.

"How are you sleeping?" Dr. Clark asked.

"Surprisingly, great," he replied. "I'm on assignment right now, so I don't have the bad dreams."

The psychiatrist typed in some notes. "That's interesting. How is your wife?"

Will shifted again. "I just found out she's having an affair with a doctor. I'm not surprised."

"What are you going to do about it?"

"Nothing right now. As soon as I finish this investigation, I'll patch things up."

"Why don't you go home now and deal with it?"

"I can't," Will replied, avoiding eye contact.

"Why not?"

"This undercover work, it's my career. My men are counting on me."

"What men?"

"The men at the Bureau. The ones here locally and in Washington. I'm on a big case."

"But you're living another life, one that's false," Dr. Clark said.

"But it's one I control. I can make up anything I want to be."

"That's dangerous. Especially when you lose your identity."

"Yeah, it is. But that's the nature of undercover work. It's addicting at times, like playing a life or death video game. I just need to get to the next level, and I'm done."

Dr. Clark frowned. "Okay. Let's talk about your relationship with your partner."

Chapter Nine

The alarm went off.

Will reached over and hit the snooze button. Staring at the ceiling, he tried to reorient himself.

Where am I?

He recalled the explosions at the biker bust in Arizona. From there, he'd come home to his wife and twins, spending over a month in his own bed. Then, he'd traveled to San Francisco, where he'd inserted himself into the Sterling family. From there, he'd landed back in Fort Worth and traveled to his home.

Home. My wife. Another man!

It was all coming back.

Will had gone to the offsite location and raced back here, the Sterling ranch just south of Granbury. He could've returned home and confronted his wife but had decided against it. He would have been in such bad shape he couldn't have come back. His big whale would swim away for someone else to harpoon.

Will thought about getting up before deciding to stay in bed for a few minutes. He needed time to get his brain working, to crawl back into his undercover skin.

He studied the ceiling and walls, looking for a camera.

There must be at least one in here—maybe a light or the smoke detector. I'm sure of it. No way Brace would let me stay on the ranch without having me under watch. I wouldn't.

Will remembered another undercover job when he was supposed to place a bug in the ceiling of some drug dealer. Things had been going well until he fell through the dropdown ceiling tiles. It had been a huge mess to clean up. He'd barely finished before security came in to check out some movement on their monitors.

Later, he'd planted a camera in a doll's eye. That worked fantastically. And the face of the defendant at trial when Will testified where the camera had been planted was priceless.

Eventually, Will swung his feet out of bed and turned off the alarm before the snooze time ran out. Slowly, he showered and dressed in one of his suits, continually looking for cameras but finding none.

It was already hot outside. Will closed and locked his door with the key Anders had given him. Looking around, he spotted a wall-mounted circular exhaust fan used in commercial kitchens on the ranch house. He headed for that.

Even though the paved sidewalks went in this direction and that, he managed to find the back entrance. As he pulled the door open, he spotted two men already seated and eating.

The kitchen area was large and open. A woman worked at the stove while another woman assembled some pastries on a stainless-steel counter. A tall stainless-steel coffeepot with a spigot sat next to a tray full of mugs. Will grabbed one and pulled on the tap, assuming it was coffee. It was.

Since he didn't know the two men, he walked over to an empty table and sat down. Sipping on his coffee, Will studied the place, careful not to raise any suspicions. The police interview comment from Anders still bothered him.

Will was half finished with his coffee but still hadn't figured out how to get food. Did they place an order? Fix it themselves?

He was preparing to get up and ask when one of the women put a plate down in front of him. Startled, Will said, "You must be Mrs. White."

"I am," she said, the morning sun highlighting her hazelnut skin.

He looked over the plate. It was covered with fried eggs, toast, and yogurt.

"I know you don't like pig, so I left it off."

"Oh," he said, "that's right. Thank you. I'm Will."

"Honey, if I knew you didn't like pig, don't you think I know your name?"

"I guess so," he said, grinning. "I have a feeling you're not your average cook."

"And you are no detective," she said, patting him on the back before returning to the counter.

Will considered her comment as he dove into the breakfast. He was hungrier than he thought. Before he could get up for more coffee, the other woman refilled his cup.

"I'm Lupe, Will," she said.

"Nice to meet you. I'm... oh, you already know."

She smiled and went to the other men, refilling their cups. There was no doubt the Sterlings hired excellent help.

Green, his ballcap back in place, came through the back door and joined him. "How do you like the chow?" he asked.

"It's great," Will replied. "Do they always fix it for you?"

"No. For the field hands, they have a buffet out back on the patio. Sometimes, they'll have a buffet in here for us."

"Do we eat lunch in here too?"

"All your meals will be right here. For lunch, they'll have a spread of cold cuts or a pot of soup—something we can serve ourselves. For dinner, it's real nice—steak, tacos, fried catfish.

If you're hungry and they aren't around, just make yourself something from the fridge. If it has a note that says don't touch, that's for a later meal. Trust me, there's always plenty of leftovers."

"Wow," Will remarked. "These two women sure work a lot."

"They do. In a few minutes, a young Hispanic girl, Sylvia, will show up. She cleans the dishes and kitchen while Mrs. White and Lupe take a break. Usually, lunch has already been prepared, so that's easy for them. They'll take some downtime. Then Lupe and Mrs. White hit it for dinner, starting around two. It's a full day," Green said, sipping on his coffee.

"I guess Mrs. White is the boss."

"That's right. She supervises, but only cooks for Grayson and the kids."

"Huh," Will said. "She handed me my breakfast. She didn't cook it, did she?"

"No," Green said, chuckling. "I'm sure Lupe did."

Will wasn't so sure. "What happens now?"

"When we're finished, Brace will come in and give us our itinerary." The back door opened. "Here he comes now."

The muscular Sterling carried a pair of binoculars as he strode into the room. "Listen up. We're shooting at the range this morning. Change clothes and meet us down there."

Green, who had eaten earlier, slugged the last of his coffee. "Let's get dressed. Wait for me, and I'll show you how to get to the range."

Will followed him back to the room, changing quickly. Donning his Oakley sunglasses, he walked with Green past the large ranch house. Soon, a building on his right appeared.

"That's the Thirsty Goat. It's a watering hole, so we don't have to leave the ranch."

"Pretty slick," Will said. "Do we run up a tab or pay cash?" Green looked at him sideways. "Come on, Will. This is the Sterlings. Everything's free."

Will nodded as the corner of his mouth twitched into a small grin. Free liquor was always a nice perk.

They came to another larger building on their right. "This here is the mechanics' shop. They maintain the vehicles, ATVs, all the machinery. Hector runs it. He's in the room next to you. That's him pointing at everyone and yelling."

Will studied the stocky Hispanic who stood in the middle of a crowded shop. "That's a lot of equipment," Will said.

"This is a lot of ranch. Spans into two counties, with the Brazos River winding through it."

As the pair walked on, the terrain bent down, making it easier to walk.

"See that building?" Green said. "That's the barn. Holds forty or fifty horses. It has another crew run by Señor. He sleeps in the bunkhouse."

"Señor?" Will said, receiving a shrug in reply. "I guess some people are known by their last names and others their first."

"I don't know about that," Green replied. "There was a guy working here called Todd, which is my name. They called me Green to not confuse everyone. But when Anders joined us, Brace just started calling him Anders for some reason. So, who knows?"

Will filed that away. Maybe it would be important.

The sounds of gunshots punctuated the warm air. Both men had a solid sheen of sweat on their faces when they reached Brace.

"Green, you know what to do," Brace said through his dark pilot sunglasses. "Will, let me have your Glock."

Will handed it to him and watched as Brace placed it on a long wooden table and broke it down in five seconds. A few feet away, 100-round plastic ammo boxes were piled high.

"Can you put it back together?" he asked, stepping away from the pieces.

"I think so." Will knew he could do it in five seconds but took much longer.

"Great," Brace said, inspecting it. "Now, break it down and clean it."

Again, Will took his time. A nearby box held small rags and spray cans of Ballistol. Will applied some lubricant to the right spots and reassembled the Glock. Checking the action several times, he was satisfied.

Brace came back and inspected his work. "Good job. Grab a box of ammo and start on the close targets, increasing your distance with each box."

"How long do you want me to shoot?" Will asked.

"Until you've gone through three boxes. Then, we'll have a little contest and see who's top dog for the week."

Will shot all morning, the rising heat causing him to stop and wipe off the sweat. He liked the Glock, especially since he had qualified with it at the FBI. Instead of making headshots, he purposely landed rounds on the outer edges of the body, occasionally putting a round center mass.

During breaks, he saw other men shooting advanced laser-sighted weapons. At the far end, Sterry stood next to a man who had a Barrett .50 caliber sniper rifle tight against his shoulder. Every few minutes, he sent a round downrange.

Making a quick count, he realized there were more men present than the eight apartments in his bunkhouse. He wondered where the other men slept.

After they finished, two ranch hands replaced the targets and the shooting contest began. When it was Will's turn, he was sure he could come in the top two if he wanted. Instead, he finished near the bottom. Dr. Z would've approved.

"Okay, men," Brace said, "Mondo is the winner. He sits in the place of honor at the Thirsty Goat. Will, you're new. Whenever you're in the bar and Mondo comes in, you bow once to him, making sure he acknowledges you. He's like royalty. If you walk into the bar and Mondo's already there, you go up to him and bow. He gets this respect until we shoot next time. Got it?"

Will nodded.

"Good. Clean your weapons and head for lunch."

As Will broke his Glock down, Brace came up to him. "Nice shooting. You'll forget your Browning in no time."

"Thanks," Will said, studying the man through his sunglasses. "It's an easy gun. Well-balanced."

"This range is open during the day, weather permitting. You can shoot whenever you want. Once a month, we practice tactics in a mock house. Sometimes, we use live grenades."

Will winced when he heard the word "grenade." That last UC assignment had left a bad taste in his mouth—*literally*.

"Your itinerary is in your room," Brace said. "You're taking Sadie into town and picking up the twins from school."

"Sure thing," Will said.

Not only were these Sterlings first-class, but they worked their employees hard. Will admired that.

•••

A cleaned-up Will found his assigned Range Rover. His itinerary explained that most of the time, he would have a driver. Today, he didn't.

Climbing into the front seat, he took a few minutes to familiarize himself with the vehicle. It had all the bells and whistles. He was adjusting the mirrors when Sadie appeared in one of them.

"Let's go shopping," she said, sliding into the passenger's seat. "Drive on, Will." He cranked up the engine and took off.

They had gone a few miles when Sadie began working on him. "I want to go to the strip club and see Sandera," she whimpered.

"I can't," he said firmly. "It's not on the itinerary."

"Oh, come on, Will," Sadie said with a pout. "I got you this job."

"And I appreciate it. But I work for Green, Anders, and Brace now. I have to follow orders."

"Okay, but that's not going to stop me from working on you. I have a few weapons left to use."

Will said nothing.

"And they're good ones, too," she said, staring out her window.

Will focused on driving, thinking about the last time he had been with his wife. He hoped he had the ability and the brains to leave Sadie alone. Otherwise, he'd be joining Charlie.

•••

The pair spent the afternoon helping Sadie load up on clothes she didn't need and wouldn't ever wear. Will had seen a few price tags hanging in his wife's closet. He was sure there were a lot of tags in Sadie's closets, too.

At the proper time, Will swung by the preschool and picked up the twins. For some reason, they liked hugging Will now. Sadie stood back and smiled.

"Can we have some ice cream, Uncle Will?" Kodi asked.

"You're getting to be like your mother," he said. Sadie playfully hit his arm.

When he pulled into a Dairy Queen, cheers erupted from the back. He unbuckled the twins' car seats and took them inside. The little group ordered some Blizzards and sat in one of the red booths enjoying the treats. The entire time, Sadie stared at Will with a glow. He was sure this side trip had sealed the deal. If he wasn't in before, he was now.

...

Will arrived back at the ranch, escorting his passengers through the front entrance. Grayson, dressed in a fitted shirt and slacks, stood outside his office, giving Will his second glimpse of the patriarch. He seemed to be a man in control, comfortable in his own skin. Will could only imagine how he'd fair in prison after being used to all this.

As the twins dragged Grayson into his study, Will headed to the kitchen. After drawing a cup of coffee, he took a seat next to Mrs. White. She was slicing up pickles.

"Where is Mr. White?" he boldly asked.

"With Jesus," she replied.

"I'm sorry. How long has he been gone?"

"Twenty-four years. Some drug dealers shot at each other and hit my Clarence. I was working in this kitchen for the head cook Mrs. Underkoeffler, a strict German lady. With no place to go, Mr. Sterling moved me in here. When Mrs. Underkoeffler retired, I took over."

Will frowned. "Makes you want to find that dealer and put a bullet in him yourself."

"Yes. I prayed about it and asked God to forgive him. One day, a police detective called and said they'd found the dealer. He'd been bound and gagged and shot. Probably some other dealer. It never ends."

Will took a sip of coffee. "Any kids?"

"Two. Grown and gone. I hear from them now and then. I know you have twins. You're all Sadie talks about."

Before he could respond, Anders came in. "Brace wants to see you."

Will stood up, his heart pounding. In this business, he never knew if he'd been made.

Will found Brace outside of Grayson's office. "Give me your gun," Brace ordered.

Will's pulse was off the charts. This forced him to work on his breathing. He had to be ready to survive this if necessary.

"Have I done something wrong?" he asked.

"My dad wants to see you," Brace said, maintaining a serious demeanor. "We don't like to have guns in his office if we can help it. Especially with kids around."

He knew that was a flimsy excuse, but he had no choice. Will removed his Glock and handed it to Brace. Then he entered into the spacious office.

Unique, rare woods blended together to create an atmosphere that said the person in this office was highly successful. The artisan hardwood floor looked like it belonged in a palace. A full bar was situated ten feet from Grayson's desk. An unused fireplace behind Grayson would make an impressive scene during cold winters.

As jazz played in the background, Will took a seat in front of Grayson.

"I understand you have a way with Sadie," the family's leader said. "We can't keep men working with her. They don't last. What's your secret?"

Will relaxed. "She respects me because she knows I don't take her sh—*attitude*."

Grayson snorted. "Then you're the only one she respects."

"I'm her paddle."

"What?" Grayson said, leaning closer.

"I've learned the hard way that no matter who you are, there's a paddle for every ass. And for Sadie, I'm that paddle."

Grayson nodded. "Good for you." He held a crystal highball glass, swirling its contents. "Just make sure that paddle stays in your hand and not in her ass. Got it?"

"Got it," Will said firmly.

"Those twins are my most prized possessions. If you have a choice between saving the twins and Sadie, choose the twins. Understand?"

"I understand."

Grayson got up and poured himself a single malt scotch. His gray hair was even more impressive up close. When he retook his high-back leather chair, they talked horses, ranching, and hunting.

"You're smarter than your record shows," Grayson said. "Tell me about your education."

Will clicked on the reel of his undercover script. "I dropped out of high school. It was too boring. I started running with the wrong crowd. Got in trouble. I picked up a GED in prison, along with more education. Nothing else to do. I had time to focus."

"Do you read books?"

"Everything I can get my hands on," Will replied.

"Leaders are readers. I'm a big reader." Grayson shifted gears. "Brace says you're a good shot. Someone teach you?"

Will kept the script going. "I fell in with a Texas militia group. Kind of a cross between doomsdayers and seceders. Claimed they were their own country. It was security work at first, but then they taught me how to shoot. Later, I learned a few tactics. That's where my first murder rap came from."

Grayson held his glass up, inspecting the ice. "Sounds like you're well-rounded."

"Something like that. At least I learned to tell good scotch from bad," Will added, hoping he could enjoy a glass with the man and pick up more intel.

"Me too," Grayson said, laughing. But he didn't take the bait. "Thanks for your time. Please send Brace back in."

Will got up without saying a word and found Brace just outside the office. "He wants to see you now."

Brace handed his Glock back. "Listen," he said, invading Will's personal space. "No one moves up in the family as quickly as you have. Don't fuck it up. We're watching. I'm bumping you up to $3,000 a week."

"Thanks," Will said, showing genuine surprise.

"You've earned it. Just don't let me down."

Brace stepped into Grayson's office and pulled together two heavy wooden doors on rollers. A metal click told Will the magnets had aligned. From what he could tell, the doors not only provided soundproofing but protection as well.

Will walked back to his unit, chuckling inside. When Schneider found out how much he was making, he'd keep Will on the job just so he could use the money to fund other operations. Wouldn't that be a new day for the FBI?

Chapter Ten

Will's phone buzzed. "This is Will," he answered.

"I heard you got a raise," Green said, slapping him on the shoulder with his ballcap. "Time to celebrate. You up for the Thirsty Goat? I mean, unless you're reading the Bible or something."

"Not hardly, unless you told me the Sterlings wrote it."

"Don't put it past them," Green said, chuckling. "See you there."

Earlier, Will had eaten dinner with the rest of the men. Juicy slices of premium roast beef with homemade horse-radish and fresh sourdough rolls were on the menu. Sides of garlic mashed potatoes and a fresh salad were followed with a generous slice of coconut cream pie. He'd wolfed it all down.

After leaving dinner, he had patted his gut then made a note to watch his waistline. There was no better way to get bounced out of the FBI than gaining a ton of weight. And he didn't want to see what Brace would think of a man with a big gut.

Will hustled down the sidewalk, the sky still filled with sunlight. Pushing into the bar, he spotted Mondo sitting in his special chair. Will walked up to him and bowed. Mondo grinned before dismissing him with a wave.

"Over here," Green said from a secluded corner table. Country music streamed through ceiling speakers, giving them even more privacy. An extra beer stood at Will's spot.

"This for me?"

"You bet," Green replied. "I need to start kissing your ass, so you'll treat me well when you're my boss."

"I doubt that," Will said, tipping the bottle back.

"I don't. Listen, we have some business to discuss. A family meal is coming up."

"Okay. What's that like?" Will asked.

"Each month, Mr. Sterling insists the family get together for a weekend. They all fly in from wherever they are."

"Sounds important."

"It is. They eat Friday and Saturday nights and are required to leave their phones in a box outside the dining room. They share a breakfast Sunday morning before they're released."

"Okay. What's my responsibility?" Will asked, tapping his chin with the longneck.

"Just driving Miss Sadie around during the day. But make absolutely sure you have her back in time for dinner."

"Anything else we have to do?"

"Not really. While they're eating, we'll eat. A separate team guards the perimeter. After dinner, we're done for the night. We can relax at the Thirsty Goat, or we might go into town and sow some seeds. They'll provide a driver. No DWIs around here."

Anders came running into the bar, signaling to the bartender to cut the music. "Hey! We've spotted someone in the woods. It looked like they were gathering intel. I need you guys to meet outside right now. And I sure hope you have your weapon with you."

Will jumped up, feeling for the Glock in his holster. He and Green hustled outside, joining a growing crowd as Brace came sprinting up.

"I have some men looking in the woods," Brace said, breathing hard. "We need to lock this place down before it gets too dark. Green, take these three men and check out the gun range—and circle back to the west along the edge of the forest. Anyone you find, try to take them alive. But defend yourself if necessary."

He pointed to Anders. "You take these four and head north. Start with the Range Rovers. Check each vehicle. When you've cleared them, go to the eastern edge of the woods and look for any movement. Go now!"

"What do you want me to do?" Will said, standing alone with Brace.

"Go inside the ranch house and find Sadie and the twins. Put them in a room and stay with them."

Sterry came running up. "I just got your text. The war room is booted up and ready for you."

"Change of plans," Brace said, turning back to Will. "I'm going to protect Sadie and the twins. Go with Sterry and check out the mechanics' shop and the horse barn. Then work east to the thicket. Don't go in too deep unless you have more men."

Sterry and Will took off together, jogging to the mechanics' shop first. "You go right," Sterry said. "I'll go left. And stay on the outside."

Will pulled out his Glock. Pointing where he looked, he checked out several open areas, finding nothing but ATVs waiting to be repaired. He came to a window and looked inside. Nothing.

Slipping around a short wall, he saw a door swinging open in the breeze. Something wasn't right.

As he continued, a quick movement to his right caught his attention. He glanced around the building. Sterry was nowhere in sight. Quietly, he left the shop and moved into the fading light of dusk.

The forest, fifty yards away, gave up nothing. As he crept closer, a cluster of tall grass moved. This sent him into a full run. In seconds, he'd covered the distance.

Two figures raced across his field of vision. "Stop!" he yelled.

One of the figures dropped to the ground. The second figure stopped, reached down to grab the fallen comrade, but gave up and ran. Will sighted the running target and shot. A loud moan came back. Will moved forward cautiously.

Through the scrub brush and mesquite trees, he spotted the first figure. Crawling on his knees, Will reached a man with his hands tied behind his back and a rag wrapped around his mouth. Rolling him over, he recognized him as Hector, the mechanics' manager.

Will removed the rag. "There's two of them," Hector whispered, trying to catch his breath. Then, his eyes grew big as saucers.

Will turned to see a man approaching. The man had placed a red laser dot on Will's chest, twitching his gun barrel several times, signaling him to move away from Hector. Will's gun in his right hand, up against Hector's body, was hidden from the approaching man. In a split second, he weighed the odds of bringing his Glock to bear and firing versus his opponent's chance of missing.

A shot rang out.

The man fell to his knees, leaned forward, and buried his face in the tall grass. Sterry stood behind him in the distance, her laser-sighted M-4 assault rifle gripped with two steady hands. Will raised his arms, causing her to continue toward him.

Sterry reached the man she had shot, checking for a pulse.

"There's one over there," Will said quietly. "Check him out while I take this rope off Hector's hands."

Quickly and efficiently, Sterry located the second man and confirmed he was dead.

"Are there any others?" Will asked Hector.

"I don't know," he said, rubbing his wrists. "I just saw these two. They took me at the shop. I'd be a goner if you hadn't got that first guy."

"We'd both be goners if she hadn't saved us," Will added.

"Let's get back to the shop," Sterry said, rejoining them. "I'll cover your retreat. When you get there, cover me."

"Got it," Will said.

The two men ran to the shop. Will pushed Hector through the door and took a position facing the wooded area. When he signaled Sterry, she got up and ran like a deer, slipping in the door past him. As Will withdrew into the shop, Sterry was on the phone. After a few words, she hung up.

"Brace is sending men down here. He wants us to check out the barn." Turning to Hector, she said, "Do you have a gun?"

"No, but I can grab a wrench."

"You stay here and show them the two bodies," she ordered Hector. "But don't get shot yourself. Let's go," she said to Will.

They jogged down to the barn and searched it thoroughly. After finding it empty, Sterry pointed to an opening. "You take a position there and cover the east. I'll be on this side, covering the west."

It was a good move. They could see outside while covering each other's back.

Will took his position and stared out at the empty field and the woods beyond. The gray dusk was fading fast, which triggered the exterior lights. Soon, large areas of land were bathed in incandescent light. Yet beyond those, dark patches took over, an excellent place for a shooter to hide.

Will and Sterry manned their posts for close to an hour, seeing nothing. Several spotlights crisscrossed from the north, darting into the dark areas. It was Brace and company.

"We found the two bodies," Brace told Sterry, "and nailed two more. Cobra shot one dead and nicked the other. I'm going to get some answers from him here in the barn. Get your gear set up. He's on an ATV. We'll bring him down when you're ready."

He turned to Will. "Good shooting. You saved Hector."

"Don't thank me," Will said, pointing to his partner. "I'd be dead if Sterry hadn't dropped the other one. She made a hell of a shot."

"We expect a lot from her. That's why she's one of the best. I'm just glad we got you some target practice this morning. It paid off."

"It sure did," Will said, nodding vigorously. "What can I do to help?"

"Go back to your room or the Thirsty Goat. Stay in one of those two places. Don't go wandering around outside. I have my men in place. We're going to sweep the entire ranch tonight with infrareds, and I don't want them picking up the wrong man. And keep your weapon on you."

Will walked back up the hill, finding Hector standing outside the shop. "Drinks are on me," Hector said.

"I tend to drink a lot," Will said.

"Then let's hope we have enough alcohol," Hector replied, putting his arm around his new amigo.

The pair made their way up the hill to find the saloon mostly empty. Country music was on, giving a façade that everything was back to normal. They grabbed a Corona and scotch from the bar and settled into a booth.

"Thanks for saving my life," Hector said, clinking glasses with Will. "I owe you a big one."

"It's my job," Will told him as he sipped on his scotch. "What was that all about?"

"I have no idea. I'm just a mechanic. You have more pull than I do."

"Not really. I'm just the guy driving Sadie around."

"Maybe I can pay my debt to you right now." Hector moved closer, bending slightly over the table. "Be careful with that one. She's burned through a lot of men."

Will frowned. "That's what I hear. But no one tells me anything."

"I'll tell you a story you won't believe. But let me grab another beer."

Will watched Hector shuffle to the bar. He could hardly contain his excitement. Strange men scouting the ranch. Three dead. One being tortured. And now some big story? He would be writing another incredible report if he could find the time and space to do it.

When Hector returned with his beer, Will put him back on track. "You said she had burned through a lot of men. What did you mean?"

Hector spoke quietly, barely loud enough to hear over the music. "She turns them into lovers. They make mistakes. Then we don't see them again."

"Why does she need other men? Is Cole not holding up his end of the stick?"

"Apparently not. This is going to blow your mind," Hector glanced around to make sure no one was close enough to listen.

"One day, Sadie grabbed her Mercedes and left for lunch. I guess Brace tracks the cars and probably our phones, too. She drove to a local family Mexican restaurant off Highway 377 in Granbury but didn't go inside. Instead, she left her phone in the Mercedes and some wannabe cowboy picked her up. She was gone for about three hours. When she returned, she and this dude went inside and sat at the bar, eating, drinking, and acting like they didn't come in together. The waitress recognized Sadie and saw her rubbing the guy's crotch. They finished at the bar, went outside, around the building and out of sight. Then the waitress called her cousin, Noe. He's a ranch hand here. She ratted Sadie out."

"How did you hear about this?" Will asked.

"I'm friends with all the ranch hands. I smuggle beer out for them. They tell me everything."

"Clever. What did you do with the information?"

"I gave it to Anders. He's my boss. He and Brace got a PI on it and found out she was seeing this guy, Seth, at his house.

"So," Will said, stroking his chin, "Sadie was trying to trick Brace by leaving her phone in the Mercedes, thinking that the GPS wouldn't give her away. But when you shop, you walk around. The phone should be moving."

"Right, and it didn't, so the PI tracked them to his ranch out in Brock."

Will concentrated, trying to memorize all this. "Where's Brock?"

"About thirty minutes from Granbury. The PI kept digging and found out this guy, Seth, liked young girls, thirteen- to fifteen-year-olds. Mr. Sterling hates pedos. A little girl of one of his ranch hands was molested. Martín, you know him?"

"He's the supervisor of all the groundskeepers," Will replied.

"Right. He went to Mr. Sterling, looking for help. He thought a schoolteacher was molesting his granddaughter, and maybe others were too. Martín told me that Mr. Sterling said he could identify his enemies. He could see them coming. But he couldn't pick out a child molester in the crowd. Since then, if there's a pedo and Mr. Sterling knows about it, they're gone— *desaparecen rápidamente.*"

"Go back to Seth," Will said.

"Oh, yeah. The PI followed Seth around and caught him meeting young girls at fast-food restaurants. He'd leave them twenty-dollar tips while he flirted and groomed them. He sent a nudie of himself to a fifteen-year-old waitress. The girl's father found it on her phone and immediately called the police. Seth paid the girl's family big bucks, $175,000. They didn't charge him."

"He was also caught with a fourteen-year-old girl in the backseat of his truck. Seth paid her family $100,000 to make it all go away."

"Where does he get his money?" Will asked.

"Worked on oilfield equipment, I was told. But his family, they got plenty of money. They know he likes those real young girls. It's been going on since he was a teenager. The guy is sick." Hector's nose wrinkled in disgust. "He even has a daughter in grade school."

"I'm guessing Mr. Sterling wasn't too happy about all this."

"After he was told about what the PI found, Mr. Sterling was afraid Sadie might bring that kind of trash around the twins. He told Brace he didn't want to hear Seth's name again and to just handle it."

"That doesn't sound good for Seth," Will commented.

"No," Hector said, shaking his head and looking down. "It wasn't. Brace had me sit in my work truck in front of Seth's house, watching until he left. You know, no one bothers a Mexican on the side of the road checking his tires. I followed his truck and called Anders to let him know where he was. Next thing you know, a sheriff's deputy is following him. Two deputies stop him, get him out of his truck, and find something in his truck."

"*Find* something?" Will said.

"Yeah." Hector winked at Will. "So, he ends up in handcuffs in the patrol car, and they head out to the ranch. They meet Brace in the far back forty along with Anders. They say Anders handed one of the deputies a big wad of cash. The deputies took the money and immediately left. Those guys didn't ask any questions.

"The story is that Anders grabbed the cowboy's phone and downloaded all of his pictures. Bunch of pictures of Sadie and this guy going at it in every way possible. There were lots of photos of the cowboy with little girls. He was a pedo all the way. Brace confronted him, and he admitted it. I was told he went straight to the boneyard."

"Scratch another victim to Sadie, I guess. Where is this boneyard?" Will asked.

"I don't know, and I don't want to know," Hector said, diving into his beer.

"I'd think they would bury him on this place instead of transporting him somewhere else. This ranch is so big. No one would ever find him here."

"They don't need anyone digging up anything here," Hector said in a whisper. "Too much to lose. They did send his truck to Mexico where it will get lost."

"Did they take care of the waitress?"

"Brace went in for a meal at the Mexican restaurant and left a $2,000 tip on his credit card."

Will shook his head. "Is everyone around here related to someone on the ranch?"

"Pretty much. The ranch hands have family and friends with eyes and ears everywhere in Granbury. They know there's a bounty on information with Sadie. The ranch hands funnel all tips to me, and I give them to Anders."

"How did Sadie deal with the loss of her wannabe cowboy?"

"I don't think she ever knew. Maybe she thought he was just another creep who stopped returning her phone calls." He grabbed Will's arm. "What do you call that liquid stuff that explodes?"

"You mean nitroglycerin?"

"Si. You be careful. They call her that. She'll explode in your hands."

Will held his hands out, palms down. "I guess I just need to keep my hands steady."

"Steady, and to yourself," laughed Hector.

Will smiled and sipped on his scotch. He needed to make a call to his handler and report all this, especially about killing that man. Maybe the family dinner would give him a chance to slip away.

Chapter Eleven

The Range Rover came to an abrupt stop. Will flung his door open and then went to Sadie's door.

"Come on. You have five minutes!" he said much too loudly.

"Okay," she said. "Don't rush me. I won't get fired from the family if I'm late."

"No, but I might."

Sadie stopped and smirked. "Again, Will, so much drama."

Will ignored her comment and escorted her through the main entrance. A few more steps down the hall and the dining room came into view. Standing at a long table just outside it was one of Brace's men. He held out a box with Sadie's name on it. Without saying a word, she dropped her phone into the box and locked it, taking the key with her.

"You're done now," she said, waving at Will. "Oh, and don't forget to drop off my packages."

"Whoops!" a man said, running flush into him. "Sorry about that."

Stunned, Will stopped and stared at Declan Sterling, aka Dallas Dillon. He was holding hands with a man beside him.

"Sorry," Will said.

"No worries," Declan replied, removing his cell phone. He and his partner used their free hands to put their phones into one box. His partner winked at Declan as he slipped the key into his shirt pocket.

"After you," the partner said, allowing Declan to enter first. Will glanced at the guard, who shrugged. As Will left, he passed a nice-looking couple—Victoria Sterling and her husband, Evan Cox. She was a tall, thin brunette with blonde highlights. Her long, smooth legs were as dazzling as her figure. Evan was less impressive. He looked like he was simply thrilled to be next to her.

For Will, he'd committed it all to memory. In less than a minute, a lot of blanks had been filled in.

He walked to the kitchen, where Mrs. White held a cup of coffee. Looking around, he put his hands on his hips. "Are we supposed to make our own dinner?"

Mrs. White grinned. "You can. Or you can hop on the bus into town. They usually go to Smokey Joe's. Can you handle barbeque tonight?"

"Do they serve beer?"

"They do."

"Then yes, I can handle it," Will said.

"Better hurry. They'll leave without you."

Will walked back to the barndominium that was his residence. He found Hector, Green, and Anders leaning against the wall.

"Are you joining us?" Green asked.

"Of course, I am," Will replied. "I just need to unload all of Sadie's stuff. It would go faster if I had help."

"All right," Green said reluctantly. "Hector, you want to come too?"

"Since we're not leaving until he's done, why not."

The three men carried hangers full of clothes and shoeboxes into the main house. A maid escorted them up to Sadie's room, where the goods were put away.

Will led the pack back outside just in time to see a Range Rover racing down the drive and sliding to a stop in the parking area. Out jumped Cole, who ran to the ranch house.

The three men stepped aside, with Hector holding the door. Before they could utter a word, Cole was gone.

"I'm guessing he was late," Will said.

"Grayson hates that," Green said. "Glad it's not me. Now, let's go into town and get liquored up."

The minibus took nine men to Granbury. Will learned several of them were on Brace's team. The rest worked on the ranch in various capacities.

At Smokey Joe's, the group had several large tables reserved. After loading up on beef ribs and chicken, Will sat next to Hector and Green. Will had a beer while both Hector and Green enjoyed cocktails.

"Where did you get those?" Will asked.

"We know the owners. They have a special bar hidden from the public. They don't have a liquor license for hard drinks, so we tip well if they pour well."

The group ripped through the food, replacing rib bones with toothpicks. As the drinks flowed, so did the intoxication level. This was what Will had been waiting for.

"I gotta hit the head," he announced as he made his way to the bathroom. To his surprise, there was a payphone at the end of the short hall, right next to the men's room. He quickly loaded in coins and dialed his handler, reaching the answering service.

"Bailey and Sons Plumbing," the lady said.

"Hi. This is Will Roberts. I have a loose gasket in my showerhead. Do you have a plumber with half-inch plumber's tape?"

"How many feet do you need?" the lady replied.

126

"Four hundred and twenty."

"Confirmed. How can we help you?"

"Connect me to my handler," Will said hurriedly.

A minute went by. It was a long minute. Will watched as some teenager went into the men's room and left. At least he was quick.

"This is Rodgers," a scratchy voice said.

"This is Will. Are you ready?"

"Go for it."

Will brought him up to speed—the gun range, the family dinner, and the Mexican scouts captured and killed. He explained his role in killing a man along with the information Hector had given him about the death of Seth, the wannabe cowboy. When he was done, he asked if Rodgers had it all.

"Yeah, I got it. This sounds more like a novel than real life. And I need to tell you that we checked out that Oakland house. It was clean—super clean."

"Figures," Will muttered.

"I'll get this report entered in tonight so the boss will have it first thing in the morning. He won't believe it—especially the part about Dallas Dillon being gay."

Will frowned. He had killed a man. Shouldn't that be more important? "Listen, connect me to my wife."

"Sure thing," Rodgers said.

Will looked over his shoulder to see a staggering Green coming his way, his ballcap off-center. He couldn't take a chance being caught on the phone, so he hung up and pushed into the men's room, beating Green to a urinal. As he stood there, he wondered if Green had heard him mention his wife. If so, that would be a death sentence.

Will washed his hands and considered walking away. This would be his best chance—maybe his only chance. He could grab a ride into Dallas and disappear.

Green finished up and slapped Will on the back. "Come on, buddy. We have more drinks to drink," he said, slurring his words.

"Let's do it," Will replied. He'd stay and take a chance. It was too big of an investigation to let go.

•••

Monday arrived, and a caravan departed. Cole went back to Virginia. Victoria and Evan flew down to Houston. And Declan and his partner hit the road again, traveling to Biloxi for a concert on Tuesday.

With the chaos gone, Will enjoyed his coffee, sitting in the sunny kitchen and talking to Mrs. White.

"I bet you're glad they're gone," Will said.

"I have more help for the family dinners, but it's still a lot of work. I'm always glad to get back to normal, even if I love seeing the kids."

"You've probably known them since they were babies."

"And pooping in their britches," Mrs. White said, snickering. "Cole and Declan were always the two who wanted the most attention from me. I was like a second momma to them."

Anders opened the back door. "Green, Will—I need you."

Will slugged down the last of his coffee. "Time to punch in."

"Have a blessed day, Will," Mrs. White said, getting up from her chair and grabbing his mug.

On the way out, Will snatched a banana and joined Green on the patio, who was finishing a piece of French toast.

"Let's go to Charlie's old room and have a sit-down," Anders ordered.

Anders unlocked the door, and the men found a place to sit. "Okay, here's the deal. Our job is about to get harder. And it all has to do with Carlos Santos."

"I heard that name in Oakland," Will offered.

"Good memory. Santos used to be Mr. Sterling's partner. They split amicably, but now things might not be so amicable. Something has caused a rift. I don't know what it is."

"Were the dudes scouting us out part of Carlos Santos?" Green asked.

"Possibly. They were checking us for weaknesses. Santos will know what happened when they don't report back. But he won't know if they told us anything or just got shot."

"What can we do?" Will asked.

"Keep your eyes and ears open. They may try to snag Sadie or the grandkids. Both of you be extra sharp. And if you grab someone, make sure you collect their phones and other electronic devices. Our guys can pull the data off and analyze it. We get great intel from that stuff."

Will remembered them collecting the electronics in Oakland. The Sterling's sophisticated operation rivaled the government's own agencies.

"Okay, gentlemen, meeting's over," Anders said, getting to his feet. "Get on with your assigned duties."

As they walked out the door, Green slapped Will on the back. "Have fun driving Miss Sadie."

"Gee, thanks," Will grunted.

•••

The Range Rover eased into a parking space, and Will cut the engine. "Okay, Sadie, let's go."

She sighed and exited the SUV.

As they stepped through the main entrance, an assistant greeted them. "Right this way," she said, leading Sadie and Will through a labyrinth of halls until they reached the doctor. One thing Will had learned working for the Sterlings was that they rarely waited for anything.

"Sadie," the doctor said, shaking her hand. "So glad to see you. Please, take a seat over there."

Will remained at the entrance, saying nothing. It was obvious the doctor was used to her security personnel being around.

For the next ten minutes, the ophthalmologist flipped through a series of lenses before pushing them away. "There's nothing wrong with your eyes. Your eyes are perfect."

"But all the celebrities are wearing glasses," Sadie moaned.

"I can fit you for glasses and make the lenses neutral," the doctor said. "No one will ever know the difference."

"Maybe I could get some colored contact lenses—blue, green—something special."

"Since you don't need them, I can't prescribe them," he said. "Nor would I recommend contact lenses. There's always a risk of infection."

"I want to be attractive to men. I want men to find me attractive."

The ophthalmologist smiled. "You're very attractive, Sadie. You don't need any of this. Just ask your husband what he thinks."

Sadie stared at the ceiling. "Cole doesn't care, nor would he notice the difference."

Sadie and the doctor bantered back and forth over this subject before Sadie finally gave up. With the appointment over, Will escorted her to the SUV. "It's time for lunch," he announced. "I've got just the place."

They drove to a Thai restaurant in North Fort Worth. After they were seated at a secluded table, Will offered up his opinion. "You don't need glasses or contact lenses. You're just being crazy and vain."

"Really?" she said. "You're not attracted to me."

"Why don't you just focus on Cole? You know, have more kids."

She lowered her head. "We were lucky to have Kodi and Brooke. I went through so much to have them."

Will leaned back. "Can you have more children?"

"It's a long story," she said. "Let's order first."

After the waitress left, Sadie launched into the tale. "We'd been trying to have children for a long time. I had five miscarriages because of the drug use and abortions. Grayson sent Cole and me to a fertility clinic down in Houston. We needed to find out if it was him or me. After three days of tests, the doctors said he was fine. I was the problem.

"Grayson was disgusted to hear that I'd had three abortions. I'm not proud of it, but it happened."

"How did it affect you?" Will asked gingerly.

"I always remember the day each one would've been born."

"No, I mean physically."

"I was heartbroken, in a panic. The doctors told me it would be tough to have children, but not impossible. I knew that was important because Grayson hated me. He couldn't believe Cole had picked me. Yet I was Grayson's only chance for grandchildren."

"Why not Victoria?"

"She's all business. She tells Evan when to jump. And Brace is just a psychopath. He'll never settle down. That leaves Declan and me. Which really leaves me. So, I spent a week in Houston having in vitro. The first several times, it didn't take. Then the fourth time, it worked. And we got twins. But it cost Grayson over $500,000 to get them."

"Where did you have them?"

"Oh, that's another story. When they found out I was pregnant, they brought me back to the ranch. I didn't have to do anything but exercise and bed rest. Cole went to Alexandria and worked. He flew back every weekend to see me, but there was no sex or anything. It was tough on me.

"Grayson hired four registered nurses to work eight-hour shifts, checking my vitals every hour, unless I was sleeping. They even put an OB-GYN nurse in a guest room in case something happened. And a driver sat in the SUV for the last three months, ready to rush me to the hospital."

"Man, that's thorough," Will said, shaking his head.

"And I didn't mention my OB-GYN they flew in by helicopter to check on me every week. He put me on vitamins and medicine, giving a nutritional list to Mrs. White to cook. I couldn't eat anything if it weren't on that list."

"What about ultrasounds?"

"They brought the machine to me. The OB-GYN did them. And when I went into labor, Grayson insisted I have the twins here, like all his children. He didn't trust a hospital and didn't want to risk the trip. And no way he was going to let the twins be born in Virginia. They had to be born in Texas on the ranch."

"What did your parents think about that?" Will asked, hoping to gain more information.

"My mother is a nut job—a psychopath, a schizophrenic. My family has a lot of problems, like the Sterlings. I never really knew my father. He ran off with another woman when I was three."

Will sat there in silence, pursing his lips. "I was surprised to learn Declan is gay, being a country-western star and all."

Sadie reached over and covered his hand. "Honey, there's a lot you'll be surprised to know. If you're good, maybe one day I'll tell you about the tattoos we all are required to have."

• • •

The day had been a very long grind on Will. After driving for several hours, taking his passenger from one store to another, Will was tired. As he waited outside each dressing room, he mused about Sadie.

She was vain but insecure. She wanted to be held and babied, yet also demanded complete control. He could only imagine the challenge to Cole, keeping her on the team. Now that Cole had some kids out of the deal, it seemed like he was okay if she left for someone else.

"I don't see anything here," Sadie announced. "Let's go to the Boardroom."

"No," Will said, heading this off. "We're not going to the strip club. It's not on the itinerary. See?" He waved a document in her face.

"Wait a minute," she said, snatching it from his hand and pointing to a line item. "It says shopping. I'm going to buy something there."

Liam Stone

"They don't have anything there to buy but lap dances and puntang."

"You're wrong," Sadie said, putting her hands on her hips. "They have nice ballcaps that say *The Boardroom*."

"Ballcaps?"

"And condoms. Come to think of it, they also have t-shirts."

Will found the SUV and clicked the security off. "The only thing you want to buy is Sandera."

"So? I've been a good girl. Show me some compassion, *Wiiilllll*." She drew out his name, saying it with a whine.

Once in the Range Rover, he listened about the Boardroom for the next thirty minutes before finally turning the car around and pointing it in the direction of West Dallas. Sadie clapped excitedly. At least he didn't have to worry about a deadline. The family dinners were over.

Sadie put on some music— Keith Sweat—to get in the mood. She listened to "Nobody," "My Body," and "Twisted," all in succession. The music had Sadie moving and shaking in her seat. Will could see she was getting lathered up for Sandera.

•••

"Did she have a good time?" Will asked.

"Of course," Sandera replied, standing next to Will at the far side of the bar. "She's in the restroom, putting herself together. You know you owe me big-time, mister. Are you getting something out of this?"

"Maybe. Enough to cover a few more cases you might pick up."

"I hope not. I hate going to jail."

"Here she comes," Will whispered.

"There you are," Sandera shouted above the music. "A shining princess."

"A princess who is ready for her carriage. Driver?" Sadie snapped her fingers.

"Take care," Will said to Sandera, roughly grabbing Sadie by the arm and escorting her out.

"Hey, you're hurting me," she said, trying to undo Will's grip.

"And you're hurting me," he said, staring directly into her eye. "I have a reputation with those people. A tough one. You calling me a driver hurts that. Understand?"

"Okay, I understand. Now, let go."

He released her arm. "Get in the vehicle. We're heading back to the ranch."

"Yippee," she said sarcastically.

•••

Like always, the evening dinner was a treat. Moist meatloaf with a side of turnip greens and French fries, all washed down with several glasses of sweet tea.

With a toothpick wedged between his teeth, Will made his way to the SUV so he could prepare it for tomorrow. As he worked over the vehicle, he spotted a roll of money on the ground. He picked it up and looked around. There was no one in sight.

He thought about counting it out, maybe keeping it. In the real world, he probably would have. But this was undercover.

It might be some test. With the cameras they had everywhere, he could be on TV right now.

Dr. Z had put him through many such tests. During one, he'd accidentally left the answers out for Will to use. Once Will pointed the mistake out, Dr. Z quickly removed them.

Or had *that* been a test?

Later, when a married recruit came into his hotel room to borrow a pen, she was soon undoing her bra looking for more than a ballpoint. Had that also been a test? At the time, Will had thought so, especially since Dr. Z had warned him about such relationships. But years later, he wondered if the FBI would allow an agent to go that far. He doubted it. Maybe she had been missing her husband. *Who knows?*

Will kept the money outside his pocket and walked toward the ranch house. If he was being watched, he wanted there to be no doubt what he was doing.

Instead of going to the front door, he walked around the back, holding the money out like it was a prized goose. Inside the kitchen, a teenaged girl cleaned the dishes. He moved past her through the hall, looking around for Brace and Anders. As he neared Grayson's office, he heard some loud talking. For some reason, the guards were gone.

"We need to move now!" Brace said. "Strike first."

"We don't know what he's going to do—if anything," Grayson said.

"But we know he knows."

"No. We think he knows. That's a big difference."

Will knocked on the doorframe, startling the men.

"Yes?" Grayson said. "What is it?"

"I found this money by the Range Rover. I don't know who it belongs to."

Brace moved to intercept Will. "We'll take care of it," he said as Will placed the money in his hand. Will turned to leave, but Brace stopped him. "Did you deviate from the schedule today?"

Will swallowed hard. "The itinerary said shopping. We went all over the place, and she shopped."

"Did you take her to that strip club she adores?" Brace asked, his chest puffing out.

"Yes."

"Why?"

"First, she convinced me she would shop there. Sure enough, she bought a ballcap. Second, to control her, she has to see a carrot every now and then. Otherwise, she becomes totally uncooperative and tries to elude me. And she's good at it. I feel like I'm reeling in a marlin with light tackle. I have to be careful or I'll lose her."

"Where are you going tomorrow?" Brace asked.

"The itinerary says shopping and meet a friend. That's it."

Brace angrily shook his head.

"Thank you for the money," Grayson said. "Is there anything else?"

Will hesitated before speaking. "Shouldn't she be with Cole in Virginia? Wouldn't their marriage be better if they were together?"

Brace smirked as Grayson loudly exhaled. "Yes. But then I couldn't see my grandkids. And it would be a lot tougher keeping track of her there in the city. She can get lost easier. You said it yourself. She's a fish that knows how to get off the hook. Here, it's a bit harder to lose her."

"But she can't get off this ranch unless you approve it," Will said. "Right?"

"This isn't a prison," Grayson replied. "We must walk a fine line between holding someone here for their protection and holding them against their will."

"Okay," Will said. "I understand."

Grayson's patience was wearing thin. "Anything else?"

"No, sir."

"Close the doors."

Will closed the doors, hearing the distinctive click. He walked back to the bunkhouse, wondering when Brace would have confronted him about the strip club. Then, he spent the rest of the night committing the conversation he had just heard to memory.

Something was coming. He could feel it in his bones.

Chapter Twelve

Will was once again in a small boutique dress shop, staring at Sadie sliding clothes on a rack. It was so frustrating watching her day after day. He wasn't getting any closer to his targets doing this. But unfortunately, this was undercover work.

He recalled Dr. Z telling the story of an agent who'd worked as a short-order cook in a diner. The Bureau thought it would only be a month or so before he could gain the keys to open or close. This would give him the freedom to install bugs in a back storeroom where the mafia bosses often met. Instead, he'd worked there for a full year before a freak snowstorm allowed him to get permission to sleep in the diner. He installed the bugs that night, helping the agents eventually snag some mid-level key players. But a year of making meals was the price.

Dr. Z never said what happened to that agent. Will wondered if the Bureau valued that kind of commitment. Would a short-order cook be pushed up the FBI ladder, or sent on similar operations?

"I'm going to try this on," Sadie said to the sales associate.

The pair walked to the back as Will followed. Before Sadie went in, Will checked out the small room. There were three stalls, each with a tan curtain. The other two were empty.

"Just call out if you need me," the associate said. "I'll be sorting some new merchandise." She pulled the curtain closed and slipped past Will.

He took a position at the entrance to the dressing area, turning his back to Sadie. He watched the associate move clothes around near the main entrance. Including the associate, they were the only three people in the store.

A few minutes had gone by when he heard the curtain slide open.

"What do you think?" Sadie asked.

Will looked around and stopped breathing. Before him was a captivating goddess. Sadie had managed to slip into a skintight bloodred pantsuit, one that exposed her left shoulder. The outfit was absolutely stunning, showing off her firm body.

"Well, don't just stand there," she said, hands on her hips. "What do you think?"

Will swallowed hard. "It's fantastic on you. I'd buy it."

Sadie smiled as her eyelashes fluttered. "Thank you for that compliment." She moved back inside the stall and closed the curtain.

Will rubbed his face and resumed his post.

"The zipper's stuck," Sadie said. "Can you help me?"

Will gave no response.

"Will, did you hear me?"

"I did," he said, moving toward the curtain. "My job is to protect you, not change you."

Sadie let out a short laugh before opening the curtain. "Don't be a baby," she said, pulling him into the dressing room. "Unzip me, please."

Will knew he should leave and bring the sales associate back. But he couldn't. Instead, he pulled down the zipper, revealing a red push-up bra and red lace panties. Suddenly, the urges he'd been fighting to control let loose. It felt like Niagara Falls—an unstoppable force.

"Do you like this?" she whispered.

"What's not to like," Will replied, slowly and quietly.

Sadie grabbed Will, pulling him closer and kissing him passionately. Will gave in, the desire fueled by his loneliness.

"Close the curtain," she whispered, her lips touching his ear.

Will shook his head, but she lowered her hand, unzipping his resolve. Visions of Charlie being taken to the mythical boneyard bounced inside his brain, fighting against his boiling blood. He was about to come to a decision when her long, thin fingers slid into his open fly. Without warning, he pulled away.

"I'm sorry. I can't do this," he said.

"No one will know," she whispered.

"I can't do this to your husband. You're married. Remember?"

"But not happily. Make me happy, Will. I know you want me." She grabbed his arm and pulled. "I want you so bad right now. I can do so much more for you. Open more doors."

"I know you can," he replied, "but I can't. I'm sorry." He grabbed her shoulders and finally used his strength to control her arms.

"Are you going to hold me against my will?" Sadie asked. "Or are you going to hold me against you, Will?"

Slipping under his grip, she reached around his waist and pulled herself to him, grinding her pelvis into his groin. Will felt a tap on his shoulder.

"Do you need some assistance?" the sales associate asked, clearly upset about this new development.

"No," Will replied. "She's fine. Just a stuck zipper." He turned away and walked out of the dressing area, readjusting his trousers.

Finding himself near a three-way mirror, he stared at his face. *You just came super close to signing your death warrant. You'd better get your shit together, or Brace and company will gut the crap right out of you.*

•••

The SUV rocketed along through the streets of Fort Worth. Sadie was fresh off a visit to the nail salon. The Vietnamese owner had showered her with red wine and attention—two things she loved.

Both the manicure and pedicure had included the works. Will had watched as a small Vietnamese man massaged her shoulders and a woman worked on her fingernails. Another woman, much older, had addressed her toes.

After a long debate over colors, Will broke the tie by selecting a light purple. It looked great with her skin tone.

"Who are you meeting?" Will asked.

"Ellie Gaetti, a friend of mine," she replied from the backseat, staring disinterestedly out the window.

"How long have you've known her?"

"Brace didn't give you a file?" she asked sarcastically.

"No."

"Do you get to know everything about my life?"

"I'm here to protect you," Will said, glancing at her in his rearview mirror. "I like to know what I'm walking into."

"You're walking into a hotel. I'm seeing a friend who is here visiting. Is that good enough?"

Will let it go. He didn't need her ragging on him the rest of the afternoon. Besides, he'd see this woman soon enough.

They arrived at the Omni Fort Worth Hotel. The valet parked the Range Rover while they entered the lobby.

"Where are you going?" he asked as Sadie took off.

"To the restroom. Is that okay?"

He studied the area. "Yeah. I think I'll go too."

Will watched her enter the ladies' room. Once the door closed, he dashed into the men's room and did his business quickly. Coming out of the restroom, he spotted Sadie walking fast down the hall. Before he knew it, she was in the elevator.

Will ran to stop her but was too late.

"Dammit!" he seethed, pounding the marble button.

He stared intently at the display until the elevator stopped. The eighth floor. At least he knew where she was.

He took the adjoining elevator to the eighth floor and searched the hall. Placing his ear up to each door, he listened for Sadie's voice. After ten minutes of this, he had struck out. Will moved to a stairwell and called Green.

"I lost her," he said, trying to hold down the panic in his voice. "She's supposed to be meeting Ellie here at the hotel, but she slipped up to the eighth floor."

"How did that happen?" Green asked.

He told him.

"Stay put. I'll call back with instructions."

Will waited an agonizing ten minutes before Anders's name popped up on his phone.

"Will, here."

"Stay on that floor," Anders said. "See which room she pops out of and report that to me."

"Got it," he said as the call disconnected.

An hour later, the door to room 804 opened. Sadie emerged, smoothing her clothes. As she walked toward the elevator, she spotted Will.

"Spying on me again?" she asked.

"Shut up!" Will snapped. "Who were you seeing?"

"I told you, a friend. Why do you care?"

Will gripped her arms, hard.

"You're hurting me," she cried.

The door to 804 opened again. Out walked a white male, his tight shirt showing off his steroid-defined muscles. "Is there a problem, Sadie?"

"Is there, Will?" she replied.

"Let her go," the man barked.

Will continued to hold on to her arm. "I'm her security. Who are you?"

"Don't answer that!" Sadie said. "He's not the police."

The man moved closer. "Come on, Sadie. I'll walk you out."

She glanced up at Will. "Is that okay?"

"No," Will said. "It's not okay."

"That's it!" the man said. "Turn her loose or prepare to get your ass kicked."

"You don't want to do that," Will said coolly. "Trust me on this. It'll be the last thing on this earth you ever attempt."

He could tell Will meant business by the intense look of anger in his eyes.

Seeing the situation escalating and knowing Will's criminal past, Sadie intervened. "It's okay," she said to the man. "You go on. He works for me. I'll handle it."

The steroid-filled man backed away slowly, retreating to his room.

"You lied about meeting Ellie," Will said. "That's a man, not a woman."

"No, I didn't. Brace's people can't spell."

"What?"

"L.E. Gaetti," she said smugly.

Will jerked his head back. "L.E. I get it. Aren't you clever," he said sarcastically. "So you two got to have your little fun. I hope you enjoyed it. No telling what Brace will do."

"If you would've satisfied me, none of this would've happened. I have certain needs, after all."

"Come on," Will said impatiently. "It's time to get you home."

•••

The air was still and filled with the smell of cut grass. The sun had just dipped below the trees, bringing a coolness to the firing range.

Will stood at the bench, disassembling his Glock. He had just shot one hundred rounds, hoping to remove the day's events from his mind. What he really wanted to do was go for a long run. But that wasn't possible.

With his gun cleaned, he started back. The dying light allowed a glow from the mechanics' shop to catch his eye. He wondered if Hector was working overtime.

As he neared the large opening, he saw a weapon lying on a bench. Its parts were scattered everywhere. He briefly thought of moving on to his small apartment but decided to check it out.

"Can I help you?" Sterry asked, catching Will off guard. She leaned against a wall just inside the opening.

"No," he replied. "I thought Hector might be working late."

She nodded.

"But can *I* help *you*?" he asked.

"You can put this back together," she said, pointing to the collection of parts. Will recognized it as a Barrett M82 .50 caliber sniper rifle. This rifle was one of the best and most expensive sniper rifles in the world. Only the Sterlings would have something like that.

"I've never done a gun like this before, but I'm willing to try."

She moved toward the bench. "You seem smarter than the average Green or Anders. Let's see what you can do."

Her comment took Will aback. He wondered if he should say something but decided against it. "A vehement denial often gives you away," Dr. Z had preached. "Liars will dramatically deny the lie to cover up the tells their face and body send out. Sometimes, the best approach is to say nothing."

Will picked up the barrel and set it on top of the stock. Even though he could put it back together in a minute or so, he drew it out, studying each part, putting it up to others as if he was solving a puzzle. He took five long minutes before stepping back and waving a hand, inviting her to check out his work.

Sterry effortlessly picked up the heavy weapon and checked the action. "Nice work."

Will grinned. "I never told you, but that was nice work you did back at Oakland. Fast, too."

She looked away. "I don't know what you're talking about. Perhaps you are confusing me with another woman."

"Perhaps I am," Will said, hesitating. "Where are you from?"

"Persia," Sterry said, placing the rifle in a hard metal case. "My family left the country before I was born. The revolution, mainly. And you?"

"I was born in Texas but moved around from place to place for several years."

She looked up at him, studying his eyes. The corners of her mouth turned up. "Goodnight, Mr. Will."

"Goodnight, Miss Sterry," he said, turning to go.

"Please see Brace in Mr. Sterling's office," she added. "He's waiting for you."

Will stopped. Again, he was going to say something but nixed it. A meeting with Brace surely wouldn't be good. "Okay."

He hustled up the slope and into the ranch house. Once inside, he padded down the hall, hoping not to find anyone there. His hopes were dashed when he saw Brace sitting on a couch in Grayson's office.

"You wanted to see me?" Will asked.

"Yes," Brace said, looking up from a packet of papers. "Close the doors."

Will pulled them together until he heard the click. Then, he turned around and stood still.

"Tell me about this guy you saw with Sadie," Brace asked.

Will told him everything, including the confrontation in the hall.

"Was Sadie surprised to find you there, or did she not care?"

"It's hard to tell," Will replied. "She seemed surprised at first, but then acted like she didn't care. Just the fact that she gave me the slip says she was trying to hide who she was with. If I hadn't seen her get on the elevator, I would've never known where she'd gone. So, I'd say she was surprised but tried to hide it."

Brace nodded. "Is she scared of me?"

"You want the truth?"

"Of course."

"No," Will said. "She's a frightened little girl, but not of you or Mr. Sterling."

"Then what's she afraid of?"

"Being alone."

Brace leaned back and digested that comment, twisting his skull ring. Eventually, he dismissed Will.

Will found his apartment and closed the door.

Heads are going to roll, he thought to himself. *And I pray one of them isn't mine.*

Chapter Thirteen

For three days, explosions rocked the landscape. Teams of men continually assaulted the same structures, kicking in doors and taking prisoners. On the fourth day, they conducted reconnaissance. Brace taught the men how to stalk a target while remaining invisible. Will soaked it up. Much of the curriculum had not been part of his FBI or Marine Corps training.

On the fifth day, they took turns with various foreign and domestic automatic weapons. During the last few hours, they handed Will a live grenade. He studied it for a moment, recalling the ones he had thrown during a brief firefight in Afghanistan. He could've died in the desert. But he didn't.

Now, he pretended to be unfamiliar with the weapon. Eventually, he tossed the Pineapple Putin at a target, ducking under sandbags before the explosion slammed in his ears. It was both frightening and exhilarating.

Around five o'clock, Brace thanked the men for staying focused. "Hopefully, you've learned new tactics and are familiar with new weapons. Think about what you've learned and commit it to memory. You may have to use it soon."

The men nodded.

"Now, head up to dinner and enjoy yourselves at the Thirsty Goat. Drinks are on me!"

"Yay!" the men yelled half-heartedly, clapping as they headed to the ranch house.

"Hey, Will," Hector said. "Want to join me for a beer?"

"Sure. I'll meet you there after I eat and take a shower."

The men filed into the kitchen. They were served a meal of Southern fried chicken, Mrs. White's special coleslaw, onion rings, and giant pickles. Afterward, Will passed on the apple pie, opting for a hot shower instead. Once he had changed into fresh clothes, he found his way to the Thirsty Goat ahead of Hector.

"One scotch—neat," he said to the female bartender. Caressing the drink, he found a booth and waited.

Will was sipping on his second scotch when Hector arrived. With his beer in hand, he pointed to Will's half-empty glass. "Hey, I've got some catching up to do."

"Then you'd better get busy," Will said, holding up his highball.

Soon, the bar was filled, and the noise level increased.

"Are you relaxed?" Hector asked.

"As much as I can be," Will replied. "And you?"

"Definitely. And I plan to stay relaxed all night. It's been a long week."

"I had no idea you mechanics train on weapons," Will said.

"When I first came here, we didn't. But recently, Brace changed that."

"What do you think about that?"

"I like it," Hector said. "Learning something new is good. Never know when it might come in handy."

Will drained what was left of his scotch and got up to grab another one. As he walked to the bar, he bumped into Green, who had just come in. Suddenly, the music stopped, and the bar went silent.

"Listen up!" Green yelled, waving his ballcap around. "I need Will, Ford, and Ramirez to gear up."

"Are you kidding? Will said, standing close to Green.

"No," Green replied. "Meet me out front in ten minutes. Casual, with a jacket."

Will sighed and set his glass down. Then he headed to his apartment to get dressed.

• • •

The coffee pot clicked off, signaling the brew was done. Will needed to clear his head after two quick drinks in the bar. He had so been looking forward to a night of relaxation that his mental state had punched out. Even though the coffee wouldn't make the alcohol leave his body, it would provide some stimulation. That's what he needed right now.

While the coffee had brewed, he'd splashed some water on his face and changed. Now, he grabbed his metal Yeti to-go container and filled it with the freshly made liquid. He checked his weapon, then slipped it into his holster, put the jacket on, and stepped outside.

The August air was thick and heavy. Stray pollen floated around, giving a few men sneezing fits. Will was one of them.

Green and Anders stood next to two men—Ford and Ramirez. Ramirez was a slender Hispanic—an excellent marksman. Ford was a typical beefed-up SpecOps warrior—either a SEAL or Ranger. Brace stood at a distance, talking privately to Sterry. She said nothing, only listening.

Will considered all this. It had been two weeks since Sadie had given him the slip. After that, he had kept a tight leash on her.

The past week, he'd been in training. He'd heard Sadie was confined to the ranch. Will had noticed that her white Mercedes was gone. He had an idea of what was going on but didn't ask any questions. All he wanted to do was stay alive and make a report back to his handler, which was way overdue.

Brace pushed his sunglass up on his nose and turned away from Sterry, waving his index finger in a circle.

"Saddle up," Anders ordered. "Green, you ride with Brace. I'll take Will and the boys."

The group climbed into two black Range Rovers and took off. As they drove toward their destination, the sun was just above the horizon. For some reason, Will had a bad feeling about this.

The two SUVs stopped in a decent lower-middle-class neighborhood in Addison. The homes were more than twenty-five years old and crammed together. The cookie-cutter architecture caused one house to look like another. Will lived in an older neighborhood, much like this one. If you were tired and not paying attention, you could pull up to the wrong house. He'd done it before.

Anders pressed the speaker button on his phone to send Brace's voice throughout the vehicle. "Sadie was at the target's house for two hours. He's just arrived back from dropping her off at the Galleria Mall, where her Mercedes and cell phone were located. The target is a white male steroid bodybuilder. He's divorced with two kids who possibly live with him. We believe he's alone right now.

"I'm leaving two men in the Range Rover out front in case he flees. The rest of us will approach the house from the rear alley. Ford, you drive the SUV. If the target escapes, you forget us and stay with him. Eliminate him if necessary. Now, let's all get in position."

Will's SUV rolled to a stop in the alley. He took the last slug from his travel mug and readied himself.

Five men formed up behind the target's house. As they watched Ford back the SUV out to get into position, Brace whispered instructions. "He's got a wooden fence from the alley to the side of the garage. Ramirez, go around the right side of the garage and look for any trouble. The rest of us will hop the fence and enter through the back patio. Be ready for whatever goes down. And, for God's sake, check your weapons. We don't need one coming loose when you jump over."

Will felt his holster. It was secure.

The sky was now a dull blue as Brace crept up to the fence and peered through the slats. Will noticed the automatic floodlights attached to the side of the house. The fading sunlight would soon trigger their sensors. Hopefully, they were inside before that happened.

Brace removed his sunglasses and pocketed them, taking a quick twist of his skull rung for luck. Then he gave the signal and jumped the fence. The rest of them followed. Out of nowhere, a barking dog came running toward them. Just as Brace was about to shoot it, Will stepped in front and dropped to his knees. The dog, confused, let Will grab its collar and stopped barking.

"Go!" Will whispered. "I've got the dog."

Brace nodded and continued to the sliding glass door. A quick jerk on a slim jim and the men were inside.

"That's a good boy," Will said, keeping the dog calm. Despite seeing strange men in the backyard, the dog was willing to accept it so long as Will continued rubbing his ears.

The dog appeared to be a cross between a collie and German Shepherd—a total mutt. Will spotted a chain and hooked him up. After rubbing the dog's muzzle for good luck, he rejoined the men inside.

Brace saw Will coming and signaled him that the target was getting out of the shower. Sure enough, a man with a towel wrapped around his waist strutted into the living room. When he saw the visitors, he jumped back, slamming into a wall.

"What the…?!" the man yelled.

"Calm down, Gaetti," Brace said, loosely pointing his pistol at the man. "We're not here to harm you."

As fear overtook his face, Gaetti stared at all the weapons aimed at him. "Okay," he said, breathing hard. "Why are you here?"

"Sit down and I'll tell you."

Anders came into the living room. "The house is clear," he said.

Gaetti reluctantly slid into a recliner. Instead of relaxing, he leaned forward.

"Alright," Brace said, "here's the deal. You've been with someone very dear to us. Her name is Sadie Sterling. Her family has a reputation to maintain."

"Look, we met online through social media. She sent me a friend request. I promise never to see her again." Gaetti thrust out his hand, hoping Brace would shake it. He didn't.

"She's the least of your problems. Take a look at this." Brace handed him a document. "This arrest and search warrant will be served this Tuesday. It charges you with dealing steroids and HGH. The DEA will be busting down your door with this federal search warrant, getting your phone records, business records, and anything else tying you to selling steroids and HGH. They'll come to my dad's ranch and question Sadie, his daughter-in-law. We don't want that."

"Okay, I'll destroy the phone," Gaetti said in his high-pitched voice.

"You can't destroy the records at the phone company, dumbass. Stop talking!" Brace yelled.

Gaetti nodded.

"Next up is the IRS. They'll freeze your bank accounts and assets while the DEA hammers on you. With no money, you'll get a free lawyer. While you're in jail awaiting trial, the DEA will go through your phone records and call all those teenage boys—the ones who trade sex for your steroids. Who knows what a teenager will say when the feds are holding a gun to his head?"

"Oh, God!" Gaetti moaned.

"Exactly. And what will the community say about you? You'll be in prison for many years with men who don't have access to steroids but do have large muscles."

"You're a pretty boy," Anders said. "You'll definitely be in demand."

"Oh, shit." Gaetti was freaking out. "What can I do?"

"We have lawyers who can reduce or eliminate the charges," Brace said.

"How much does it cost? I don't have money to fight these charges, but I'll find what it takes to pay you." Gaetti joined his hands like he was praying to Brace. "I have women followers on my social media accounts who give me money and expensive things. I can get the money."

"So, you live off these women followers of yours?" Anders asked.

"Look, you don't understand. They follow my other bodybuilder friends and me, too. They're lonely and crave a man's attention. They'll give me whatever I want."

"You're a sick bastard and a parasite," Anders replied, his bald head growing red.

Brace held up a hand to quiet Anders. "How did you meet Sadie again?" Brace said.

"Like I said, she contacted me through social media wanting to be my friend. We started flirting for about a month until we decided to meet me at the Omni Fort Worth Hotel."

"Did you know she was married?" Brace asked.

"I figured she was by the way she flaunted her wealth around. She sent me photos of her trips, cars, and jewelry. Since she didn't work, she had to get it somewhere." Gaetti's eyes started watering. "Please, I beg of you. Let me get you the money to take care of this."

"We don't need your money," Brace said. "We're going to put you in a safe house in another state so our people can contain this, put a lid on it. It won't cost you a dime."

"Are you kidding me?"

"This is your lucky day because you just happen to be fucking the right person. We can't have her involved in any of this. We need time to settle things down. It doesn't cost you anything other than your promise never to deal steroids, be a pedophile, and never ever see Sadie again."

"I'm not a pedophile," Gaetti said.

"You have sex with underage boys in exchange for steroids, and that's what makes you a pedophile," Anders said through a clenched jaw.

"They've never complained. And we both get what we want." Gaetti said. "But I promise I'll stop."

Growing impatient, Brace raised his weapon and pointed a red dot directly between Gaetti's eyebrows. "What's your answer?"

"Deal!" Gaetti replied. "What about Waylon?"

"Who?" Brace asked.

"Waylon, my dog. Everyone knows I don't go anywhere without him. They'll get suspicious. I have to take my dog."

"We're not taking a dog," Brace said.

"I can't leave here without my dog."

Brace glanced at his men before lifting his gun to Gaetti's face. "Okay, you got it. Get on the ground."

Gaetti kneeled before Brace and said, "Just promise you'll leave some food for him and plenty of water."

Brace pulled back the slide. "Any final words?"

"No, don't. I can get you the money," Gaetti said, crying.

Brace's face twisted in anger. Will knew Brace didn't want nor need another cleanup job. Too many variables. Young boys coming by looking for steroids and sex. They'd have to be neutralized. And Gaetti's kids driving up to see him. Maybe even more hookup girls. The body count could get out of control.

"Fuck," Brace said, carefully releasing the hammer. "We'll take the dog with us." Brace turned to Will. "You got the dog. You handle him. That means you're coming with us."

"Thank you," Gaetti said, sobbing as he grabbed Brace's pant leg.

Brace kicked his leg free. "Get the fuck off me. Be a man for once, you worthless piece of shit!"

Gaetti let go.

"Now, stand up and get dressed," Brace said. "Plane's leaving soon."

• • •

The Gulfstream tilted to the right, straightened up, and landed smoothly in Bloomfield, New Mexico. Except for a few airport lights, it was dark. Very dark.

Two SUVs loaded up the group and took off in a northwesterly direction. With each passing minute, all traces of civilization disappeared. Wherever they were headed, life was scarce.

Will sat in the first SUV, holding Waylon. By now, they had a good understanding of each other. Waylon knew Will was in charge and would take care of him. Will had even brought plenty of dog food and water. Still, Waylon kept looking for his master.

At 2 a.m., they arrived at an open-air shack illuminated by portable floodlights tied to generators. Coming out to greet them were three Iranian men.

Brace jumped out of the second SUV and talked to the Iranians for a few minutes. Then, he pointed to Gaetti.

The Iranians took a zip-tied Gaetti and led him to the shack. This gave Will time to study the entire boneyard.

The portable lights created long shadows everywhere. But the light was bright enough to illuminate most of the layout.

A large brick furnace sat a football field away. Two four-wheelers were parked nearby. At another location, dozens of brown fifty-gallon metal barrels sat in clusters. Next to those was a pigpen with maybe ten hogs. Off to the side, two backhoes rested close to a Port-a-Potty. A large concrete slab occupied the center, which Will guessed was a heliport. Yet a nearby crane stuck up twenty feet, making it hard for anything to land on the slab. That was a mystery.

"Here's a cooler with some water," Brace said. "Keep yourself hydrated out here. Even though it's dark, you can still dehydrate." Brace pointed to several chairs scattered around the concrete slab. "Make yourself comfortable."

Will led Waylon to a chair facing the crane and sat down.

An Iranian came up to Brace. "When do you want to start?"

Brace studied his watch. "Satellite's clear. We're good."

Another worker brought out a hog and shot it in the head. The sound stiffened the men, awakening them if any had been sleeping.

With the help of another man, they lifted the hog into a large barrel. A worker drove out a Ford F-150 pulling the massive barrel on a double-axel trailer. It stopped in the center of the slab.

The helper jumped off the truck and placed a hose into the barrel with the hog, pumping liquid in it. A sizzling sound reached the group. Wisps of steam followed. Gaetti twisted in his restraints, assuming this was not good news for him.

With that done, two Iranians lifted Gaetti from his chair and walked him to the crane. Then they zip-tied his legs. As soon as they had him hooked up to the crane, he screamed and cried. "You promised you'd put a lid on my case, send me to a safe house. What is this?"

The crane operator engaged the chain and lifted Gaetti ten feet into the air. His bound hands pulled and stretched above his head.

"Hey, you!" he cried. "What are you doing? You promised me!"

When Gaetti was lowered to within a few feet of the barrel, he furtively looked down at the opening, then back up at Brace, and back down again.

Brace finally spoke. "We checked your phone. You were sending nude photos of yourself to Sadie and those underage boys."

"They sent me nudes first!" Gaetti pleaded. "I swear I'll leave them alone. You promised me. Where's my safe house? You're a liar."

"No, I'm not," Brace said casually. "I never said the safe house was for *your* safety. It's for ours. And as for putting a lid on the whole matter, don't worry. We have one ready to put in place."

Brace signaled the crane operator. The structure lurched, and Gaetti's body slowly dropped. His bound feet disappeared in the opening as he struggled to avoid his fate. Soon, a sizzling sound preceded his yelling. The sizzling grew louder but was mostly drowned out by Gaetti's agony-filled screams.

Waylon barked and pulled at his restraints, trying to help his old master. But he couldn't. Will had his leash securely gripped.

Will wanted to throw up but knew he couldn't. Since he couldn't look away without drawing suspicion, he had no choice but to push his mind onto something else even though it was impossible. Gaetti's screams were too loud.

Gaetti's cries eventually stopped, and the dog calmed down.

Will remained at the shack as Brace talked to the men, giving orders. He then walked over to Will.

"I always love to hear them scream. It means the job was done right," he said, chuckling. "Listen, my team needs the jet to go in another direction. Sit here in the shack and wait for a call with an 818 area code. A pilot will give you directions. Then drive yourself over in the other van to meet them. The plane will take you back to the ranch."

"What about the dog?" Will asked.

"Leave him," Brace said. "They'll dispose of him."

The two SUVs took off, leaving Will with the Iranians. He watched as they sealed the barrel with Quickcrete. Then, they used the crane to drop the barrel in the bed of the Ford F-150. The pickup turned on its headlights and took off for the desert, leaving Will and Waylon all alone.

Chapter Fourteen

Pollen floated through the air and landed on Will's jacket. The nearby forest seemed to be laughing at him. He sneezed a few times, futilely hoping each sneeze would be the last.

Waylon wasn't affected by the pollen. He sauntered along, sniffing and checking out his new world.

Will and the dog had arrived an hour earlier, back from the boneyard. With no one watching over him, Will decided to take Waylon back to the ranch. He assumed a man like Gaetti would've chipped the dog. Having the dog here meant tying Gaetti's murder to the Sterlings. As for what he'd say if they found out about him disobeying orders, he'd figure that out later.

Will led Waylon to the rear entrance of the mechanic's barn. Sticking his head in through the open door, he spotted Hector.

"Hector, can I see you a second?" he asked as quietly as possible.

Hector turned away from an ATV and grabbed a rag, wiping his oily hands as he walked toward Will. "What's up?"

"Come outside for a sec."

Will stepped back and held Waylon by the leash. When Hector saw the dog, his eyes lit up. "Where did you get him?"

"On a trip to the boneyard," Will whispered. "His owner didn't make the return trip."

Hector nodded, raising his eyebrows and pursing his lips.

"Look, I need a favor," Will said. "I couldn't leave him out there to be shot or die of starvation. Any chance you could use a dog around here? Maybe keep him for a while until I figure out what to do."

Hector squatted down and petted the dog. "I always had a dog growing up. I love them. What's his name?"

"Waylon."

"I could use an assistant," Hector said, rubbing the dog's neck. "Someone to chase away the varmints."

"Here's a package of his food," Will said, handing him a brown sack. "It'll last a few days."

"When it runs out, I'll have one of my men bring some dog food from town," Hector offered.

"And there's one more part," Will said, looking around. "Brace told me to leave the dog at the boneyard. I couldn't do it. Can you keep him undercover for a while?"

"No problem," Hector said, standing up. "We've had dogs and cats around here before. I know they had a dog at the horse barn at one time. No one will care if we don't make a big deal about it."

"That's what I was hoping."

He handed the dog over and caught up on any news before heading to the ranch house. It was after one, so he'd have to scrounge around for something to eat.

Will walked along a pavestone path, thinking about how Waylon represented a key piece of evidence against Brace Sterling. He also thought back to the sickening way Gaetti had died. As much as he'd wanted to pull his gun out and start shooting, he knew the surest way to get back at a psycho like Brace was to be the best witness possible. Seeing Brace hunched over at the defendant's table would be sweet revenge.

Will pushed into the kitchen to see a young Hispanic girl cleaning the dishes. Mrs. White sat at a table, going over a to-do list.

"Look at you," Mrs. White said. "Working hard and skipping lunch. You must be pushing for a raise."

"It's less hard work and more bad luck," Will replied. "The plane took five hours to pick me up. What did I miss?"

"The usual. You want some?"

"Sure. Where is it? I'll get it out."

"No, I'll fetch it," Mrs. White said, getting up. "You grab something to drink. Let Mrs. White wait on you."

"That puts me in rare company," Will said.

She put her finger over her lips. "I won't tell anyone if you won't."

"I can keep a secret. It's the people I tell who can't," Will said, laughing as he headed to the soft drinks.

After a few minutes, Mrs. White brought over a plate of small sandwiches. On the side were German-style potato salad and her homemade pickles. She grabbed a cup of coffee and joined him, making small talk while he ate.

"You want some coffee?" Mrs. White asked him after he was done.

"No, thank you," he replied. "I'm headed straight to my room to shower and crash. I'm exhausted."

"At least you have a full belly now." She patted him on the back. "Sleep well."

Just as he was leaving, an older woman he'd never seen before appeared with a note. "This is for you," she said.

Will opened it up and read the contents. He glanced at Mrs. White. "Looks like I'll miss supper too."

"Would you like me to pack you some food to go?"

"No, thanks," Will replied. "I'm sure they'll take good care of me in first class."

Will hustled to his apartment and changed clothes. After checking everything over, he went to the parking area where a Range Rover idled.

"Sorry I'm late," he said, getting in.

"No problem," the driver replied. "We have plenty of time."

Twisting around, Will saw Sadie in the back, checking her phone and ignoring him. He decided not to say anything to her. There would be plenty of time on the plane.

The trip to DFW Airport was smooth. Will loved it when he didn't have to drive.

At the curb, he helped the driver with the luggage while keeping an eye on Sadie. She stood a few feet away, checking her texts. When the last bag was out, the driver handed Will a brown envelope. "Don't open this until you get to D.C.," he said.

Will stuffed it in his jacket before hailing a skycap to check in what looked like fifteen pieces of luggage. He had already put his zip ties, gun, and spare magazines in a duffel bag and given it to the driver. No way he could take it on the flight.

At the counter, Sadie ignored him. The cold shoulder continued all the way to D.C., which was okay with Will because he slept most of the trip.

When they arrived at Ronald Reagan National Airport, two men in an SUV greeted them. They loaded all the luggage while Sadie climbed into the front seat. This left Will in the back with the other man.

Twenty minutes later, the SUV stopped in front of a brownstone in Alexandria. As Will and the man next to him exited, the driver went to the door and knocked. Cole appeared. Sadie bounded up the steps, brushing past him like he wasn't there. Cole walked down to the curb as Will and the two men unloaded the luggage.

"Would you like us to take all this inside?" the driver asked Cole.

"No," he replied. "Will and I can handle it."

Will tensed up. Why not let the men carry the bags into the house? It would take longer without their help. Did a bullet await him inside? But then he had this thought: *If they wanted to kill me, they would've done it at the boneyard.*

Still, he was on high alert.

Both Will and Cole grabbed two pieces and made the walk up the steps. They repeated the trip three times. With all the bags sitting in the foyer, Will turned to leave.

"Wait a minute," Cole said. "I need to talk to you."

"But I have a flight back to Dallas in an hour," Will said, anxious to get out of the house.

"Is Sadie having an affair?" Cole whispered.

Will grimaced and said nothing.

Cole moved closer. "Come on, think about it. Has she been having an affair?"

Will considered how this might fit into his operation. Depending on what he said, there was so much that could go wrong. "Yet chaos always breeds opportunity," Dr. Z had told him. "If you sow chaos in your enemy's camp, you may be able to gain more in one day than a thousand calm days. Just look for your opportunity."

Will made eye contact with Cole and answered firmly. "Yes, she has."

"Did my dad or Brace tell you not to say anything?"

"No."

"Did Anders or Green tell you not to say anything?"

"No."

Angry and distraught, Cole looked away.

Will put his hand on Cole's right shoulder. "Look, I'm here to protect her. I don't want to get caught up in anything. This is personal between you and Sadie. No one else needs to get between you two."

"I know what she did," Cole said as he stared at the floor. "I know what happened."

"Then you don't need me connecting the dots."

"You're a loyal employee to the family," Cole said, looking back up at Will. "I admire your loyalty because I know what that takes."

Will nodded.

"And there's something about you that I understand. It's like we're part of something. I don't know what it is, but I'm going to figure it out."

For the second time in minutes, Will was afraid he'd been made. "I'm sorry, Cole, but I've got to get back to the airport."

"You haven't heard the last of me," Cole said.

As Will turned to leave, he wondered what that meant. It may be time to end this operation.

He opened the door to the SUV and got in.

"You're fifteen minutes late," the driver said.

Will raised his voice. "Look, buddy, I was helping him tote all that luggage up the stairs and into his bedroom. Cut me a break."

Will ignored him the rest of the way. The driver dropped him off at the check-in curb, speeding away before Will could close the door. He watched as the SUV dodged passengers who were crossing from the parking garage and wheeling luggage behind them.

Reaching for his ID, Will remembered the envelope in his jacket pocket. He found an unoccupied bench inside the terminal and opened it up. Inside was $5,000 cash. At the bottom of the envelope was a little scrap of paper. It read, *Call this number*. Will pulled out his cell phone and dialed.

"Yes," a man said. It was Grayson.

"Mr. Sterling," Will replied. "This is a pleasant surprise."

"Where are you at?"

"I'm here at Reagan National."

"Did you drop Sadie off?" Grayson asked.

"Yes."

"Did you talk to Cole?"

Will hesitated. "I helped with the luggage and had a brief moment with him."

"Was he in good spirits?"

"He was happy to have Sadie back. I mean, he was thrilled."

Silence.

"Okay," Grayson said, "get on the plane and come back here. We'll talk some more."

The call ended. Will leaned back on the bench and wondered what was coming next.

•••

It was almost one in the morning when Will arrived at the ranch. He was exhausted, especially from having to find a rental car after his ride failed to show. It was yet another crack in the Sterling armor of perfection.

Will had solved the problem by using his fake ID and paying cash. Despite his calls, no one told him why the ride failed to show.

After making the long drive to the ranch, he exited the rental car and walked toward his apartment. A man on an ATV came from the direction of his apartment and flagged him down with a spotlight. "Mr. Sterling needs to see you. Go through the front entrance."

Exhausted, Will's shoulders drooped. But he followed instructions and went through the front doors, taking a seat in the vestibule. He used this time to take inventory.

He had no gun. The driver had taken it before the outbound flight. If a driver had been waiting for him on the return flight, he'd have his weapon back. But the driver no-showed.

He'd seen Gaetti killed at the boneyard. And he knew the approximate location of the boneyard in New Mexico. So did a lot of other people and they hadn't been eliminated... yet.

He'd disobeyed orders by bringing the dog back to the ranch. Did they know about that?

Cole suspected something. Maybe his cover was blown. There were so many ways this could go south.

The British butler appeared and asked if he'd like a drink.

"Yes," Will said, "give me a shot of a single malt scotch." He needed a little calming down.

When the drink arrived, it was delicious scotch—smooth and expensive. Will took a sip, followed by a deep breath. He felt better.

He had been sitting for almost twenty minutes when the butler motioned for him to come. Will followed the man to Grayson's office. There stood another man, a real monster. At six-foot-nine-inches and hair past his shoulders, this steroid freak was a frightening sight.

Without saying a word, the tough guy waved Will into Grayson's study and closed the doors behind him until he heard that distinctive click.

"Take a seat," Grayson said.

On one side of his desk was Brace and the other Anders. They all faced him. Over in the corner, almost hidden, was an attractive woman with blonde hair. She seemed to be an assistant or a scheduler.

The speakers played Don McLean's "Starry, Starry Night." It set a soft, sensitive mood. Will hoped it stayed that way.

Grayson started the questioning by asking about the car trip to DFW International Airport and ending with their arrival at Cole's house. Will gave him every detail he could remember. Since Sadie had said nothing to him, it was a short rendition.

"Do you like working on her detail?" Grayson asked.

"No, not really," Will replied. "She's one promiscuous bitch."

The corners of Grayson's mouth turned up. Brace and Anders were unable to hold it in. They laughed out loud. The monster remained stone-faced.

Grayson switched to Cole. "What was his demeanor?"

Will told them, leaving out Cole's words.

After a few minutes of this, Grayson leaned forward and placed his palms on the desk. "Tell me all about the strip clubs Sadie visits. Leave nothing out."

Will gave it to them. When he finished, they peppered him with other matters.

"Is she a lesbian?"

"Do you think she spends too much money?"

"How hard does she try to elude you?"

Again, Will answered all their questions.

When they moved on to the cell phones, Will surprised them. "She has all these burner phones. I thought she was getting them from you. If not, I'm guessing she has one or two others you didn't provide her."

Grayson glanced at Brace, who frowned.

"Do you trust her?" Grayson asked Will.

"I don't trust her at all. Not one bit."

The room fell silent. Grayson swirled his drink as he sat in his large chair, pondering everything Will had told him. Then, he pushed back from the desk and turned to his fireplace to stoke a log. That was when Will noticed the temperature. Despite it being August, it was frigid in the large office.

Grayson poked at the fire several times, staring at the embers. After a minute of this, he put the poker back in its place and poured himself another drink from the bar.

"Would you like a refresher?" Grayson asked Will.

"I'd like Glen Fiddich if you've got it."

Grayson cocked a sideways glance at him. "I like a man with good taste."

The two talked about scotch for a while, with the other four watching and observing. As Grayson ended his questioning, Brace immediately began his.

"What did you think about what happened at the boneyard?"

Will turned to face Brace. "You don't pay me to think about things like that, so I don't."

Brace grinned. "Good answer. Listen, we're going to keep the twins here for the rest of the summer and into the new school year. That will give Cole and Sadie some time to be together. Much of the time, the kids will remain here on the ranch. When they go into town, you will always have a driver. The two of you will protect them at all costs. Understand?"

"Absolutely," Will replied.

"Good. During the time you're not watching the kids, I'm putting you on Anders's team. They handle special jobs. What do you think about that?"

"I'd love to, but I don't know that I can compete with those young guys. They've been trained by professionals from an early age. I've been trained by nonprofessionals."

Grayson spoke up. "Sometimes, there's wisdom beyond youth. And experience on the street can come in handy in more ways than one."

It was quiet again.

Finally, Anders spoke. "I want you to take tomorrow off. Okay?"

"Sure," Will said. "I need to shop for some personal items. Maybe catch a movie. Can I borrow a vehicle?"

"Of course," Anders said. "Whatever you need."

With the meeting over, Will was escorted out of the ranch house by the muscle-bound gorilla. A few minutes later, his head hit the pillow and he was out. It had been a very long two days.

• • •

Later that morning, Will awoke refreshed. He joined the other men for breakfast, then grabbed a Range Rover and headed into town.

His destination was a Walmart in North Dallas. This would be suspicious since he could easily find one in Fort Worth. If they had a tracker on his vehicle, they would see where he was going. But he had to take a chance.

After entering the Walmart, he lingered in the men's clothing area, looking for a tail. Satisfied there was none, he slipped his phone above a ceiling tile in a dressing room stall. Then he made his way to the manager's office. His friend happened to be in.

"Hey, I need to make a call," Will said. "Can I have your office for thirty minutes?"

"Why, sure," the manager replied. "Just promise to tell me some spy stories one day when you retire."

Will sat there for twenty minutes, telling his handler all he'd seen. When he was done, his handler told him they'd researched Carlos Santos.

"He's an under-the-radar drug lord," Rodgers said. "Small, but very effective. The D.C. guys want you to get in deep and see where this goes. They're handling this investigation directly. But this news is going to upset you: Schneider has been promoted to D.C."

Will held the phone away from his face. "Figures," he groaned. "Connect me to Dan."

Dan answered and asked for a plan.

"Let's meet at the usual Cinemark theater," Will said. "I'm heading there now."

Thirty minutes later, Will emerged from a rear exit of the theater and spotted a silver Chevy truck.

"Good to see you again," Dan said as Will climbed in. "And the better news is that you won't have to deal with Schneider again. He's moving on up."

"Yeah, I heard," Will replied as Dan drove away from the theater. "I'm sure they'll plug in another blue flamer turd soon enough. Just take me home. I can only use this ruse for another two hours or so."

"Why don't we catch something to eat first?" Dan said, ignoring his comment.

Will sighed. "That doesn't sound good. Something must've happened. Why don't you just rip the Band-Aid off?"

"Okay. Jennifer has filed for divorce. I've arranged for Sid Benton to be your lawyer. Sid said you could pay him his retainer once the investigation is over. He said you're good for the money."

Will looked away, noting the gray sky and biting his lower lip.

"You want to talk about it?" Dan asked.

"No. It's over. Let's just talk about this operation."

"You sure?" Dan said. He allowed some time to go by before changing the subject. "I've been hitting the computer and talking to sources. The Sterlings are into sex trafficking—overseas, mostly. They move drugs, mainly heroin, but not like a drug cartel. They do everything smart while staying way below the radar. One source said they're also into black-market luxury cars and smuggling weapons. That would explain the top-of-the-line weapons and explosives they have. They seem to touch every known industry. And no real trouble from anyone. They offset this low profile with a ton of philanthropy work." Dan turned to Will. "I'm not exaggerating when I say this is a major case, maybe the biggest the Bureau has ever seen. But you can't lose Jennifer over this. Right?"

"I already lost her," Will said sullenly. "I might as well make it count for something. Let's go somewhere private. I need that drink."

"I know just the place."

Dan hit the freeway exit and did a U-turn. As he straightened out, his phone rang. It was D.C.

"Rockton, are you there?"

"Yes," Will replied, sitting up taller.

"Your handler just entered your report. This is so unbelievable! I feel like I'm reading a novel."

"I totally agree with that," Will said.

"You've snagged some great evidence on Brace. We already have enough to bring in those Iranians at the boneyard and get them to talk. They may roll on Brace."

"Good luck with that," Will said, "They don't seem the type to roll. And the muriatic acid makes it even harder."

"Our lab experts are telling us that mixing an animal's DNA with a human gives them an argument in court that it's nothing but an animal in the barrel, that the pig ate something with human DNA on it. Either way, we would have to explain how an animal's DNA is mixed with a human. We'll have to inspect any DNA that's left."

"You won't even find the barrel," Will told him.

"That's why we're leaving you there. We need to see if you can get Victoria, Cole, and Grayson. Or at least see if you can find any weak links in their chain, guys we can roll upward. Video and audio evidence. Anything. We can still make the case with the missing pedophile bodybuilder. Maybe we can get that county deputy who stopped the wannabe cowboy to roll. We already have his name by checking the GPS in the patrol cars. Just keep digging. If we get a search warrant for the Sterlings' ranch, I want to know we'll hit the jackpot for sure. We only get one chance at this. If we swing and miss at these guys, well… I don't want to tell you how bad that would be for all of us."

"I understand," Will said. "I'll do my best."

Dan put the phone away. "Come on. Let's take an hour off. Dinner's on me."

Will picked up a blue file from the console. "Is this the divorce stuff?"

"It is."

"I'll look through it while you drive. Maybe I can sign everything before you get there. Then, I can shut my mind off for sixty fucking minutes!"

Dan nodded and drove.

Chapter Fifteen

The first strong cold front of the year blew a piece of ivy into the glass. Will watched as it fluttered and flailed, its withered leaves barely attached to the vine. Standing in the living room, he looked out the bay window past the ivy to Sashay's, a shop near the park. Its purple awning flapped wildly.

Behind him, Cole banged away on his computer. He had four computer monitors set up. Above them were three TV screens mounted to a wall. Several clocks displayed the time in London, Brussels, Moscow, Beijing, and Sydney.

Will held a black composite clipboard, reviewing tomorrow's itinerary. The second item caught his attention: Sashay's. It reminded him how deep he was into this investigation.

Two months earlier, he had been flown with the twins to Alexandria. He and a team of three other security professionals watched over Cole's family. If Sadie went out, so did Will.

For living quarters, Cole put him in an upstairs spare bedroom. The idea was to have someone on the premises ready to take a bullet for the twins. The reality was somewhat different because Cole needed a close confidant—someone to talk to about his problems.

The minute he'd hit Alexandria, Sadie complained to him about Cole. It was like hearing in stereo all the problems with their relationship. For the first weeks, Will wasn't sure he could take it.

While Cole told his problems to Will because he wanted advice, Sadie told Will her problems with Cole because she wanted Will. He had mostly resisted her advances. But three weeks earlier, she had shopped at Sashay's. This was where his career had almost gone off the rails.

The regular driver had called in with a family emergency. Because the twins were in daycare with their own guard, Will drove Sadie around. They visited Sashay's.

In the dressing area, Sadie touched, probed, and grabbed Will below the belt. For some reason, the sales associates left the store. Later, he assumed Sadie had paid them. Without a third party to worry about, Will's worries coagulated even more.

In a familiar move, Sadie asked Will to assist her with a stuck zipper on a pair of super skinny jeans.

"How did you get these on in the first place, girl? Paint?"

"Very funny," Sadie replied. "Just help me. They hurt my stomach."

Will moved in to assist Sadie, and she pulled him even closer to her taut body. As she loosened his belt, his remaining ability to resist had been whittled down by months and months without a physical companion. Somehow, Sadie knew how to reach into his body with those thin fingers, grab his soul, and squeeze it. His eyes rolled back in their sockets, and he lost consciousness.

In a vision, there was Dr. Z. He was telling the male recruits, "Women can give you three things: sex, freedom from having to carry a badge, and a new career. And it all happens in the blink of a zipper."

Will and the other recruits had laughed.

"Everything you worked so hard to accomplish can be extinguished in a few seconds," Dr. Z had said. "Especially you agents in UC work. Don't cross that line. Too many agents have lost cases in court due to infidelity with subjects or lying under oath about it."

Will's eyes opened, and he immediately pulled away from Sadie.

"What's wrong?" she asked.

"I'm here to protect you. Not have sex with you." It had been a close call. Very close.

After he had composed himself, they left the store and strolled around. As a consolation prize, Will had caressed her hand and held it, feeling euphoric as he floated down the sidewalk. The possibility of consequences had faded again.

Two young men from a nearby university walking toward the happy couple smiled at him. One of them gave Will a headshake, acknowledging that he had bagged a trophy. For an hour or so, Will felt alive. The words *boneyard* and *divorce* didn't exist.

Will noticed Sadie relished the attention too. Older women sized her up, grimacing at her figure and the distinguished-looking man on her arm. She knew she was something special and that other women hated her. She also knew she was from the wrong side of the Granbury tracks. But now, she'd made it to the major leagues and wanted the other snobs to know.

During his time in D.C., Will noticed Sadie was never invited to events unless it was with Cole. The D.C. and Northern Virginia society women knew all about Sadie, so they avoided her like the plague. That meant their husbands had to as well.

Of course, that night in bed, the exhilaration was long gone. The crushing weight of thinking of sleeping with Sadie landed hard on his chest. He was still married, even though it was to an unfaithful wife. Evening the score wouldn't make him feel any better. Instead, he would only feel worse.

As Will tossed and turned, he worried about the mistakes he had made. Holding her hand in public was stupid. He wondered if he'd be able to have an open casket or no funeral at all. Would he just disappear in some barrel of acid like all the others?

Will blinked a few times and looked up from his clipboard. He was no longer standing by the window. It was 11 p.m. Cole had moved from his desk to a brown leather overstuffed chair, a pamphlet of papers piled high in his lap.

Will looked around the room. The door was closed to keep the twins out, although they were already in bed. Cole's office was sparse by most standards. There were numerous accolades and photographs with presidents and other world leaders hanging on one wall. Sitting near the desk in a place of honor was a bronze bust of Winston Churchill, Cole's favorite world leader. The office was functional but tasteful, not ostentatious or showy.

Several low knocks on the door drew Will's attention. He moved to open it, but Sadie appeared before he could.

"Can I speak to you for a few minutes?" she asked Cole.

Will stood up to leave, but both Sadie and Cole urged him to stay.

"What do you need?" Cole asked in a slow Texan drawl.

"I'm worried about you working so hard," she said in a concerned voice. "And for what? This government doesn't care at all about you or what you do for them. All you are is a garbageman handling their dirty work when no one else will do it."

Cole looked directly into her eyes. "That's my choice, not yours. Is there anything else?"

"Yes," she said, turning sweet and pleasant. "You're working so hard you deserve a vacation. I'm tired of being here in cold D.C. I want to see some sun and lay on a beach for a few days. Come on. Let's go."

"Sadie, you know I can't leave D.C. right now. I have to prepare for that intelligence conference in a couple of weeks in Brussels."

Sadie continued the sweet voice. "Well, I want to go."

"I'm sorry, I can't. We'll plan something for later in the spring."

"No need to wait," she said, her eyes wide with excitement. "I've booked rooms at the Playa Rico Resort. Kodi, Brooke, and I are leaving in a couple of days. I would love for my husband to be there with his wife and family."

Cole shook his head. "I can't. Besides, it's too short notice. You'll just have to cancel the plans."

A change came over Sadie. Her eyes turned angry, her nostrils flared, and a dark crimson crept up her face. She threw the vacation itinerary on the desk and spun to the office door, slamming it hard.

Cole spilled his papers onto the floor as he got out of his chair. "I don't fucking believe this!" he shouted. "I need to be on my game at this conference, and now I'm going to have to put up with this mess for the next two weeks." He stalked around the office, hands on his hips, cursing. "What do you think?" he asked Will.

Will calculated the possible outcomes and how they might move this investigation forward. He had no real option. "You've been working hard, Cole. Your eyes are glazed over and bloodshot. You could use some sun and relaxation for a couple of days. That's the best way to be in shape for your conference."

"No!" Cole snarled. "I meant sending her to Key West without me. I can't leave here."

Will stepped closer to Cole and doubled down. "If you're going to have a family, you have to spend time with them. Or one day, you'll come home and the family isn't there. Your wife will belong to another man, and the kids will be playing with a different father."

"That sounds like a lesson you learned the hard way."

"I'm divorced, so yeah, I know it all too well." It scared Will how fast his undercover role was morphing into his personal life.

Cole rubbed his jaw. "You know, I could get a ton of work done if I didn't have her sniping at me all day long. I guess I'll have to send you down there to make sure she stays out of trouble."

Will closed his eyes and gritted his teeth. "Cole, you really ought to go. Trust me. Be with your family." Visions of a master suite and a large bed filled Will's brain. There was Sadie, slipping out of her bathing suit while tugging on his belt. It almost made him shiver. "I mean it!" Will said forcefully one last time. "Go."

Cole put his hand on Will's shoulder and smiled. "You'll have to go and take one for the team. Don't have too much fun. Those sunny Key West beach babes can make a man forget his name."

Will shook his head. He didn't need a beach babe when Sadie would be happy to fill that role. If he weren't already dead, he'd be a goner soon.

"I guess I'd better get busy coordinating the team we'll need," Will said, picking up the itinerary from the desk. "Should I tell Sadie, or do you want to?"

"You can," Cole said, turning back to his work. "Just keep her out of here the rest of the night."

•••

Will disassembled his gun, spreading the parts over a special gray cloth. As he cleaned each one, he stared out the window at Key West. Tourists snaking down Duval Street mingled with cars. Frozen drinks in plastic cups. Topless men. Girls in tiny bikinis. Everyone was enjoying themselves while Will pretended to be a criminal so he could catch a bunch of criminals. And, of course, stay alive.

Across the hall from Will's room was Sadie's luxury suite. She looked out over a gorgeous beach and the crystal-blue ocean. She had it good. But getting her here almost didn't happen.

First, Brace was not willing to provide any security for Sadie. Sadie responded by saying she'd take Will and the men in D.C. "If they're good enough to protect us at home, they can handle the job in Key West."

Brace passed her off to Grayson. After a half-hour of back and forth on the phone, he'd made no progress with his daughter-in-law.

Left with no options, Brace agreed to provide a team from his vaunted Echo One Nine. But he needed four extra days. To that, Sadie agreed.

On the appointed day, J.D., Nate, and Hannah loaded up the Echo One Nine team in the Gulfstream and flew down to Key West. After dropping them off, they jetted up to D.C. and picked up Sadie, the twins, and Will's men. A quick return trip to Key West and everyone was cozy. Luckily, Will had found a spare moment to call his handler before leaving D.C. That gave him some comfort.

Will reassembled the gun, checked the action, and loaded it. Satisfied, he holstered the weapon. That was when he noticed a problem with the lime-green rubber bracelet around his wrist.

Liam Stone

Wearing it signified he belonged on the resort. However, it caught on his holster when he tried to draw. That could be fatal.

As he moved the bracelet to his left wrist, the phone rang.

"We're going to the pool," Sadie said bluntly. "Meet you out in the hall."

Will checked his gear and appearance before stepping out to meet them. Not surprisingly, the twins had matching pink swimsuits with opposite patterns. Then Sadie appeared. She wore a one-piece turquoise, black, and pink swimsuit painted onto her body. The palm leaf pattern appeared strategically over her private parts. There was no way a man could look away from that.

"Come on, girls. Let's go get some sun and have some fun," she said, patting Will on the chest. "Relax, you'll get to enjoy this all week."

Will grimaced, glancing back at the guard who stood outside Sadie's suite. He wanted to make sure the guard knew he was disgusted with her comment.

The pool area was crowded. The twins were the first to get wet. Will stood under an awning as they mingled with other kids their age, splashing and having fun.

Sadie found an open cabana next to the hot tub to her liking. Two men with Will fanned out behind it, making sure it was safe. Will moved in to help her arrange the towels, snacks, and waters on one of the two small teakwood tables.

"Would you put some sunscreen on me?" she asked Will as she undid one of her straps.

Will knew Anders was watching from a hotel window. It would look wrong being that intimate with her.

"I'm here for your security, not to oil you up," he said, loud enough for one of the security detail men to hear.

"Fine!" she said. "I'll call that cabana boy over to do it then." Will moved back to his prior spot and watched as a Latino male took great pleasure in rubbing it in. When that was over, Sadie took her time spreading two blue-striped white towels over a lounge chair, bending over several times and making sure the men around the pool noticed her tanned and toned body.

Straightening herself up, she pulled her long brunette hair back slowly, tying it with a red scrunchie. A young waitress stopped by and asked if she would like a drink.

"I think I'll have a mojito to kick off this vacation."

"Good choice," replied the waitress.

Will glanced up to the balcony of room 504. Anders sat there, using a pair of his favorite Steiner binoculars. Will knew he was taking notes for Brace, documenting Sadie's every action. Will also knew Anders had a Nikon camera on a tripod to photograph any discrepancy she might indulge in.

Before long, Sadie struck up a conversation with Jane, a woman from Fort Worth, on vacation with her older children. Even though Jane appeared to be in her mid-sixties, she wore a one-piece white bathing suit that had seen better days. Like Sadie, she wasn't beyond trying to earn the men's attention at the pool, hot tub, or on the beach.

Will listened in on their conversation.

"My husband's family has the F Bar A Ranch just outside of Granbury."

"Oh!" Jane said. "Then, Grayson Sterling is your father-in-law?"

"Yes," Sadie replied smugly.

"My daughter went to Stanford with your sister-in-law, Victoria. I can't remember her married name."

"Cox," Sadie quickly answered. "Victoria Sterling-Cox."

"What's she doing now?"

Sadie filled her in, explaining how Tori lives in both Houston and London.

"I always knew she'd excel in international business," Jane said. "She has that killer instinct like her dad. I feel sorry for whoever tries to screw with her or her company."

The women gossiped and gabbed as time drifted on and on. Before Will knew it, he'd been standing in the exact same spot for three straight days.

During the morning's briefing, Anders reported to Brace on a speakerphone that all was well except for Sadie's flaunting and flirting with almost every man at the resort.

Will chuckled silently, recalling the women who had glared at Sadie as she displayed her tight body around the resort. She thoroughly rubbed it in when she strutted around in three-inch heels, searching for more towels or a cabana boy to apply sunscreen to her strapless back.

"I need more photos," Brace demanded.

"You got them," Anders said, wrapping up the FaceTime meeting.

As he watched Sadie flirting with another man in the hot tub, Will could imagine the Nikon going off. Brace would get all the photos he wanted.

• • •

With two days left on this vacation, Will had some serious decisions to make. As he stood at his post on the pool deck, he wondered what came next. Should he walk away and let D.C.

bring the wrath of God on the Sterlings? Or should he stay and gut it out, hoping for the grand slam of evidence?

Leaving now seemed like dropping a half-eaten Snickers bar on the men's room floor. Unsatisfying.

He didn't want to spend the rest of his life wondering "what if." He had to stick it out and hope for something to break soon.

It would.

Chapter Sixteen

Sadie leaned back, giggling. A plate of fresh barbeque chicken sat in front of her, mostly untouched. Jane, on the other hand, had wolfed down several ribs and a chicken breast. She was enjoying herself.

The Playa Rico Resort knew how to keep their guests happy. A beach cookout was one way.

"I'll get us a refill," Jane said, heading back to the bar.

Will watched as she swayed from side to side. Jane had matched Sadie drink for drink. If she looked like this with a plate of food in her stomach, Sadie had to be flying.

The bartender greeted Jane but spent most of his time focused on Sadie. Will had been studying him. Since their first day, the Cuban bartender had kept the drinks coming to Sadie, occasionally taking time to rub some lotion on her. Sure, he was working for tips. But did this guy have something else in mind?

It was getting close to ten. The event would be over. Will couldn't wait to park Sadie in her suite and take a soak in his room's large tub. His feet hurt from hours of standing.

When the drinks were ready, the bartender helped Jane carry them back to the table. As he set them down, Sadie whispered something to him. He pointed to an area and helped her up. Will assumed she needed to go to the restroom.

Sadie staggered as the bartender held her up. He spent most of the trip eying her black beach dress, especially the elastic top clinging to her chest just above her breasts.

A few steps from the restroom, she grabbed the bartender's shirt, pulling him with her. He glanced around, clearly considering the proposal until he found Will a few steps behind him. The bartender jerked her hand loose, setting himself free.

Sadie reached to grab him again, but Will was there. "Come on," he said. "Let's get you into the restroom all by your little ole self."

Sadie scowled at him but went inside. Obviously, she had to go bad.

A few minutes later, Sadie exited the restroom and staggered back to the bar. She said something to the bartender, who answered her. Then, she made her way to the table.

"Will," Sadie said, using her index finger to signal him. "Come here."

Will moved to the table. "What is it?" he asked, withholding a tired sigh.

"Get the car. We're going to a topless bar."

"No, I don't think so. We need to get you to your room."

"Call your boss," she said condescendingly.

Will, feeling anger welling up, pulled out his phone and dialed Anders. "She wants to go to a strip club. The bartender must have told her about it."

"Hang on," Anders said.

Will waited a few minutes, holding the phone to his ear.

"Okay, it's a go," Anders said. "The twins are locked down for the night. Brace said he's okay with her going to one. We'll have the SUV out front. I'll have an Echo One Nine team follow you."

"You're kidding, right?!"

"No. Let her go, as long as you take her," Anders replied.

A frustrated Will hung up. "Okay, Sadie, you're going to a topless bar."

Will escorted her to the lobby. "Where are your friends?" he asked.

"Her daughter wants to go. They'll meet us there."

Will helped Sadie into the SUV, making sure she had her seatbelt fastened.

The drive to Timba's took approximately sixty minutes. Once inside, Will counted eleven men watching dark-skinned dancers from various islands on elevated stands throughout the club.

Sadie plopped down on a dirty navy-blue couch and immediately attracted a lead dancer's attention, offering to purchase drinks for her. She also wanted a lap dance from the slender Jamaican woman.

Jane and her daughter, Kyndall, arrived and sat on either side of Sadie, watching her give them a masterclass in strip clubs.

The dancer immediately spotted Sadie's bankroll and was more than willing to perform for her. When Sadie whispered something in her ear, the dancer boldly pulled down Sadie's top and sucked on her breasts. Will looked around to see Anders snapping photos with a minicamera. Brace would be thrilled with these photos for sure.

Before the Rihanna song "Pour It Up" ended, a second dancer came over to feast on Sadie's cash buffet. Working with the first dancer, they rubbed and sucked Sadie raw. Jane and Kyndall looked stunned. With nothing to do, they sat there and watched.

Kyndall soon attracted the eye of several drunken men willing to buy her drinks. She moved to a bar and cozied up next to a beach bum with long stringy hair. Jane stayed on the couch, taking it all in and pounding down the highballs. And Sadie rotated through the dancers, making each one rich.

It went on and on. The girls from the Playa Rico Resort were having the time of their lives. Will looked at his watch and saw it was well after 1 a.m. He knew the club closed at two. He couldn't wait to be back in his room and asleep.

Out of the corner of his eye, he spotted two new arrivals. It was the dark-haired bartender. And he had brought a friend. Before Will knew it, the pair had ingratiated themselves with the women. Sadie was curled up with the bartender on the couch while his friend had cut out Kyndall from the beach bum. He was busy cleaning her teeth with his tongue. Jane, close to death from alcohol poisoning, had her head back on the couch, mumbling to herself. She was spared her companions' obscene behavior.

Will moved away from the orgy and toward Anders. "Can you believe this?" Will said. "I need to stop this before it gets out of hand."

"No, let it play out," Anders said.

"What?!" Will replied.

Anders stared directly at Will. "You spend more time with her than anyone else. Be grateful she hasn't tried that act on you."

Will nodded and looked away, avoiding further eye contact.

"Anders, is that you?" a deep voice cried out behind them near the front door.

Will turned around to see a man coming through the entrance.

"Well, I'll be damned. It *is* you!" the man said. "What the hell are you doing here? Last I heard you were working contracting jobs in Afghanistan and Iraq."

"Sully!" Anders said. "It's great to see you."

The two men embraced.

"See that brunette over there on the couch, making out with that Cuban?" Anders said, pointing. "I'm here to protect her for my employer."

"The one licking his cheek?" Sully asked.

"That's the one."

"Then you're doing a shitty job," Sully joked.

"I'm here to protect her discreetly, not get into her business," Anders said. "This here is Will. He works with me."

Will shook Sully's hand.

"Listen up, old friend," Sully said. "I didn't mean you were doing a bad job by not being close to her. The hombre she's with is on the National Terrorist Watch List. So is that other guy over there with his hand up that girl's shirt. The Bureau is watching those two very closely."

"What the fuck?!" Anders said. "Are you kidding me?"

"No. Trust me on this Anders. Those guys are hardcore Cuban terrorists. They took menial jobs at a resort near here to work their way into wealthy women's lives. We're guessing they want to get some money and maybe a green card. They got off a small boat near Key West. Even though they're classified as Venezuelans, they originate from Cuba. I'm here with Homeland Security assisting the Bureau. These two may be working with some guys who run this club. We already know they have contacts at the resort."

Anders slapped his leg. "I can't believe it! If you hadn't come along, these fuckers might have ruined my day."

"For sure," Sully said. "But it's worse than that. This place is getting ready to have a federal search warrant executed on it." He glanced at his watch. "In eighteen minutes, to be exact. The Miami Division's SWAT team is taking this place down.

Get her out now. You can thank me later by giving me a job when I retire next year."

Anders grabbed his arm. "You got one for sure, Sully. But do you mind if I take those two motherfuckers with me? I may be able to extract some information out of them the hard way."

"That would sure make my life easier. But if I agree, will you get me a summary of the intel gathered?"

"You got it, brother," Anders said, "along with a case of your favorite expensive bourbon." He turned to Will. "Figure out a way to get those two terrorists and Sadie out in one package. And make it quick."

Will walked briskly to the couch, slowing down to avoid alerting the two men. Leaning down, he whispered to Sadie, "I've arranged for a bar down the road to stay open after hours. They have a steaming hot tub available, too. They're ready to keep this party going for you."

Sadie smiled and whispered a drunken, "I love you," to Will.

She spent the next four minutes telling the two men and women they could continue the party at another bar. Once they all agreed, the group slowly got to their feet, stretched, and worked their way to the exit. During all this, Will watched Anders stare a hole through his heavily scratched Omega watch as the minutes ticked off.

Finally, the party group left the club. But they still had to get out of the parking lot.

To speed them up, Will grabbed Sadie's arm, and Anders grabbed Jane's, hustling them to a waiting panel van. The drunken happy group climbed in.

Will slid the door shut and went to the SUV. Anders climbed into the driver's seat and closed the door.

"Great work," Anders said. "I don't know how you convinced the two terrorists to come along, but it worked."

"It was easy. I just promised a hot tub and an open bar right down the road."

"You're a genius. The shit you come up with…"Anders checked his phone's display. "Good. The two men have been tased and zip-tied. And all five have been juiced. They'll be out for hours."

The SUV led the van away from the strip club. Will looked out the windshield as five SWAT vehicles sat along the road, poised for a strike.

"What about the video in the bar?" Will said. "They'll see all of us and be on our ass in no time."

"Don't worry," Anders replied. "Sully will take care of it."

Anders pulled out his Iridium satellite phone. "Brace, we have a major malfunction here in Key Largo." He laid the entire situation out. "What are your orders?"

"Hang on," Brace said. "I'm getting my bearings."

Anders led the caravan south on Highway 1. Fifteen minutes later, Brace spoke up. "Okay, take everyone to LZ-378. I'm texting you the coordinates. Park there and stay out of sight. Wait for further instructions."

"What about the two female civilians?" Anders asked.

"We'll handle that issue when I get there. Look for me in about four hours. Maybe longer. Out!"

Anders studied the coordinates and drove on. Approximately twenty-five miles north of Key West, he pulled into an abandoned gas station. Anders left the SUV idling while he went to talk with the driver of the van. Will watched in the side view mirror as Anders held a device high over his head for a few seconds. When he lowered it, Anders stared at the device, then pointed north.

Anders came back to the SUV. "We're almost there," he said.

The two vehicles drove on a gravel road through the sawgrass marsh and pine flatwoods. Finally, they stopped.

Will gazed out at the moonlit marshland. It was utterly desolate. There were no lights or signs of life.

"What's the plan?" Will asked.

"We have to wait for Brace. He's coming here."

With permission, Will reclined in the SUV and took a nap.

It seemed like only a few minutes before Anders jostled him. "Up and at 'em, cowboy."

Will rubbed his eyes and checked his watch. Five hours had disappeared. The sky was a dull gray, with sunrise not for another thirty minutes. Taking in a deep breath, he exited the vehicle to see Brace standing near the van.

"I've got some food and water for everyone," Brace said. "Take a quick break."

Four men exited the van and joined Will and Anders. They sucked down half the water and most of the food. It was a surreal scene.

Brace clapped his hands. "All right, men. Huddle up." They formed a semicircle around him.

"We've checked their phones and fingerprints," Brace said. "Sully was right. The two men are definitely hardcore terrorists. Apparently, they targeted Sadie. The other two women are collateral damage." Brace stopped talking and looked to his left as a maroon Ford F-250 truck pulling an airboat eased near the group. Brace gave hand signals to the driver. "Get Sadie and those two sluts out of the van," he said to Anders, "and bring them to me."

Anders ordered Will and another man to help him.

"Put Sadie over here," Brace said, pointing to a lawn chair he'd set up near the van.

Sadie was barely coherent. "What's happening here?" she slurred.

Brace ignored her and walked directly over to Jane. "Do you remember anything from last night?" he asked her loudly.

"Why? Are you a cop?" Jane said arrogantly. She was more alert than the other two women.

"No, you vodka-soaked bitch. I am your judge, jury, and executioner all in one. What do you know about Sadie?" Brace asked.

Jane rubbed her face. "She said her father-in-law is Grayson Sterling. Kyndall went to school with Tori."

"Did you call anyone and tell them that?"

Jane shook her head. "No. But I took some photos. I planned to post them on all of my social media accounts."

Brace tensed. "Did either of you post anything about Sadie and the strip club on social media last night?"

Both Jane and Kyndall shook their heads.

Brace pulled out his phone. "I need a photo of both of you. Go stand over there," he said, pointing to where a mangrove marsh started.

The two women shuffled their feet, slowly moving to the edge of the marsh.

"Farther," Brace said, waving at them.

"But we're in the weeds," Kyndall cried. "There might be snakes here. Or maybe gators. We could get eaten."

"I'm counting on it," Brace replied.

A team member handed him a silenced Heckler & Koch 416 assault rifle. As soon as the stock hit his shoulder, Jane screamed out, "What did we do?!"

Brace aimed at Kyndall. "You were in the wrong place at the right time with the wrong people."

Psst. Psst.

Kyndall fell backward into the marsh.

"Or vice versa," Brace said. "I can never get that saying right."

Jane, staring at her dead daughter, tried to scream, but nothing came out.

"Your turn, bitch."

Psst. Psst.

She joined Kyndall, falling on top of her. Sadie, watching all this transpire, passed out.

"Pull the two terrorists out here," Brace told Anders. "And Will, get some water and revive Sadie. I want my dear sister-in-law to wallow in the pain and suffering she's caused."

They removed the two men, leaning them up against the van. Somehow, they had immediately sobered up.

"Is she back with us?" Brace asked Will.

"Yes, she's conscious," Will replied.

Brace turned back to the men. "I know you work for the Santos organization. What are you doing here?"

They refused to say a word.

"I think you two are brothers. You seem like the oldest," he said, pointing to the bartender. "Move this one over there to give me an angle downrange over the ocean."

One of the team members cut the thick zip ties from the man's legs and helped him walk to the edge of the marsh. Then he moved away.

Brace raised his weapon and took aim. "Last chance, amigos. Anything to tell me?"

Both men looked like they were about to spill their beans but didn't. They assumed Brace was bluffing.

Psst. Psst. Psst.

The younger man crumpled, falling next to Kyndall's blood-soaked body. Sadie moaned in disbelief.

"So, amigo," Brace said, making eye contact with the older bartender, "I'm back to you."

Before he could say anything, another SUV drove up. A man got out and pulled a heavyset woman from the passenger's seat.

"What's this?" Brace asked the man.

"It's the twins' babysitter. We caught her loading up on Ms. Sterling's jewelry and LV purses."

Brace's shoulders sagged. "Fuck. We've sure done a piss-poor job here. If this was a test, we'd all fail it."

The man handed Brace something shiny. Brace walked toward Sadie and tossed it over to her. She was in no shape to catch anything, so it landed in the dirt at her feet. Will picked it up and handed it to her.

Sadie looked it over and moaned. She lifted her head and stared at Brace.

"Don't look at me, you bitch," he said. "That's the bracelet Dad gave you on your wedding day. It was my mom's. She rarely took it off."

"Why does she have it?" Sadie mumbled.

"Because you were lazy and didn't lock it up in the safe."

Brace, now fully enraged, motioned for the babysitter to be placed in the same spot as the others. When she looked around and saw the dead bodies, she took off running into the marsh. She was near the ocean when Brace double-tapped the trigger sending her face-forward into the shallow marsh.

Sadie screamed and dropped to her knees. "Stop!" she begged Brace. "Just stop it. Stop it!"

"That's up to your Latin lover boy," Brace said. He walked over to the bartender and pulled him away from the van. "Okay, amigo, it's time to pay the piper. Why were you at the resort?"

The bartender, his voice cracking, gazed at the dead bodies and began answering Brace's questions. "We were sent to make contact with Sadie Sterling."

"You speak good English. Where did you learn it?"

"Cuba."

"How did you know which resort she was at?"

"I don't know," the bartender said, looking down at his feet. "My boss just told me where to go and get close to her."

"Why?"

"They needed her to leave the resort so they could provide a babysitter. They were going to kidnap the kids."

"Wait!" Brace said. "Was that babysitter part of your team?"

"I've never seen her before, but I knew they were arranging a woman to watch them."

"Aw, fuck me!" Brace yelled, spitting into the dirt. "And I just shot her." He turned to his men. "That one's on me, guys. My bad. She may have had some intel." He turned back to the bartender. "Okay, Jose Cuervo, anything else?"

"We were going to take her back to our house after the strip club," he said.

"And do what exactly?"

"Whatever we felt like doing. But we would've been respectful."

"Sure you would've. Unfortunately, that's my sister-in-law, and I have to protect her husband—my brother—and my family honor."

"Are you going to cut me loose?"

"Close. More like cut you up."

Psst. Psst. Psst.

The bartender dropped to the ground. When he coughed, Brace fired a single shot to the forehead.

The sun was just peeking above the horizon. Brace put on his sunglasses and circled his finger in the air. A door opened from the F-250, and Sterry jumped out.

Will and Sadie watched as she unrolled black plastic, making a large area. As each body arrived, one man stripped off the belongings before passing it to another who cut off the arms and legs. It was quickly a bloody mess.

In thirty minutes, each body had been stripped and chopped into neat plastic packages. The men loaded the packages onto the airboat. Sterry and one of her men started the airboat and took off into the marsh.

Sadie continued crying. Seeing this, Brace yanked her close to his chest. "You're racking up quite the body count, sis."

"Please stop it," she begged.

"Oh, I'm stopping because there are no more people to kill right now. At least until you go out and grab some guy's dick, you promiscuous bitch. Then we'll be right back here. Or... *somewhere else.*"

Brace pulled Will aside. "You take her to a private airstrip near Lakeland and wait for a plane. I'll text you the address. Take the SUV Anders drove."

Will decided to push the envelope. "Brace, why am I the only one protecting her? Shouldn't I have one or two men go with me? Are you looking to get rid of me?"

Brace stopped what he was doing and focused directly on Will. "No. Absolutely not. The truth is, we don't want to lose you. But if something unfortunate did happen to Sadie... well... we'll grieve quickly and move on even quicker."

Will frowned.

"Look," Brace said, "you're not in any danger. You're immune from the virus. Sadie is the carrier. She can't get sick herself. She just gives the virus to others, who then die. The problem with her is that she can't stop infecting people. It's sad, but each one of these souls is on her conscience, not ours."

Will nodded. "Thanks for the pep talk," he said sarcastically.

A few minutes later, he was headed north on Highway 1. As he drove, he absolutely could not believe what had just gone down.

The boys in D.C. will never believe this next report. I just need to find a payphone.

Chapter Seventeen

The drive to Lakeland was so very long. During the first hour, Sadie dozed. She had been in shock when they took off, so Will let her sleep. But after stopping for gas and some black coffee, she started talking.

"What did Brace mean when he said I was racking up quite the body count?" Sadie asked.

"Remember Seth, that wannabe cowboy you had an affair with before I started working here?" She nodded. "I think he's gone."

"Oh no. I saw the billboards in Fort Worth and Granbury looking for him but didn't think I had anything to do with it."

Will pressed forward. "And the bodybuilder? I'm sure he's gone too."

"How sure?"

"As sure as I can be."

"Were you there when it happened?" Sadie asked.

"I was. Brace found out he was having sex with underage boys. It wasn't pretty."

She turned her head to the window as tears streamed down her face.

"Sadie, these people are serious. You should stop doing this. It's like a drug to you. You're addicted."

She cried for several minutes. "Maybe I am. Aren't you addicted to something?"

Undercover work, he thought.

"Staying in the free world. I pay my child support and keep clean, and I get to stay free."

"You have it easy," she cried. "Your life isn't very complicated. Mine's a complete mess."

"It could be great if you only worked harder at it."

Sadie wiped her cheeks. "I just want somebody to love me," she said, grabbing Will's hand from the console.

He left his hand there, caressing hers with his thumb. And he enjoyed it.

• • •

Will drove hard for another hour before stopping at a Cheddar's. The restaurant was half empty, so the pair had their choice of booths. Soon, with the help of a friendly waitress, Will coaxed some food into Sadie, and she responded.

"Do you feel like talking?" Will asked.

"I guess," she said, moving her fork through a Caesar's salad.

"When are you going to tell me what F Bar A means?"

"Family Above All," she said dejectedly. "Some family this is." She went on to explain that every family member had a red F Bar A tattoo on the inside of the upper right arm. Hers was in black.

"Why red versus black?" Will asked.

"Red signifies a blood relative," Sadie replied. "Black is for everyone else like Evan and me."

"Why the right arm?"

"Right is usually the conservative side. Or maybe it's the right hand of God. Some crap like that. I hope one day I can erase it."

"Look, Sadie," Will said, touching her hand gently to get her attention, "they're protecting you, making sure nothing happens to you or the twins. Why are you screwing them over?"

She pulled her hand away. "I'm alive until they no longer need me. If something bad happened to me, they would cry fake tears and move on. That's how it is."

Will knew she was right. Brace had just told him so.

He sipped on his coffee. He wanted more information but couldn't decide which subject to try next. The wrong move might shut her down.

"How did you meet Cole?" he asked her. It was the perfect subject because it set Sadie off on a long story.

First, she detailed how she had come from a troubled family. After that horrible beginning, she fell into drugs. She was even tested for bipolar disorder. Her life was a complete mess when she met her future husband.

"Cole has this female intelligence analyst named Avery," Sadie explained. "She's his go-to analyst. He treats her like one of his daughters. One Saturday night, a guy she'd met through an online dating site beat her up. When Cole saw her busted face, he and a friend grabbed two Marine buddies and went after this guy. When they finally found him, they literally beat the crap out of him. Cole told him to stay away from Avery or he'd kill him next time.

"When they came back to his friend's office, there I was. His friend was my bail bondsman. My bond required I check in with him every week."

Sadie explained that Cole needed a project. She was it. Plus, there was something about her that turned him on. Yet even though she had sex with anyone who wanted it, she felt powerful when she made Cole wait. That made him more interested in her.

"Cole is like his mother," Sadie added. "He's sensitive and caring. The others are like Grayson. They each have a killer instinct. That's why I couldn't believe I'd found someone who was gentle with me, actually cared about my feelings."

Even though Sadie had been charged with several drug possessions, intent to distribute, identity theft, and other felony thefts, Cole wasn't deterred. He was confident he could change and mold her into his perfect woman. He even tried to instill his love of the ballet, symphony, and opera into Sadie, but it didn't take.

Cole noticed that Sadie was with men who abused her both physically and mentally. They walked all over her, and she allowed them to do it. She dated men who were fresh out of prison or with one foot in the cell. She had low self-esteem issues and slept with any man who shared methamphetamine with her. Cole set about cleaning up her entire life.

"When I had him good and hooked," she said, "he used his law enforcement contacts and court personnel, as well as Grayson's connections with state and federal judges, to get most of the charges dismissed and sealed forever where no one can ever find them. Cole even persuaded a state district judge to give me a second limited probation even though I was looking at more than twenty-five years in prison. Grayson can do anything, buy anybody, and get anything he wants."

Will listened carefully, absorbing this information and trying to commit it to memory.

Sadie explained that Cole had spent thousands to fix her teeth. He gave her the money to buy expensive clothes and shoes. He paid the best wardrobe consultants to shop with her. Cole also got her into a local university. He placed tutors and resources all around her to succeed. With his determination and her perseverance and hard work, she eked out a degree in business administration.

Throughout all this, Cole spent money keeping the drug dealers and her other lowlife friends away. He was at her beck and call 24/7 for more than four years to help her get through the difficult times.

"Cole once said it was like using a piece of plywood on the beach to hold the ocean back. No matter how hard he held the plywood up or how long he stood there, the water splashed around it."

Once she received her bachelor's degree and stayed clean for a couple of years, Cole eventually married her. They had a lavish wedding on the ranch.

"After the honeymoon, he stopped protecting me because he was sure I had changed for good. Then he found out the truth: You can take the girl out of the trailer park, but you can't take the trailer park out of the girl."

Sadie said she spent money faster than Brace went through bullets. She demanded and received the best. Always drove a Mercedes. Credit cards were magically paid. Rolls of cash available for spending. It was a great life. Until it wasn't.

"I got back into drugs—smoked a lot of meth. Cole sent me to nine, maybe ten, rehabs. When he cut off the money, I had sex with the dealers for a hit. Then came the abortions. Somewhere between the fifth and eighth rehab, my relationship with Cole changed. It was all business. I was a womb for him, something to produce his children. Once the twins came, any tenderness he had for me was gone. Now, he doesn't like having sex because he doesn't know where I've been or who I've been sleeping with."

"Can you blame him?" Will said.

"Talking it out like this, I guess I can't."

The check came and Will paid it. Silently they trudged out to the SUV and climbed in. They drove for a while before anyone spoke.

"I've never had a role model. My father abandoned us, and my mom was never around. I think my parents are alcoholics and drug addicts, but I don't know for sure. One thing I *am* sure of is that my husband doesn't love me, and my in-laws want to kill me. What a great life," she said sarcastically.

It was a lot of information, and Will took it all in. He thought her life would be so much more content and happier if she would just listen to him.

Sadie reached over and placed her hand on Will's thigh, sliding it up, getting his direct attention. "So how do I get out of this, Mr. Security Stud?"

Will glanced down at her hand, which was still moving up. "I don't know. But I'm sure an opportunity will present itself."

Sadie touched his zipper. "I'm sure it will, *Will*."

• • •

The lights of the Range Rover sliced through the darkness. Occasionally, the reflective eyes of a deer appeared. But mostly it was dirt and dark browns.

December in Texas was here. The trees had lost all foliage, sporting mostly bare limbs. And it was cold.

When the SUV stopped at the ranch's parking area, Will exited, turning up his collar. The driver helped him with Sadie, who had been unknowingly drugged on the plane.

"Brace's orders," J.D. said after Sadie had gone from babbling to drooling to passed out. "Besides, having a passenger freak out in one of these planes is much different than in a commercial jet. We just couldn't take that chance."

Will understood. He didn't feel like dying either.

The two men carried their patient to the kitchen, mainly because Will didn't know what to do with her. The Sterling efficiency was usually on display, with everything being handled. But not this evening. Or, at least, not for Sadie.

Once she was slumped over the table, the driver left quickly. Will knew where her bedroom was from bringing in the packages, so he decided to carry Sadie's small body up to her room and put her to bed. He had no other choice.

Will reached under her breasts and lifted her from the chair. Then he tossed her arm around his shoulder.

"Wait!" Mrs. White said. "Let me help her upstairs."

Will stopped until Mrs. White had a grip on Sadie. "Can you handle her?" he asked.

"I think so. Help me get her to the stairs. Maybe she can start walking a bit."

She did. Will stood at the base of the stairs and watched Mrs. White slowly walk Sadie up. Satisfied, he went back to the kitchen to rustle up some dinner.

He had just begun pulling a few items out of the refrigerator when Mrs. White returned. "Take a seat. I'll get you something."

Will grabbed a glass of tea and sat down. Mrs. White soon joined him after sliding over a plate of grilled chicken breast, navy beans, and winter squash. As Will ate, Mrs. White talked.

"Poor girl. I had a cousin who got messed up on drugs. She worked at an office job during the day, mostly sober, then hit the drugs at night. She'd leave the house and walk the streets, making extra money in prostitution. I told her, 'Some people don't know which life they are in.'"

"I think that applies to Sadie," Will said. "What happened to your cousin?"

"A crackhead put a gun to her head and blew her brains out. The only person in the family stable enough to ID the body was me. You don't get something like that out of your mind."

Mrs. White eventually left, and Will finished his meal. Since it was almost eight, he decided to stay up a few more hours before going to bed.

He walked to the mechanics' shop and found Waylon. Seeing a stick that the dog had been playing with, Will tossed it toward the forest and watched as the dog galloped to fetch it. This went on for more than twenty minutes until Waylon dropped the stick, drank some water, and came to rest at Will's feet.

"Good dog," he said, petting the animal. Will heard some voices on the other side of the shop and went to check it out.

"It's the flyboys," he said, seeing J.D. and Nate. "You heading out again?"

"No," J.D. replied. "The plane is having some routine maintenance work, and we have the next two days off."

"Then let me buy you a few rounds at the cantina," Will said.

"We were just heading over there," J.D. replied. "Nate was planning on getting sick."

Nate laughed. "Yeah, too bad I don't drink alcohol."

"That leaves more for us," Will said.

After collecting their drinks and finding a booth, Will saw another excellent opportunity to get information from the two men who had probably seen a lot. "How long have you been flying?" Will asked J.D.

"Since I was sixteen. It's all I've done. Can't imagine doing anything else."

"You get a lot of hours flying for the Sterlings?" Will said.

"Over two hundred a month," J.D. replied.

Will kept pressing. "What type of fleet do you guys have?"

"We call it equipment," J.D. said. "We have three helicopters, the Gulfstream, and some other smaller planes."

"Do you stay on the property?" Will asked.

"Not usually. Just depends on what they need. Nate and I have even slept on the plane a time or two." The two pilots clinked glasses.

"What's the farthest you guys ever go?"

"Oh, here and there," Nate replied. "J.D. captains the planes. I'm captain of the helicopters. I fly Victoria or Grayson down to the corporate headquarters in Houston. Every day is different."

"You can't be the only pilots."

"No," J.D. said. "We told them they needed more, and now we have pilots who sub in. A lot of ex-military guys."

"How much does a pilot make working for the Sterlings?"

J.D.'s brow furrowed, and he leaned back. "Man, you remind me of my brother-in-law. He's an FBI agent."

Will's heart stopped. "Oh? How so?"

"He's always asking questions," J.D. said. "I feel like I'm in an interrogation."

"Sorry," Will apologized, trying to deflect the comment. "Just making conversation."

"No, it's okay," J.D. said. "I understand. You're still kind of new around here."

No one said a word for a few minutes.

J.D. started up again. "What's funny is when you asked how much money a pilot makes. My brother-in-law can't stop bitching about money. He says the FBI is always worried about spending too much, going overbudget. It's crazy. If he wants something for his operation, he has to buy it himself."

"With the United States government behind them?" Will said. "That's hard to believe. In the movies, money's no problem."

"That's right," J.D. said. "But he says it's true. That's why I like working for the Sterlings. It's like having a job in the movies because they have the money to do whatever we need. If we blow out a strut, no matter where we land, a mechanic is there with the right part to fix it. Their money solves every problem."

Will sipped on his scotch, remembering when he had to buy an expensive Mont Blanc pen with his own money because he didn't want to show up at a meeting as an undercover business manager with a government-issued pen. Then there was the time on another operation when the FBI provided a cheap plastic briefcase that screamed government agent. A James Bond-style briefcase had set him back some cash, but the operation was a big success.

Dr. Z had prepared him for that. "In the 1800s, British ship captains of wooden frigates spent their own money for extra gunpowder. The British government gave them only enough powder to fire once or twice a month and to fight. Yet a smart captain wanted his men to practice all the time. He knew successful—and alive—captains needed crews who could hit where they aimed. It was worth it to spend money on high-quality powder. The FBI is no different. If you want to be an undercover agent and maximize your chances of staying alive, you must spend your own money."

No wonder there was always a temptation to keep a few bills from an operation.

Anders approached. "Will, can I talk to you?"

"Sure," Will replied. "Gentlemen, enjoy the drinks."

Will followed Anders to a more secluded booth. "What's up?"

"The situation that's been brewing is about to blow up big time. If you want out, now's the time, because things are going to get hairy."

"I'm in," Will said firmly.

"You sure? Because I've got to know I can count on you."

Will set down his drink. "You mean like in Oakland at the bookie's house? Or in San Francisco when I got the twins back? Or saving Hector here on the ranch? Or at the bodybuilder's house? Or when—"

"Okay, that's enough," Anders said, holding up his hand. "I hear you. Now, let me tell you what I know."

Anders detailed the dispute. Decades ago, in Venezuela, Grayson and Carlos Santos were partners. They had just started out.

A piece of property thought to have oil came on the market. The partnership tried to buy it, but another company beat them out. Now, Santos has learned that Grayson used a straw buyer to snatch it up for himself. The property eventually made Grayson a multimillionaire, propelling him into all kinds of businesses, which made him even richer.

"Santos always thought Grayson had made his money through other ventures. Even though Santos has done well and made a good living, he could've been mega-rich, too. Now, he's pissed. He wants his cut and is coming to get it."

Will asked, "What does 'coming to get it' mean?"

"As you know, those men we nailed here and in Key West were Santos's men. He'll probably hit the ranch and try to take us down. We've pulled in the troops and are setting up a strong perimeter in a few days. No one is going in or out without permission."

"In that case, I need a few days off. I have to see my kids. I've been in D.C. all this time and need to buy them some Christmas gifts."

"Sure," Anders replied. "Get that done. Then, get your ass back here A.S.A.P."

"Thanks," Will said, standing up. "I'm going to pack right now."

Anders stopped him. "Oh, and you're being bumped up to $5,000 a week."

Will shook his hand. "Man, thanks!"

"Don't thank me. Thank yourself. You earned it."

"You're really taking care of me," Will said.

"This is coming from Brace. So, he's taking care of you."

Will hustled out of the cantina to his room. If Schneider were still around, he would've ordered Will to stay on, just so Schneider could collect the money and add it to his budget.

Thinking about it made Will chuckle. Then he had another thought.

At $260,000 a year, I might just have to quit the FBI and stay here for good.

Chapter Eighteen

Will sat on the edge of the bed, staring at his open suitcase. *This is what it's come to,* he thought to himself. *Another casualty of undercover work.*

He studied his legal pad. It was full of notes and questions he had for his divorce lawyer. He would make the call once he got to the offsite location.

As the weight of losing Jennifer and his family fell on him, Will leaned back and let his head fall to the pillow. He allowed himself to cry. He vowed this would be the one and only time for a pity party.

I need to get this out of my system. Then I'll be good to go.

Will laid there for a good thirty minutes. When he was done, he wiped his tears away and washed his face. It was time to get to work.

Walking through the lobby of the La Quinta Inn, he nodded at the clerk. Outside, it was cold and blustery. He pulled his jacket collar tight around his neck and climbed into the Range Rover. His first destination was the mall.

Will drove carefully through traffic. The Christmas season had arrived. Half-crazed drivers with too many items left on their lists filled the roads. The last thing he needed was to have an accident in a Sterling vehicle.

Will arrived safely at the mall to find it packed. He had counted on that. It was part of his plan.

After parking, he walked through the main entrance and studied a map display. Then, he meandered around until he located a payphone. A quick call and he was all set.

Will continued the charade, buying a few toys for his real kids. He went into stores, lingered, pulled products off the shelves to examine them, and left. If there was a tail, he wanted a good report.

An hour into this game, he carried his packages through a Neiman Marcus store, taking its elevator to the top floor. Right next to the elevator was a stairway, which he quickly descended and exited at the ground level. Waiting there was his trusty partner.

"How's it going?" Dan asked as Will climbed into the pickup truck.

"More killings to report," Will replied as he fastened his seatbelt.

"If this case gets any bigger, you're going to need a building the size of the Pentagon to hold all the agents working on it."

"It's getting pretty big," Will muttered.

"What's got you down?"

"I need to call my lawyer and ask him some questions. I'm not looking forward to it."

"I suggest you do that before you enter your report," Dan said. "It sounds like you'll be busy once everyone finds out what you've been up to."

Dan was right. After he talked to his lawyer, Will hit the save button, locking his report into the system. Then the calls came.

"Another blockbuster report," Coleman said over the speakerphone. "Any weak points you recommend exploiting?"

"I'm in good with Sadie Sterling," Will said. "I believe I can get her to flip. I'm just not sure how much she actually knows."

"She did witness the killings," Coleman said. "With you, that makes two."

"See if you can find a good moment to flip her," Ashcroft added. "Obviously, you'll have to be ready to leave the ranch fast if she says no."

"I understand," Will said, "but it won't be an easy thing."

"If you can let us know when you might pop the question, we can have agents in the area ready to pick you up," Ashcroft said.

"That might be dangerous," Will said. "They're already on the lookout for Santos's men. But I may have a way of phrasing it, telling her I know a guy who can get her a deal with the feds. Something like that."

"You're the quarterback," Coleman said. "Whatever works."

"And is safe," Ashcroft added.

They ended the call a little after 8 p.m. Dan took Will to a French restaurant and grabbed a secluded booth.

"You need a steak au poivre," Dan said. "Heavy on the cognac."

"Okay," Will said quietly.

"How did the call with your lawyer go?"

"Jennifer is willing to give me a sweet deal. She doesn't know I know, so I can only assume she's head over heels with this doctor. Since he's loaded, I'm like a dinghy. She needs to cut the rope loose so she can hop onto his luxury yacht. I guess 'for better or worse' doesn't count much."

The waitress took their orders and left. This gave Dan a chance to change the subject.

"Do you think this Santos character is going to attack the ranch?"

"I don't know, but Brace thinks so," Will replied.

Dan rubbed his hands together. "If that happens and there's shooting, it could be a great excuse for us to come onto the property and snoop around."

"That might be the best way, so long as you hear about it. There aren't any neighbors around. And forget the cops calling it in. The Sterlings have the Granbury law enforcement in their pocket. We practice at the range all the time and no one sets off any alarms. There could be a war on the ranch and you'd never hear about it."

"Good point, not to mention you could be shot. Do you have to see the shrink?"

"Yes," Will said. "Tomorrow."

"Are you getting some relief?"

"Nah. She never offers any help other than more pills."

"In that case," Dan said as the drinks arrived, "let's try some holistic healing. Have some scotch. I'm driving."

"Thanks," Will said, taking his glass. "I think I will. Just shoot me in the foot if I start crying."

"I can do that," Dan chuckled. "I cleaned my gun last month."

• • •

"How are you sleeping?" Dr. Clark asked.

"That's the first question you ask me every time I'm here."

"It's a good question," she said. "Tells me a lot about you."

Will shifted around in the chair. "When I'm at the ranch, I don't have the nightmares. When I'm back in my real life, the nightmares return."

"And last night?"

"Return? Of course, they did," Will answered. "It didn't help that I dealt with the divorce lawyer yesterday. At least Jennifer is turning all the lights green for me."

"I don't understand."

"She's making it easy for us to get a divorce. She's probably surprised I'm taking it so well."

Dr. Clark removed her glasses. "Have you talked with her?"

"Not since I started this assignment in June. What's it been? Six months?"

"Is it a dangerous assignment?"

"Yes," Will said, "but they treat me like a king. I've done some things for them, so they're happy with me."

"Do they treat everyone else as well?" she asked.

"Maybe not like a king, but at least like a prince. Top healthcare. Raises all the time. Bonus money. Excellent food and equipment. I'm making a hundred and fifty grand more than at the Bureau. I might just stay on." Will laughed.

She put her glasses back on and made a note. "I see."

"Come on," Will said. "That was a joke."

"But they are a major criminal enterprise, right?" She had a serious tone in her voice.

"Absolutely, they are. They do some horrific things. But to cover up the bad deeds, they do gracious things, too."

"Like what?"

Will glanced at the ceiling as he searched his memory. "Like one of the ranch hand's kids. She has dyslexia. So the patriarch of the family offered to pay the salaries for two special ed teachers at the local school district. But the school district lawyers turned him down because it would require paying the other teachers the same amount of money he was going to pay these two. Instead, he had them work with the kid at the ranch. Stuff like that."

"These people are criminals," Dr. Clark said firmly. "It sounds like you're justifying their actions."

"I'm just telling you how they get away with it. They're very clever. I admire smart criminals. Makes me work harder to nail them."

She made more notes on her iPad.

"So, are we good?" Will asked, clapping his hands together.

Again, Dr. Clark removed her glasses. "Will, I'm independent of the FBI. That means I can tell you the truth. I think you're in way too deep. You need to get out."

Will slumped in the chair. "I'm not sure I can. I've lost Jennifer and my kids dealing with this big case. I can't just let go of the rod. I feel like that fisherman in *The Old Man and the Sea*."

"You *can* get out. But do you want to, Will?"

"I have to. D.C. wants me to find the exit quickly so they can bring down the wrath of God on them. Trust me, we are really, really close to making our country safer."

She sighed and typed in more notes.

"Are you going to rate me unfit?" Will asked.

Dr. Clark hesitated. "Not yet."

•••

After two hours of forcing his eyes to stare at a binder filled with Sterling photos and details, Will made the long drive back to Granbury. The first to greet him was Kodi holding a game controller.

"Can you play with us, Uncle Will?" the young girl asked.

"I might have some time," he replied, picking her up. "Let me check in first, see my schedule. I'll come and get you if I can play a game with you." Kodi seemed satisfied and went off to find her sister.

Will went to the kitchen, where lunch—an hour away—was being prepared. He looked around for Green, Anders, or Brace, but saw no one. After drawing a cup of coffee from the spigot, he made his way to the patio. Sitting at the farthest table near the pool was Sadie.

"Mind if I join you?" he asked.

Sadie waved dismissively at a chair next to her. She unfolded the newspaper and pulled a Bloody Mary closer to her lips.

"A little early for happy hour," Will said, sipping his hot coffee.

"I need it after all I've been through lately. Where have you been?"

"Buying Christmas gifts for my kids," Will replied. "Brace told me the place is going on lockdown, so I wanted to see them one more time, pay some child support."

"My God, Will!" Sadie yelled, banging her hands on the metal table. "If I hear one more thing about your child support, I'm going to scream."

"Maybe you need to enjoy your Bloody Mary by yourself." Will picked up his coffee to leave just as Sadie stretched out the front page of the newspaper. Below the fold was an article about two missing local women in Florida. Color photos of the billboards in Key West and Key Largo showed their faces.

"Oh no!" Sadie cried. "It's them."

"Who?"

Will snatched the paper from her hands and studied the article. He sat back down. "Jane and Kyndall."

"All I wanted to do was to have some fun that night," Sadie moaned, tears streaming down her face. "Now, I've killed them."

Will gave her the napkin from his cup. After she had calmed down, Will leaned closer and whispered, "I told you this is the real deal, Sadie. Real-time. Real-life. You have to listen, really listen to me for once," Will said sternly.

"What am I going to do?" she asked, wiping her eyes.

This was the moment he'd been waiting for.

"Oh, Will," she said before he could speak. "I have even more problems. I talked to one of my relatives. My worthless father is in jail again. DUI—third strike. And with possession of a controlled substance, he could go to prison for the rest of his life. I need your help."

"I don't know. I'd have to run it past Anders."

"No!" she blurted out. "He would say no, anyway. Sandera told me you have some underworld law enforcement contacts. Can they help my father?"

"I could get in big trouble by helping your dad out."

"Please," she begged, shoving her big brown eyes with tears streaming down her cheeks closer to his face.

Will sighed, hoping to sell it hard. "I'll see what I can do. But you'll owe me big time."

"Of course. Whatever you want."

"Where's he located?" Will asked.

"Durango, Colorado."

Will pulled a pen and pad from his front pocket. "Here, write down his details. I'll need a burner phone from you." He grabbed her wrist and squeezed. "A real burner phone. Not a Sterling special, because I'm destroying the phone after I make the call. Understand?"

She stared at his hand on her wrist before shifting her gaze to him.

"I mean it, Sadie. If I get caught doing this favor for you, I'm a dead man."

She nodded. "I'll get it for you."

"Good," Will said, releasing her wrist. "I don't know why you want to help someone who has hurt you so much."

"It's complicated," she replied, rubbing her wrist. "I don't suspect you'd understand."

"I might if you'd be straight with me for once."

Sadie's eyes met his again. "If you'd take me out of here, run away with me, you'd see I could be all yours."

"You don't mean that."

"But I couldn't leave the twins behind," she said, looking away. "They'd have to go, too."

"If you ran away with the twins, Brace would hunt you down and kill you—boneyard-style. Me, too, if I decided to come along. I'd give us two weeks max. Grayson is not going to lose those two girls."

"Could you leave your kids?" she asked.

"I already have. And believe me, they're better off." Will was trying to set her up to leave the ranch without her children and become a cooperating witness. But when he closed his eyes, all he could see were the images of his real kids, not the computer-generated fakes.

"I'll get the phone and slip it to you next time I see you," Sadie whispered.

Anders leaned out the kitchen door. "Will, Brace wants you."

"Be right there," Will replied.

"Got to go," he said to Sadie. "While I'm gone, stop drinking and clear your mind. I have a feeling you're going to need it."

Will jogged inside and was taken to Brace's office, a place he hadn't seen before. It was a smaller affair than his father's.

"You wanted to see me?" Will said.

Brace, sitting at a desk, looked up from his papers. "I need you in D.C. to cover Cole. I'm sending three men with you."

"Okay," Will said.

"You and another man stay inside and rotate watching Cole. The other two men will rotate outside—twelve-hour shifts. You'll sleep in the condo. Can you handle it?"

"Yes, of course. When do I leave?"

"Two hours. Get packing."

So much for getting a burner phone from Sadie, Will thought to himself. *I'll have to find another way to make that call.*

•••

The Sterlings' Gulfstream and two local Range Rovers transported the men, luggage, and their weapons to Cole's townhouse. After getting everything set up, Will worked the noon to midnight shift. His replacement followed, working the next twelve hours. This went on for several days until Will slipped away before his noon shift.

He located one of the few payphones left in the area and called in. Once he was screened and cleared, he reported the new information to his handler. Then he talked to Dan.

"I need you to do me a major favor," Will said. "I need to address some charges on Sadie's father. This might be the edge I've been looking for so she can become a cooperating witness."

Dan took down the details. "I'll get on it and let your handler know. Now look, you need to be careful. There's been someone probing on your background. They may be sniffing you out."

"I'll be careful. So far, I haven't seen anything that's setting off any alarm bells."

"Nevertheless, be careful," Dan urged.

Will promised and hung up. He bought a few toiletries before hustling back to the house to begin his shift.

A few hours later, Cole got up from his desk and closed the door to his study. Will, who had been standing at the window checking on Lance, the man on duty outside, turned to go.

"No, you can stay," Cole said. "Sit down."

This was strange. With Sadie not around, it usually meant Cole had to make a private phone call.

"Listen," Cole began, "I've been doing a lot of thinking. I couldn't figure out the connection between us, but it finally came to me. Dr. Z."

Will's heart stopped. His right hand eased back to his holster. Breathing deliberately, he said, "Who's Dr. Z?"

"The man who trained both of us. He didn't show me your file, but he did confirm my suspicions after some serious arm-twisting."

Will imagined Dr. Z hanging from a chain at the boneyard, his body spinning around in the wind. He assumed there were several men just outside the study, waiting to stick a needle in his arm and transport his body to New Mexico. He quickly reviewed his options.

Jumping through the huge bay window. He would be cut up bad and likely tumble all over the sidewalk. Lance, a few feet away, would put a bullet in his skull. The probability of survival: low. He decided to try another option.

"So, you think I haven't been to prison?" Will asked.

"I know you have," Cole said with confidence. "I was there, too. It was part of the tradecraft training. So was the course in Black Bag Entry. My time beat yours. And I scored higher than you in all the classes, although Dr. Z said you had other skills. 'Criminals don't care who makes the best grades,' he often said."

Will felt sick. Everything Cole said was accurate. But there was absolutely no way Dr. Z would give up another student. They must have accessed Will's file. That was the only solution.

"If what you say is true," Will said, "why am I here?"

"Because Dr. Z told me I needed protection. He knows I'm not involved in Brace's or Dad's world. In fact, years ago, he told me he'd send someone to watch over me."

"Why?" Will asked, sticking to safe responses.

"Because I'm a very valuable asset, just like you. But you're much better at the underworld cloak and dagger stuff, and the guns. I'm more into databases and information."

"I see," Will said.

"We make a good pair, I think."

Will decided to continue this noncommittal track. "Are you happy with the job I'm doing?"

"Absolutely. Not only do I have a fellow colleague here, but a good friend to bounce ideas off."

"I'm glad you feel that way," Will said. "Like you said, my job here is to protect you. So, let me do my job. I need to walk around, make sure Lance is doing his job out there. Which reminds me, I need to relieve him for a bathroom break."

"Sure," Cole said. "Go ahead. And listen, I'm not going to say anything. I'm just glad to have someone to talk to, someone who thinks like me."

"Thanks for the chat," Will said as he got up and headed to the door. He turned the knob with his left hand while moving his right hand to the Glock's butt. *This might be how my life ends*, he thought.

He pulled the heavy door open. No one was there.

He moved into the hallway and found it empty. Then, he slowly pulled the front door open to feel a blast of cold air. He had not put on his jacket and decided to go outside without it.

"Lance," he said to the man eight feet away. "Coffee break?"

"I need one." Lance bounded up the steps and inside, closing the door behind Will.

The cold air instantly reached his chest. His body was on fire, so it felt good. As he stood at the base of the steps, he tried to slow his heart rate down. He needed to process everything that had just occurred.

First, it was clear no one was about to kill him. This led to the next conclusion: Cole meant everything he said. Maybe his talk wasn't a setup? At least, not right now.

Will replayed the conversation in his mind. He had never really acknowledged Cole's facts. If Cole had been recording their conversation, there was no way a judge or jury could hold it against him. Unfortunately, the Sterlings did spend a lot of time in court.

A vigorous tapping on the window drew his attention. It was Cole.

"Come in here!" Cole mouthed, his face distraught. "Emergency!"

Will looked up and down the street. Nothing was out of place. This was his chance. He could walk away and head to the nearest FBI field office if he could make it. Or he could go back inside and roll the dice.

Months of painstaking work hung in the balance. If he walked away, it would all go down the drain. His sacrificed marriage would yield nothing in return. *Maybe I can still finesse this*, he thought. *And I can still deny everything to Brace, at least until they drop me in a barrel of acid. If that happens, I don't like my chances of keeping my mouth shut.*

Will heard the tapping again. He turned and ran back up the steps.

"What is it?" Will said, bursting into the study, his right hand plainly on his holster.

Cole motioned him to close the door. "Don't worry, I'm safe. It's my sister Tori. Her husband, Evan, has been killed, and she's been taken hostage."

Will blinked several times. "Where?"

"Venezuela," Cole said, his face sweating. "We need to lay this out and make a plan. I need your help."

"Okay," Will said. "What can I do?"

"Get her back!" Cole snapped.

Chapter Nineteen

Ten minutes raced by while Cole and Will waited on a conference call. Cole was out of control until Will told him that whatever was going down, the family needed his A-game.

Finally, the call began.

"Listen," Brace said, "Evan and Tori were on the family yacht celebrating their tenth anniversary. They were anchored off the coast of St. Vincent. Tori has been working on an oil deal in Venezuela with some government officials. She received a call to come over and meet with the decision-maker. She and Evan flew down to Caracas, hoping to close the deal. At our office there, Evan was killed, and she was taken hostage. We're certain it's Santos. We're putting together an all-star team to go down there and look for her."

"What can we do?" Cole asked.

"I'm sending the plane to pick you and the men up. Pack up your files and computers because you're going to be here at the ranch for a long time. Bring anything you need. Destroy any files there since we can't protect your house."

"How long do I have?" Cole asked, running a hand through his thick hair.

"J.D. and Nate are leaving for Meacham in ten minutes," Brace said. "You can do the math from there."

"Okay. Anything else?"

"We'll know more by the time you get here. Just focus on sterilizing your place and bringing everything with you." Brace disconnected the call.

Cole jumped up and pointed at Will. "Grab all the file boxes you can find. Then round up all the luggage. I may need you to get some more boxes. Organize the men while I go through my files."

"Consider it done," Will said.

He and the men quickly gathered everything Cole had requested. He had a man pick up a dozen more boxes, rolls of tape, and dispensers at a nearby rental truck store. An hour later, they were stuffing boxes full of files while Cole disassembled his computers.

Thinking ahead, Will arranged for five SUVs to pick them up. Cole's files and luggage and five men with their own bags barely fit into the SUVs. When J.D. saw the large load, he said the plane would be overweight. He ordered Will and the three men to fly commercial with their luggage but agreed to carry the weapons and other protective equipment. After helping load the plane, Will and the men headed to Reagan National.

Will snagged the only first-class seat left. The other three flew coach. This gave Will time to relax and think about the last four hours. It was a lot to process.

By the time he touched down, Will knew he was at another crossroads. Cole may have spilled the beans to Brace and company. If so, he'd be executed on the ranch. If Cole had kept his mouth shut, Will might still see this case reeled in. When the Range Rovers arrived at the passenger pickup, he hesitated.

"You coming?" the impatient driver asked.

Will stared at him and stepped forward. "Sure. Sorry about that. My mind was somewhere else."

Once again, Will was all in.

•••

A warm light filtered in between the curtains. Will rolled over and tried to focus on his watch. When he could see straight, it was time to get up.

After a shave and a shower, he felt refreshed. He headed to the kitchen for a much-needed breakfast.

Inside, the ranch house was decorated for Christmas. A tree in the living room stood in the corner, tastefully covered with ornaments. Stacks of presents sat on the floor, waiting to be opened. Frilly trim adorned the walls. There were even scents of cinnamon, cloves, and pine needles coming from hidden dispensers. At any other time, it would have felt wonderful.

In the kitchen, Will noticed an unusual buzz. The place was crowded with men, three of whom carried H & K 416s. They leaned the guns against the table while they ate. A distinct trepidation hung in the air. Everyone knew that bullets could start flying at any moment. Life was definitely getting serious.

The previous night Will had learned he would stay at the ranch to watch Sadie and the twins. He had met with Sadie and learned her father had been released from all his charges. She couldn't thank Will enough. He'd wanted to try to flip her right then, but with everything going on, he couldn't do it. The risk was far too great.

After dinner, he had found Hector and played with Waylon while they talked. Hector had told him about all the activity going on at the ranch. "Lots of men and lots of guns," Hector said. "A storm's coming, just in time for Christmas."

With the Thirsty Goat closed, Will had turned in early and crashed. He needed the sleep.

Reenergized and ready for a new day, Will finished his breakfast and grabbed a second cup of coffee. He headed to the patio, hoping to find Sadie, but she wasn't there.

As he stood gazing over the long field, he heard his name. It was Anders.

"We need you for a moment," he said.

Will's heart pounded in his ears. He looked around and realized there was no place to run. *I hope Cole meant what he said.*

Brace was at his desk, furiously twisting his skull ring and looking more stressed than ever. Behind Will stood Anders and another man.

"You wanted to see me?" Will said.

"One of my team members going to Venezuela has problems with his gallbladder. I'm a man down. Can you go?"

"My passport hasn't come in," Will replied.

When Will had started working for the Sterlings, they'd helped him fill out the application and take his photo. That was the last he'd thought about it.

Brace held up a small blue booklet. "I have your passport, and it's good to go. We checked."

Will looked around, mainly to buy time while he considered this offer. *Are they trying to get me on a plane to the boneyard?* he thought. *Maybe this passport has to do with the recent check on my background.*

"Sure," he finally said. If they were going to kill him, they didn't need a plane to do it.

Brace shoved Will's passport in a bank deposit bag and zipped it up. "Anders will tell you what gear to pack."

Will went with his boss to his apartment. "Man, this is some serious shit."

"You have no idea," a somber Anders replied. "Let's get you fitted out and on the plane. I don't want you getting down there and not having what you need."

...

The Echo One Nine team rolled through Venezuela in two SUVs. Will rode with Brace, who had plugged in some up-tempo songs like Guns N' Roses' "Welcome to the Jungle." Brace cranked the volume up and mouthed the words to the song. He was getting ready for whatever they had to do.

The day before, they had landed in Bogota with nine men and lots of gear. They were the best of the best—Colby, Savalas, Sparks, Van Zandt, Bolton, and Jenkins. Anders, Will, and Brace rounded out the team.

The second the Gulfstream's engines died, Brace had bounded down the stairs. He had met with someone wearing a white Panama hat in a beat-up old Jeep on the tarmac. After twenty minutes, Will had seen Brace fold up some papers and head back to the plane. They had taken off and landed in Cúcuta. From there, they had boarded a special bus that breezed through the border into Venezuela. After driving all night, the crew had arrived at a bedraggled warehouse around 6 a.m. Brace had ordered the men to get some sleep while he waited for the remaining SUVs to arrive.

Will hadn't waited on anything. He had unfolded his sleeping bag and was out before anyone else. When Brace woke him up, it was one in the afternoon. A spread of metal containers had caught his attention.

"Eat up," Brace had ordered. "Once you all are awake, we'll organize and check our gear."

They had eaten and spent an hour recleaning the weapons and repacking the equipment in special backpacks. Will had been amazed at the Israeli-made bulletproof products. These desert-brown packs would stop most handguns and a few assault rifles.

Around seven, more food had been delivered with plenty of strong coffee and water. The men had lingered around until eight, when Brace explained they would check out the company office with infrared gear to make sure they weren't heading into an ambush.

Now, it was dark outside save for a few bright stars in the sky. And they were strangers in a strange land.

With nothing else to do, Will took in the sights of Caracas. There wasn't much. Buildings crammed next to each other. No urban planning. The facades were mostly drab, faded colors. Socialism at its finest. It looked like a dreary place to live.

Or die.

The nightlife should have just begun, yet the cafes had few to no customers. The recent economic collapse had stopped many events in this once great city. From Will's perspective, the quicker they got in and out, the better.

Brace reached over and turned off the radio. "Okay, men, get your war face on."

Will jumped out of the car and followed Anders. He studied the two-story building they were about to enter. Painted gray plaster covered the exterior. The street level was made of concrete block walls with either no windows or solid metal bars and security grating at the main entrance. An old tree hung lazily over the sidewalk, its limbs scraping the side of the building. Everything was dark and foreboding.

Will and Anders moved into place. They were responsible for the left side of the office.

"Let Brace do his thing first," Anders said. "He's looking for heat signatures. Keep your eyes peeled."

After about ten minutes, Brace brought everyone to the car. "Weapons locked and loaded. We're going in."

The men picked up the H & K 416s. As Will grabbed his rifle, Brace pulled him aside. "I want you to stay here on the street. Look for any trouble coming up on our six. I doubt there's anyone inside, but be careful. You never know if someone might jump from a window. Be ready for anything. No one gets away. Got it?"

Will nodded.

Brace unlocked the sliding metal gate, followed by the front door. He and his men went inside, muzzles pointing this way and that, disappearing from Will's sight. Will turned his back to the entrance and took up his post. He hoped they wouldn't be long.

•••

Will checked his watch. They had been inside for an hour and forty-five minutes. Will felt conspicuous standing in the shadows holding an assault rifle. Like Oakland, he wondered how he'd explain this if the Caracas police rolled up. It would probably involve Brace and a roll of bolívares.

A noise behind Will startled him. He turned to see the men coming out. Two of them had green military-issue duffel bags.

Brace locked the door and pulled the metal gates shut. After he locked those, the team climbed into the two SUVs and headed back to the warehouse.

Along the way, Will learned that they had recovered some surveillance tapes even though the perpetrators had taken the disks and destroyed the system. Brace now had a secret backup the perpetrators hadn't found. He seemed highly confident.

They reached the warehouse and left Brace alone. He sat in a corner, uploading the video to Cole. Then he snapped his laptop shut and declared no more work for the night.

The men were well-rested. They stayed up playing cards and munching on the leftover hallacas and asado negro. At midnight, Brace ordered lights off. Will took full advantage and again, was out before anyone else. He was determined to bank some extra sleep.

• • •

Three days later, Brace was fit to be tied. The team had not located Tori. They didn't even have a clue where to look.

Back at the ranch, Cole had dissected the tapes and analyzed the attack. Three men dressed in official garb had entered the office and were escorted to the conference room. As Evan and Tori met with them, one of the men said something to Evan. Evan had pointed, possibly to the restroom. The man feigned ignorance. As Evan walked ahead to show him where it was, the man shot him in the head from behind. The two men in the conference room zip-tied a screaming Tori and chased the rest of the employees out the door. Then they damaged the surveillance equipment, and the tapes stopped transmitting. Or so they thought.

A tiny surveillance camera in the ceiling had survived. It sat high in a hallway, displaying the lobby to the back offices. This camera had not been on the main system. Instead, it operated on its own, recording over itself every seven days. Because Brace had gotten there quickly, he had some footage of additional men who came in after the shooting to ransack the place, making it look like a burglary. Cole was busy trying to ID any one of them.

Using information from the cell phones taken in Oakland and from the Cuban terrorists in Key West, Brace had set up a series of Stingrays—mobile cell phone towers—to pick up calls to and from specific numbers. So far, nothing had hit.

"How much longer are we going to be here?" Will asked Anders as they stared at a silver Mercedes van with its mast extended twenty feet above.

"Tomorrow is Christmas," Anders replied. "I think into the New Year. Why? You got a date?"

"I wish. More like I wanted to see my kids for Christmas while they're out of school."

"Don't count on it. When Brace fixates on something, he doesn't give up. And Tori is his only sister. He's not likely to leave without her—dead or alive."

Anders's phone went off. "Yes… yes… right, we'll be there."

He started the SUV. "We're headed back to the warehouse."

"And leaving this Stingray unguarded?"

"Orders. The Sterlings can afford plenty of Stingrays. They have only one Tori."

• • •

Outside the warehouse, old box trucks rumbled in both directions. Inside, it was quiet and still.

Several incandescent lights had been lowered from the roof, a single wire supporting each one. Underneath one of them, the men formed a semi-circle around Brace, who held a stainless-steel clipboard. He flipped a Bose headset mic up to his forehead and began talking.

"We've received an ID on one of the men who came to the office after the initial three. His face matched a Venezuelan named Herrera Pena. Pena applied for a taxi permit four years ago. We've done extensive research on him. He comes from El Amparo, a small town on the banks of the Rio Arauca. It's the perfect place to stow a captive—remote, with lots of trees to thwart air surveillance. For what it's worth, El Amparo means the Protected Shelter."

"Is this still in Venezuela?" Colby asked.

"Yes, eleven hours southwest of here. Bolton, you'll stay here in the warehouse and operate the computers. You will also communicate with Cole and relay intel to us. Everyone else is going. Each team will have a Spanish-speaking guide. On the way out of town, we'll pick them up. Any questions so far?"

There were none.

"Good. When we arrive in El Amparo, we will first visit all the relatives of Pena. I can't imagine they'll give us any information. But the hope is for them to contact Pena and put him on the move. I'm having additional men relocate two Stingrays to the Amparo to try and pick up something. Each team will have plenty of bolívares. The locals might want to make some extra money for information.

"Let's get the gear ready. Roll up your sleeping bags. Grab plenty of food and water and stow it in the SUVs. And bring everything—we may be gone a week or more. Liftoff is in thirty minutes. Get to it!"

Will moved fast, arranging everything in fifteen minutes. He lingered around, watching the other men work. Some checked their weapons and loaded ammo. That made Will wonder where this would lead. The last thing he needed was another firefight.

When everyone was loaded up, the Range Rovers took off. At a nearby street corner, two men who would serve as the interpreters stood waiting. Once they were fastened in, the group headed south for El Amparo.

•••

The drive was long but uneventful. Will was able to get some sleep in except for the three stops for fuel and restroom breaks.

The team arrived at the small town early in the morning. Cole had arranged a vacant wooden structure to be used as their base of operations. Because Will had slept most of the way, he took the first watch.

The men had their gear unloaded and bedrolls laid out in minutes. Before Will could situate himself for the watch, the snoring began. Soon, a chorus of noise filled the room.

Will made it to 8 a.m. By that time, Brace and Anders were up ordering food and checking in with Bolton back in Caracas. After the food arrived and the men were digging in, Brace made some announcements.

"Okay, guys, we're going to finish breakfast and spread out across town. Since we have two interpreters, we'll go in two teams, four men each. Will and Van Zandt will stay here and watch the gear. I don't need it stolen. Besides, I don't want someone coming here while we're gone and rigging up a couple of explosives. I'm not dying in some shithole town in Venezuela because I failed to post a watch."

"Do you foresee any trouble here?" Jenkins asked.

"I don't know," Brace admitted. "In 1988, the town had a massacre here. A group of Venezuelan military soldiers teamed with local Amparo police and battled sixteen Columbian guerillas armed with machine guns and grenades. The Venezuelans said they exchanged gunfire with the guerillas for up to twenty minutes at a range of thirty meters. Fourteen guerillas died with not a scratch on the other guys.

"The two surviving guerillas dove into the Arauca River and swam upstream. Turns out the guerillas were just Venezuelan fishermen headed to a picnic. Investigators found weapons among the fishermen, but an informant said those were planted. One victim was found shot in the back with his skull crushed in. For good measure, his face was disfigured by acid. So, somebody went off the rails. That means they might still be around and not take kindly to gringos like us. Stow your weapon and have it handy. Real handy."

A few minutes later, the men were gone. Will let Van Zandt take the watch while he hit the sack. *It looks like easy duty*, he thought to himself. Then, he drifted off.

•••

After two days of questioning all their leads, they hadn't picked up the trail. Brace was dejected.

Will remembered an investigation that had taken him to a small town. He had run into roadblocks. Late one day, he had looked in the mirror and noticed his shaggy locks. Walking down the main street, he'd found a barber and pulled on the door just as the man was locking up.

"Got time for one more?" Will had asked him.

He did. With no one in the shop, Will struck up a conversation. The information the man provided broke the case open. Will had learned a valuable lesson: barbers and beauty salons heard lots of information. They were almost as good as prostitutes and strippers.

Will pulled Brace aside. "I've got an idea. My uncle used to be a barber. He'd hear about everything in town. I noticed there are two barbers in town. Why don't we have the interpreters go to each one by themselves and get a haircut? Let them take some cash and see what they can find out."

Brace's eyes opened wide. "That's an excellent idea."

"But make sure it's the last appointment of the day so they have the place to themselves," Will added.

Brace glanced at his watch. "It's just after four. Let's find out when they close and make it happen."

A few hours later, one of the translators hit pay dirt. Brace grabbed the computer for some information. He called a meeting.

"Listen up, men. Things are about to get hot. Tori may be two miles away at a camp on the Arauca River. It's on the Venezuelan side. Supposedly it's uninhabited, with dense jungle covering the area. Van Zandt, you stay here. I'll need you to call in the cavalry if we get in a jam. Will, this was your brilliant idea. You're coming along. All of you pack up for a three-day excursion. And bring your night vision gear. It'll be dark soon."

• • •

The two SUVs came to a stop just off a dirt road. Brace told Sparks to stay and watch the SUVs. He took Will and Anders and went left while Savala's team went to the right.

The light was still falling, so they didn't need night vision equipment. The three moved quickly, yet quietly, with Will bringing up the rear. It took them thirty minutes to reach the camp first. It was vacant.

"Fuck!" Brace said, looking around. "We've just missed them."

The second team arrived. Brace ordered Colby to scout for tracks and report back. Will walked fifty feet to the river and studied the scene. When he returned, Brace and Anders were sifting through the fire for any scrap of evidence while the others covered the perimeter.

Colby returned and made his report. "I can't tell, but there may have been a hostage here. They've covered up the tracks real good. No matter what was going on, they boogied out of here in fifteen minutes."

"Okay," Brace said, "let's get out of here."

"Brace," Will said, pulling him aside, "the path to the river has a lot of footprints that were covered up. They must've drawn water from the river."

"So?" Brace replied, his hands on his hips.

"I think Tori might have given them the slip and crossed the river."

"Into Columbia?"

"Yes," Will replied. "She couldn't drift down to the town. She might be discovered and taken back to the captors."

"You're making a lot of assumptions," Brace said.

"Give me a man—Savalas or Jenkins—and let us check it out."

"It's too risky," Brace said, shaking his head. "You might be mistaken for guerillas."

Will put the full-court press on. "Tori may be hiding on the other side. Let me take a lot of food, water, and gear and check it out."

Brace removed his sunglasses and rubbed his jaw as he walked to the water's edge. "I can't let you have a cell phone or radio. They might trace you back to me." He showed the map to Will. "I'll have a man wait at the junction of Highway 66 and Tame-Cravo Norte. By walking in any direction away from the river, you can find Highway 66 and get to that location. But how are you going to cross?"

"Tape those blow-up mattresses together and tie a rope to them. I'll strip down and go across first with my gear. You can pull the float back, and the second man can come behind me."

"Who are you?" Brace asked. "MacGyver?"

"What?" Will asked, his blood turning cold.

"That's a great idea!" Brace said, smiling. "Take Anders. He loves jungles. Get your gear ready. I'll tell the men."

Will secretly smiled. Whatever Brace was going to run into, Will wanted to be far away. He'd take his chances in a jungle in Columbia.

Chapter Twenty

Will and Anders had crossed the muddy Rio Arauca, lucky to find sandy ground to walk on. They had stripped down and placed their clothes and shoes in waterproof bags that rested on the air mattresses. Nothing got wet. And the water reached only their upper thighs. It was an easy trip.

On the other shore, both men quickly dressed while Brace's team had guns ready to provide suppressing fire if necessary. After waving goodbye, they disappeared over the riverbank. The two were on their own.

Anders looked back. Seeing they were out of Brace's sight, he grabbed Will's arm. "What the hell were you thinking, volunteering me for this job? I don't know anything about tracking. And I sure as hell don't want to be wandering around a Columbian jungle with all these bugs and anaconda snakes."

"I'm sorry," Will said, adjusting his backpack. "Brace asked me who I would like to share a Columbian jail cell with, and I said you. I don't know those other guys."

"What?!" Anders replied.

Will grinned. "I'm kidding. I wanted Savalas or Jenkins, but Brace said you loved jungles. I thought he was serious."

"Oh, man! At least I see where I rank in this family." Anders exhaled loudly. "Okay, what do we do first?"

"See this strip of sand following the river?" Will replied. "We're going to search it for footprints. See if we can pick up the trail."

Will found a long stick and marked a fifty-foot-long line in the sand from the edge of the bank toward the jungle. "Let's walk five minutes to the left of this line. That's the direction the river's flowing. I'm guessing Tori may have let the river take her down a ways, then crawled over the bank. It would be a good way to throw them off the trail."

"What if we don't find anything?" Anders asked.

"We'll double back. You watch the jungle for any narco-terrorists who might pop out while I'm looking for tracks. We need to hurry before we lose what light is left."

"Let's get this over with," Anders said reluctantly.

Anders raised his H & K 416 rifle and pointed it toward the jungle. Then he let Will start walking, staying fifty feet behind in case someone wanted to spray the field with bullets. In training, Brace had continually preached the importance of spacing out from each other. With men too close, one enemy with an automatic rifle could take out ten in seconds. At least this would make a killer think before shooting.

When they reached the end of five minutes, Will had found nothing. They doubled back, passing the long line Will had drawn.

Halfway into their second leg, Will had a hit. "She fooled me," he said, dropping to his knees. "She must have swum upstream a bit. Look here."

Anders came over. "What am I looking at?"

"This track is from someone barefoot. And it's small and shallow. This person weighs less. Most likely Tori."

"Come on," Anders said in disbelief. "It could be any Columbian or Venezuelan. Maybe a fisherman or a kid's footprint."

"Maybe, but over here are military-style boots, three sets."

Anders checked them out. "Okay. Maybe you're right. Maybe not."

"I'm right," Will said, getting off his knees. "Let's follow them into the jungle."

Anders looked around, hoping for another option. Not finding any, he sighed. "You lead. I'll bring up the rear. And chase away any snakes or monkeys for me."

Will made it a few minutes into the forest before it seemed like someone flipped a switch and made it nighttime. Both men clicked on the lights strapped to their heads. Occasionally, Will stopped, turned off his headlamp, and set a flashlight on the ground. This created shadows, which made it easy to see the depressions and ridges on each footprint. Anders was impressed as he sprayed mosquito repellent all over himself.

During a water break, Anders directed a cockeyed glance at Will. "You sure learned a lot in prison. If I didn't know any better, I'd think you were in special forces."

Will nodded. "I was on a seal team for four years."

"I knew it!" Anders said, slapping his thigh. "You never told us any of that."

"It's true," Will said plainly. "We had water leaks in prison from exposed pipes all the time. My job was to take a crew and seal the leak. We had ten separate teams. I was on Seal Team Six."

Anders's shoulders drooped. "Okay, smartass. You got me. Let's get moving. I don't want to be in this jungle any longer than necessary."

"At least it's more forest than jungle," Will said.

He was right. It wasn't wet or full of bogs... yet.

The pair traveled another thirty minutes, going slow, making sure they hadn't lost the trail.

"Look at this," Will whispered, urging Anders to get down.

"What?" Anders said, crawling closer.

"It's a cigarette." He held the butt up and sniffed it. "And it's still warm. I'm certain these men are tracking Tori. These footprints must be hers."

"Listen, Will," Anders whispered, "if we find Tori, we're gonna be heroes."

"I think we'll find her. But we might have to pry her loose from these three guys first. On the other hand, she may have had a head start by several hours."

"If we're close, shouldn't we switch to night vision?"

"You're right," Will said, removing his pack.

The men strapped the night vision goggles on and flipped the switch, illuminating the dark jungle.

"Let's go," Anders said. "I can't get that 'Welcome to the Jungle' song out of my mind. I'd like to say goodbye to it. Fast."

They moved quickly, occasionally stopping to flip on the thermal imaging system and drink some water. Two hours into their journey, Will dropped to his belly and motioned for Anders to do the same. When Anders crawled next to Will, he whispered, "What's up?"

"I see a light," Will replied. "It's going back and forth. I think they're sweeping for footprints."

Anders adjusted his goggles. "I see them. I think there are only two. Their light is making it hard to see. I'm going to hide behind that tree over there and find my binoculars. I might get a better view."

"Good idea," Will said. "I'll crawl forward and flip on the thermal. See what I can pick up."

Will crawled forward and found an excellent position to see both men. He watched the thermal images as they searched for footprints. But something was wrong. The men weren't moving forward or backward. They were just standing there, running the flashlight back and forth on the ground.

Suspecting a trap, Will flipped on his night vision and raised his gun, staring through the sight. Out of nowhere, the dark forest lit up with bursts of gunfire. Bullets chipped bark off the trees, sending dangerous splinters everywhere.

"Arrgghh!" he heard from Anders. "I'm hit."

Will crawled backward, trying to get to Anders on his right. Through his night vision, he spotted Anders slumped against a tree, his glasses hanging off one ear. But he couldn't locate the gunman. When he reached Anders, he whispered, "Where are you hit?"

"Everywhere," Anders moaned. "I can't move."

Will switched to thermal, desperately trying to locate the third gunman. Not finding him, he looked back at where the two men had been swinging the flashlights, but they were gone. He scanned the forest and found them. The two were approaching him from different angles.

"They've got us boxed in on three sides," Will whispered. "We may have to give up. How do you feel about that?"

"Will, who are you really?" Anders coughed out.

Will said nothing, enduring the silence.

"Anders?" Will nudged him, but he fell over on his side. Anders was dead.

Will crawled away from him, hoping to use him as a decoy. Better for his hunters to shoot a dead body than a live Will.

When he crawled forward, Will saw the two men had zeroed in on his position. One had the left flank covered. The other came from straight ahead. He was sure the mysterious man on the right was moving in. He'd have to fight this one out.

"Time to even up the odds," he whispered to himself. He aimed at the man on the left and slowly squeezed the trigger. Once again, the forest lit up. This time, six or seven guns fired in every direction, but Will had not fired a shot.

A heavy thud landed on Will's right. Then the guns stopped.

Ten seconds of silence followed.

"Drop your weapons and raise your hands," a voice said in English.

Will still had the thermal vision on and saw ten large shapes, obviously soldiers.

"Weapons down," he yelled, getting to his knees. "Hands raised."

"Don't move," the same voice commanded.

A spotlight blinded him. Sticks crunched all around. A soldier came close and kicked away his gun. Another behind him removed his sidearm and knife.

"Get up," the voice ordered.

Will got to his feet.

"Who are you?" the soldier asked.

"Will Roberts from the United States of America." Since the ID he carried said Will Roberts, he thought it best to stick to that persona.

"Who is that man?" the soldier asked, pointing to Anders.

"My partner."

"What are you doing here?"

"Looking for a woman. She may have escaped her captors from a camp in Venezuela."

The soldier ran a flashlight up and down Will's body. "Do you have an ID?"

Will produced his passport from a waterproof pouch hanging around his neck. The soldier inspected it as he shined a light in Will's eyes. Satisfied, the soldier handed it back to Will and disbursed his men into a wider perimeter.

"Take your weapons back," he told Will.

"You're Americans," Will said as he put his knife and sidearm back. "Who are you?"

"We're American soldiers, here for drug interdiction missions. We received orders to move to this sector regarding an American woman who escaped from Venezuela. We were told to find her if we could. We were also told to look for two men hunting her. I guess we found the men, but not the woman."

"Her tracks lead south," Will said.

"We didn't see any tracks. But the ground is hard where the vegetation ends. That's about another twenty minutes for you. There's a highway two or three miles south of that. She may be making her way there. Don't go left, or you'll find bogs and swamps."

"Did you see any other men?"

"No. Just the two dead guys out there and Jungle Jim, who was hiding in the tree," the soldier replied.

That's why Will couldn't find the third gunman. He'd been up in a tree.

"Listen, we have to leave now," the soldier said. "The Columbians will be here shortly, and we'd prefer not to explain why we're here. You'd better get moving, too."

"What about my associate?" Will asked.

"I've logged the GPS coordinates. I'll transmit it up the chain so you can retrieve him later, although the Columbians may beat you to it."

Will nodded.

The soldier looked at his watch. "It's after midnight, so Merry Christmas. I hope you find your present."

"Keeping my life was the best gift of all," Will said as he dusted himself off. But when he looked up, the men had vanished.

Will worked fast, transferring Anders's water and food to his pack. Slipping it on, he picked up his rifle and turned on his night vision. If he was going to make up some time, he needed to stop looking for Tori's tracks. She had to be heading south. The faster he got near her, the better chance of picking her up on his equipment. If he lingered too long, it would be daylight, and his advantage would be gone.

He took a few cautious steps before jogging slowly. In ten minutes, the land leveled out, giving him solid footing. He ran at a good clip.

Soon, the forest thinned out, making it easier to run faster. Sure enough, Will reached the open land.

Stopping on a ridge, he scanned the next mile for any signs of life. There were none. He lowered his head and started running again.

Ten minutes later, he crested another rise and stopped, taking in some water. It wasn't that hot, but with all his gear, he was sweating hard.

Adjusting his night vision, he was confident the highway was no more than half a mile away. With no cars or streetlights on it, it was impossible to be sure. But a dip in the land looked like a bridge. If he were Tori, he'd head there and hide.

Will ran fast, but not as hard as he had been. No telling who had a gun and might take a clear shot. Many a rescuer had been killed by the person they'd set out to rescue. "A drowning or desperate man will take you under," Dr. Z had said. "You can't rescue anyone if you're dead."

With nothing but an occasional bush in his way, it was easy for Will to cover a lot of ground safely. As he approached the dip, he noticed a short bridge spanning over a tiny creek. Or maybe it was a drainage ditch. Regardless, Will switched on the thermal imaging and got a hit. Someone was sending up a heat signal behind one of the columns. This had to be Tori.

Will brought his rifle level and moved cautiously, studying the ground as he took careful steps. When he came within 100 feet of the heat signature, it moved to another column directly behind the first one. Will decided to take a chance.

"Tori Sterling. This is Will Roberts. I work on the ranch."

The figure shifted but stayed at the column.

"Tori, if that's you, three of Santos's men are dead. Brace sent me."

The figure moved again. Will walked another twenty feet. "Victoria, the police and possibly more of Santos's men are on the way. We have to get out of here now!"

"How do I know it's you?" a woman's voice came back.

"Well, I came alone because Sadie thought the sand might mess up her pedicure."

She moved to the side of the column and out in the open.

Will turned off the goggles and pulled out a flashlight. "I'm going to shine this on my face. It will blind me, so if you want to run away, you can." He flipped on his flashlight, holding it away from his body so he didn't look like a monster. He heard some movement. Then, footsteps.

"It *is* you," Tori said. "Thank God."

Will shined the light on Tori as she ran to hug him. It was a tight embrace. "Where's Brace?" she asked, breathing hard.

"Still in Venezuela looking for you," Will replied.

"Get me out of here," Tori said.

"Let me check you out first." He turned on his headlamp and aimed it at her. Her shoulder-length brunette hair was dirty and matted, obscuring the blonde highlights. She had muddy and torn pajama bottoms and a damp blue t-shirt on minus a bra. Will noticed the red F Bar A tattoo on the inside of her upper right arm.

"Do you need water?" Will asked, removing his pack.

"Oh, God, yes!"

He gave her a water bottle, which she chugged. While she drank, he ripped open an energy bar and she ate it. And another.

"Okay, that's enough," Will said, taking the empty wrappers and water bottle and putting them back in the pack. "Let's get moving. Can you walk?"

"Yes. Where are we going?"

"To a junction in the road. Brace has a man waiting there for us."

Tori put her arm around Will and hugged him again. Then, she kissed him on the cheek. "I'm ready," she said. "Get me home!"

• • •

Will bowed his head and said a prayer. When he opened his eyes, a large plate of scrambled eggs, turkey bacon, nine-grain toast, and oatmeal with muesli appeared. Standing there was Mrs. White.

"I cooked it myself," she said.

"I'm moving up in the world," Will replied.

"You most certainly are. If you invent a cure for cancer, you'll be invited to the White House."

"Maybe I can get a pardon for my crimes."

"Ask for more. Like a cabinet position." Mrs. White wiped her hands on an apron. "While you're thinking about it, eat up. You have a big meeting afterward."

"Okay," he said. "I need to build up my strength."

Will sat by himself while the rest of the men stared at him. It was a new world he'd stepped into.

After piling in as much food as he could, he grabbed a second cup of black coffee and lingered in the kitchen, reading the sports page. When the woman appeared, he knew it was time.

"Right this way, Mr. Roberts," she said. Will noticed the change to mister.

He followed her to Grayson's office, where she opened the sliding doors and let him in. Hearing the distinctive click of the doors closing told him he'd arrived.

Grayson sat behind his desk with a cup of coffee. Brace sat to his right and Cole to his left.

Grayson started. "I can't thank you enough for getting my daughter home. And on Christmas day, even if there were only ten minutes left. That was the best present I've ever received."

Will nodded and kept his mouth shut.

"Tell me what happened after you left Brace," Grayson ordered.

Will detailed the entire adventure, including Anders's death. "I'm guessing Cole called the American soldiers," Will said.

"Absolutely!" Cole replied. "They owed me a few, and it was time to cash in."

"What about Anders's body?" Will asked.

Cole continued. "When I received their report of contact with you and of Anders's death, I sent them back out to recover his body. It's being flown on a DC-10 to DFW Airport with full military honors."

Will turned to face Brace. "Thanks for making sure your man was there to pick us up. I don't know what would've happened if someone would've spotted us."

"It would not have been pleasant," Brace said. "But when I give orders, people follow them."

"How's Tori?" Will asked Grayson.

"In shock and grieving Evan's death," Grayson replied. "She's been through a lot, but she's tough. She's a Sterling."

Brace glanced at his watch and pointed to Will. "I have something to say. It's December 26 at 9:25 a.m. I want everyone in here to note the exact time I stopped doubting you and your abilities."

Will grinned broadly.

Brace pulled a fat envelope out of his back pocket and tossed it to him. "That's a bonus for you. And, unfortunately, we have a job opening due to Anders's death. We'd like you to take his place."

"I don't know what to say," Will said, completely dumb-founded.

"Say yes," Brace replied. "We'd be honored. Besides, it comes with a salary of $500,000. That pays a lot of child support."

Will blinked several times. "Definitely, my answer is yes! You are my family now. You're all I have."

"Don't get misty-eyed," Grayson said. "You've got work to do. Brace will provide you with a list of the men you are supervising. Go over that and make sure you understand your responsibilities. Then, take the day off. Tomorrow, I want you and Cole to go over the intelligence and report to us in three days. On December 30, we have a family dinner planned. I'd be honored if you would attend. That is unless you have other plans."

Will nodded and chuckled. "I'll check my calendar, but I'm thinking it's wide open."

"Good. We'll expect you there. Cole will tell you about the dress code."

"Thank you, Mr. Sterling, Brace, Cole—for putting your trust in me. I won't let you down."

"We're certain you won't," Grayson said. "You're family now."

"Let's go to my office," Brace said. "I'll go over your new responsibilities."

•••

Will placed the flat envelope on the table and opened it up. He had closed the curtains to his new suite and opened a safe that came with it. After counting the bills twice, he totaled $100,000. He was stunned. Just gazing at the stacks made him understand how a cop could take a little money here and there and not worry about it.

Now that I'm getting a real divorce, I could pay this year's and next year's child support from this stack and have some leftover, he thought to himself. *And I could shift more of my paycheck to a college fund for the boys.*

He picked up a stack and held it up to his nose, sniffing it before letting his thumb release the bills like a deck of cards.

Who would ever know?

Chapter Twenty-One

The Thirsty Goat buzzed with activity. With so many men on the ranch now, the booths and tables were almost full.

Will checked his phone, then lifted his eyes in time to see Hector coming toward him with a waiter's tray. Hector carefully balanced the drinks on the tray, setting it down on the table.

"To my soon-to-be new boss," he said. "I brought a few extras."

"Thanks," Will said, "but three drinks?"

"We're going to be here a while. I want to make sure you're well taken care of."

Will removed his three drinks from the tray. "I don't know about being your boss one day."

Hector put the tray away and sat down. "We have to face reality. Tori's a widow. You're divorced. Tori Sterling-Roberts? It has a nice ring to it."

"More like Will Roberts-Sterling."

Hector laughed heartily. "Here's a toast. To Will Roberts. Part of the Sterling family now."

Will clinked his glass with Hector's beer bottle. "So, what did I miss while I was in Venezuela?"

"Not much. Just a bunch of military guys everywhere on the ranch. No way Santos gets through them without spilling a lot of blood. And Waylon barked a lot. A few of the men tossed the stick for him until he got tired, dropped it, and went to his water bowl."

"Here's to Waylon," Will said, lifting his glass. "He's part of the family now." They clinked again. "Have you been off the property?"

"No. It's locked down hard. They're letting us go home on New Year's Eve. They have a spot where we can bring the family to watch the fireworks."

"There are fireworks?"

"Big ones," Hector replied. "Same as you'd see at any of the large displays around the country—even better. And it should be extra huge because last year it was canceled due to a lack of rain. When that happens, Grayson uses the fireworks from last year and adds to them. It should be spectacular. It starts around 9 p.m."

Will's mind raced. "Can people leave after that?"

"Last year they could. There's always a lot of activity—catering trucks, guests—because Grayson has a New Year's Eve party for the staff. They bring in the food. But with this Santos stuff going on, who knows."

Will nodded as he sipped on his scotch, his mind working through a plan.

"So, enough ranch stuff," Hector said. "Tell me about Venezuela and all the bad guys. Don't leave anything out."

"It might take me these three drinks," Will said.

"Don't worry. If you run long, I'll bring more."

• • •

Will looked at his watch. It read 11:15 p.m. The night had flown by.

"It's time for me to go," Will said.

"See you around," Hector replied.

Will stood up and felt the scotch in his legs. He shook his head to get some feeling back in his face. Then he made his way to the apartment.

As he fumbled with the key in the lock, he heard something behind him.

"Pssst. Will." He spun around, reaching for his weapon. It was Sadie.

"I need to talk to you," she whispered. "Over here."

Will plodded over to her.

"No," she said, grabbing his arm. "Farther away from the building."

Once they had moved a football field away from any building or car, Will whispered, "What's up?"

"I'm ready to leave the family," she said firmly.

"What?! Are you for real?"

She nodded.

"Now?"

"Whenever."

Will's mind was getting up to speed. "And the twins?"

"I'll leave them. You're right. They'd hunt me down. You and I can have kids. If not, we can adopt. I just need to get out of here."

Will puffed out his cheeks as he exhaled. "Okay. What about New Year's Eve?"

"I'm expected at the party. It starts at ten, right after the fireworks. When do you want to leave?"

"After the fireworks. There'll be lots of cars going on and off the property. We'll make our getaway then."

"That might work," Sadie said. "We can slip out unnoticed. I'll tell Cole I'm not feeling well."

"Start the day before, when we have the family dinner. Tell him you don't feel good, but you'll come anyway because you know how important it is to the family. That will give you a pass during the fireworks."

Sadie nodded. "That's smart. I'll do that. Cole won't be looking for me during all the confusion." She pulled Will close and kissed his lips hard. "You'd better be there for me because I'm going to be there for you. In every way you can imagine."

She disappeared fast. Will had to close his eyes for a moment to make sure that had just happened. He wiped the lipstick off his lips and studied it in the moonlight. Sure enough, it had happened. Five days from now, he'd be in the FBI's Washington Field Office with Sadie as his top confidential informant. And he'd have that long to decide what to do about the $100,000.

•••

The room was filled with paper, mostly call logs from cell phones. Leftover food dotted the plates along with crumpled napkins. Stacks of files surrounded the two men. Will looked through one stack while Cole hammered on the computer. A knock on the door drew Will's attention.

"May I come in?" Mrs. White asked. "I just want to clear the dishes, dear."

"Certainly," Cole replied, not looking up from his screen.

"Was it good?" she asked Will.

"Delicious, as always."

"I hope you liked the fresh fruit," she said. "It's winter, but I can still get melons and cantaloupes."

"From where?"

"I have my sources," Mrs. White said, a tiny smile creasing her face. She set a fresh pot of coffee down between them and put the plates on a tray. Quietly, she slipped out, closing the door behind her.

The office Cole occupied shared a wall with Grayson's office. It was Grayson's far wall, the one where he had a writing desk surrounded by bookshelves. This ensured no noise leaked between the spaces.

On the walls of Cole's office were security cameras. The entire compound was covered. Brace had another room where these cameras were duplicated, so his men monitored from there. But this was the original war room of the Sterling family.

"You getting any more ideas?" Will asked Cole.

Cole stopped and looked up. "We get Santos, we kill the head of the snake. One shot and we're done."

"But how long will that take?" Will asked.

"We can play the long game better than he can. We out-asset him."

"By what? Two to one? Three to one?"

"Twenty to one, at least," Cole replied. "We have more money, which buys more weapons and men."

"That's what I thought," Will said, dropping a file he'd been holding. "Why not take a different approach? Mrs. White reminded me of fruit—*low hanging* fruit."

"Explain," Cole demanded.

"We hit anyone associated with Santos. All the low-level guys who should be easy pickings. The guys working for him will worry and hide. They won't be out kidnapping people if we're eliminating them."

"They'll plug in more guys," Cole said.

"Sure. But that takes money and training. And those lower-level inexperienced guys make mistakes. They might also run when the bullets fly. Plus, it makes the mid-level managers do the work of the lower guys. This exposes them. Before you know it, Santos and a bunch of his executives are left to do the grunt work, which exposes them. Then you take your shot."

"Hmm," Cole said, "that's interesting. I don't think it's the right strategy, but I'll present it to Dad along with mine. We'll see what he and Brace think."

• • •

At 5 p.m., Will and Cole went into Grayson's office for a strategy meeting. Will was surprised that Cole laid out both plans—treating each one balanced and fair. Neither Grayson nor Brace asked for recommendations.

"I like the low hanging fruit approach," Brace said, his hands slicing through the air. "It gets us back to doing what we do best: the extermination of pests."

Grayson nodded. "I agree. It's a good war strategy to chop off the enemy's lines of supplies, to sink boats full of ammunition and food. Before long, they'll feel the pinch." He leaned forward and pointed to Brace. "Hit everyone and everything everywhere. Got it?"

"I got it," Brace replied.

"I have some targets," Cole said, surprised at this development but not unprepared. "Can you start tonight?"

Brace looked at his watch. "The night's still young. Let's see if I can give Santos some indigestion before breakfast."

•••

Three days later, the four met again. Brace briefed them on the body count. It was significant. Will could see the Sterlings were making a big dent in Santos's operation. Grayson was pleased and adjourned the meeting so everyone could get dressed for the family dinner.

Will, already dressed, walked over to the dining room. It was closed, but a waiting area next to it was open. A skinny man stood behind a short bar, sorting out various beers and liquor bottles. Will, being nosy, went over to take a peek.

"Are you joining the family for dinner?" the man asked, eyeing Will.

"Yes. I've been invited by Mr. Sterling."

"Oh," he said, straightening up. "May I get you a drink?"

"Certainly," Will replied. "I'll take a single malt scotch, preferably ancient."

The bartender smiled. "Excellent choice, Mr. ..."

"Roberts. Will Roberts." He took the drink. "How long have you been the bartender here?"

"A few years. I'm also responsible for replenishing the inventory of wine and spirits for the ranch."

"I'll bet that keeps you busy."

"You don't know the half of it."

A loud voice echoed down the hall. "I must have at least two drinks. That's the only way I can get through this dinner."

The loud talker came into view, holding Declan's hand. He was the same one Will had seen with Declan the last time.

The man wore an ornate cowboy-themed outfit. A large silver belt buckle covered with turquoise set off the light blue in his shirt. A stringed bolo medallion took the place of a tie. Expensive slacks made of a unique material appeared as blue jeans when he moved. To Will, it looked like he had stepped out of a fashion magazine selling the faux cowboy look. It was gaudy but somehow fit together.

"I'm Russell Simmons," the man said with an effeminate voice. "And who are you?"

"Will Roberts. I've been invited to dinner by Mr. Sterling." Will repeated it because he felt so out of place.

"Well, Will, we'll be eating together. I hope you're not the main course. I've had that already." He kissed a blushing Declan on the cheek.

Will nodded, unsure how to reply.

Declan stuck out his hand to Will. "Good to see you again," he said. Will took his hand, but Declan pulled him close, hugging him hard. "Thank you so much for getting my sister back. I'm writing a song about it. I think you'll like it."

Will backed up and noticed Declan's eyes were moist.

"Mr. Simmons, may I get you a drink?" the bartender asked.

"Definitely. I'm parched. I'll take some of that designer vodka you have. With some diet tonic water."

"Of course. And Mr. Sterling?"

Declan ordered a whiskey and coke.

Once they had their drinks, Will continued the conversation. "Have any shows coming up?"

Declan nodded. "Tomorrow night in Vegas. We're performing on the strip at an outdoor venue. I'm one of eight performers."

"Oh, that's great," Will said. "Are you performing at midnight?"

"No, that's for the high-dollar acts. I go on at seven, which will likely slide a bit. I'm only a B-lister."

"But not for long," Russell said. "He'll be the top act soon. Once he comes out with that new album, he'll be there. 'Dynamite Whiskey' will be a big hit. So will 'Momma's Little Book.' That makes me cry."

"We'll see," Declan said, shrugging. "You never know if a song will be a hit or a dud nowadays."

Will made his drink last while his two conversation companions worked on their second one. Soon, Brace and Cole arrived. The small area grew loud.

When Grayson arrived, he clapped, signaling it was time to move into the dining room. Everyone dropped their phones in a locked container. Will patiently waited for everyone to enter before he did. He wanted to know where to sit.

Walking in, it didn't take long to figure it out. His place was directly opposite Grayson.

Will noticed the rectangular table was perfectly sized for eight people. On Grayson's right sat Brace. To Grayson's left were Cole and Sadie.

To Will's left was Tori. To his right were Declan and Russell. It was an interesting arrangement.

"How are you doing?" Will asked Tori.

"Still recovering slowly," she replied.

Will noticed she looked like Sadie had on the plane back from Key West. An untouched glass of red wine stood in front of her.

The room was still decorated for Christmas. A beautiful tree occupied a corner behind Sadie. The richness of the wood paneling and the table décor made this scene hard for Will to fathom. He had never been to an event like this.

Brace got up and adjusted the logs in a massive fireplace behind him. As Will looked at Grayson, he noticed flames climbed up, making it seem they were burning his back and head. For a few seconds, it was eerie.

Will nodded at Sadie. She had a glass of tonic or something clear and carbonated. That made Will happy. The last thing he needed was her getting drunk and running her mouth.

Grayson waved his hand, and Mrs. White brought in the twins. "Say hi to everyone," he told the girls.

"Hi," Kodi and Brooke said.

"Excellent. Now, go with Mrs. White. She's made some chicken tenders and French fries and that special macaroni and cheese you love."

"Goodie!" Kodi yelled.

Mrs. White led them away by the hand and closed the door.

Grayson looked at Will. "The children will join us when they are ten, in case you were wondering."

Will smiled.

"Now, I have an announcement to make," Grayson said. "The yearly family portrait will be taken on January 2, when Declan is back from Las Vegas. I want everyone to be available for the photoshoot. And, Sadie, I want you and the girls to wear those white lace dresses that we had made in France last month. Gentlemen, you will wear the tuxes we just received from Mr. Chu."

The young Hispanic woman appeared and poured water and wine into the glasses. She served everyone except Grayson. When Mrs. White came back, she filled Grayson's glasses.

With no one to talk to, Will studied the fine china and crystal. He took a sip of red wine. It was exquisite.

Will listened to the talk around the table. Current events, sports, crude oil, and cattle prices were the main topics. Sadie and Tori stayed mostly silent.

Somehow, the conversation stopped. This allowed Sadie to ask Russell where he got his clothes. Before he could answer, Declan spoke up. "He was a JCPenney boy when I met him. Now, he's a Nordstrom's man."

"Where did you get that beautiful watch and belt buckle?" Sadie asked.

"Rodeo Drive," Russell replied. "And the boots too."

Will noticed Grayson's expressions switch between a grimace, smirk, frown, clenched jaw, and finally, grinding teeth. It was obvious he disapproved of Declan's flamboyant lover.

Brace, who had been mostly silent during this exchange, cleared his throat. "I don't think they have any real rodeos in Los Angeles. Here in Texas, we only get fancy belt buckles for riding bulls. Have you ever ridden any bulls?" he asked with a sly grin.

The table fell silent. Everyone knew Brace had insulted Russell's manhood.

"No," Russell said, unfazed. He grabbed Declan's hand. "But I've had a bull or two ride me."

Sadie, who was drinking from a glass, spewed water three feet in front of her face. She just missed Russell. After coughing out the last drops, Sadie reached across the table and touched Russell. "I knew there was a reason I liked you."

They began talking about fashion. "We need to get you some mascara," she said. "I'll take you to the mothership."

"What's that?" Russell asked.

"Neiman Marcus. It started in Dallas. They have everything you'll need to get Declan excited to see you."

Russell gazed at Declan. "Oh, he's always excited to see me. His record is five times in one day." Sadie howled with laughter while Grayson turned away.

When the conversation died down, Grayson spoke up. "Let's bow our heads." He said a prayer, thanking God for bringing Tori home safely. Then the meal was served.

As usual, the food was off the charts. A slab of melt-in-your-mouth prime rib sat next to mashed potatoes and a vegetable medley. Fresh yeast rolls and ranch honey rounded out the feast. Will left nothing on his plate.

After the meal, fruit and dessert were offered. As Will finished his chocolate lava cake, he stood up to excuse himself, assuming they might want to have a conversation without him there.

"Sit down, Will," Grayson ordered. "You're a guest, but I'll decide when it's time to leave the table." His voice had a bitter edge to it, no doubt from putting up with both Sadie and Russell in one night.

The conversation continued, but more subdued. Another round of coffee was served and consumed. As Grayson finished his cup, he got up and grabbed a package from under the tree. He walked over and stood behind Will. "This is for you, Will. A token of our appreciation. We have grown very fond of you."

Will glanced around the table and saw everyone nodding their head. Declan patted his right arm while Tori kissed his left cheek.

"Well, open it up," Cole said.

Will tore away the ribbon and wrapping. He lifted back the lid and pulled out a Rolex Day-Date II President watch with an 18K yellow gold bracelet. It was gorgeous. And expensive.

For one brief moment, Will felt like he was part of this family. He pushed his other world down and enjoyed this one. And his heart smiled.

Chapter Twenty-Two

The rapid tapping of shoes on the Italian-tiled floor echoed down the hallway. Will looked ahead and guessed who was coming his way.

"Uncle Will!" Brooke yelled, leaping into his arms.

"Are you getting cuter every day?" he asked.

"Yes," the young girl replied.

"What about me?" It was Kodi.

Will set Brooke down and picked up Kodi. "Let's see," he said, inspecting her. "Yep, you're getting cuter every day, too." She smiled.

Sadie came up behind the twins, buttoning her long blue coat. "Come on, girls. Let's go outside to the bounce house before it gets too cold."

"Uncle Will, can you come out and play with us?" Brooke asked.

"I have a meeting with your grandfather. I'll be out after that's over unless it runs long."

Satisfied with his answer, they took off running.

Will stood at the entrance to Grayson's office. "Come in," Grayson said. "And close the door behind you, please."

Will slid the doors shut. Brace and Cole were already there. He took a seat between them.

"I'd liked to be briefed on the progress," Grayson said. "Brace, you first."

Brace handed thick red folders to the three men. Will took one and opened it up.

"As you can see," Brace said, "we've eliminated twelve associates in three days. All of them are low-level men except for one executive who happened to be riding with one of our targets. We scored a two-for-one hit there."

"How has that affected their operations?" Grayson asked.

"They're moving men around to compensate," Brace replied. "This has opened up more targets. A war of attrition will sap Santos dry a lot quicker than us. I wouldn't be surprised to hear something from him soon. Maybe an overture of peace."

Grayson furrowed his black brows. "It's too late for that. What about any countermoves he might make?"

Brace set his folder down. "We have men on our tanker and watching the oil fields. Our folks in Europe are on high alert. Tori is here. And we have the ranch buttoned up. There are plenty of low-level targets in our operation he could tap, but that takes men and money. And right now, he's leaking both."

"Cole, what do you have to say?" Grayson asked.

"It's going better than I thought. Brace and his team are doing a great job. We just need to be vigilant here."

"I agree," Grayson said. "Will, you'll be responsible for the ranch house security tonight before and during the fireworks. Do you have your men sorted out?"

"I do," Will said. "I may want to borrow an ATV and check the perimeter."

"Stay off the ATVs," Brace said. "You can easily hurt yourself on one of those at night. It's hard to see holes and ditches. And you can get shot. Take an SUV. It has bulletproof glass and headlights. Let the parking lot watchman know you're leaving so he can signal ahead and make sure you don't have any problems. But, really, you should let my team handle the perimeter and stay with the house."

"I agree," Grayson added. "But he has an excellent nose for trouble. Will, you do what you want. Just communicate and be careful."

They continued the meeting, discussing security details of the party as Brace picked up the folders to ensure they didn't walk out of the room. Cole mentioned that Sadie wasn't feeling well and would likely miss the fireworks. Both Grayson and Brace seemed disinterested.

Grayson wanted to discuss goals for the upcoming year, so he dismissed Will. Taking his time, Will made his way outside and found the bounce house just off the path to the barn. Sadie stood to the side, watching the kids enjoy the fun.

"How's it going?" he asked as he came up next to her.

She looked around to make sure no one was listening. "My outfit is ready. I'll look like a caterer."

"Good. Do you have a ballcap to wear?"

"Yes. I'll stuff my hair underneath it."

"I know I've told you this, but no electronic devices or luggage," Will said sternly.

"Don't worry. I'm not that stupid. I plan to come down from the bedroom with my hair loose like normal. I'll be wrapped in a long coat like this one. I'll pick up an empty tin from the kitchen and walk out through the door and past the patio. Once I'm outside, I'm going to stuff my hair in the hat and remove the coat. Underneath, I'll be dressed as a caterer. I'll casually stroll to the SUV with the tin. You have your men cleared out from the patio and the front. I'll take care of the rest."

"That tin had better be empty," Will said. "No mementos, because someone might search the tin. Once we're free, we'll buy everything on the fly."

"I'm bringing my driver's license and passport, and all my cash."

"Fine. I'll put the backseat down and toss in several dark blankets. Put your tin on the floor behind the front seats so it's hidden and climb under the blankets. I'll turn off the interior lights in the SUV. It'll stay dark when you get in."

"What time do you want me there?" Sadie asked.

"Right before the fireworks. I'll be opening the door to the SUV at 8:55 and driving off. You come five minutes earlier at 8:50. I'll have a window cracked so nothing fogs up."

"I'm scared but excited," Sadie said. "I can't believe we're actually doing this."

"Believe it," Will said. "But listen to me. At 8:55, I'm leaving with or without you."

"I'll be there," she said. "You just be there for me."

Will nodded. "Let me play with the kids. I need to make this look real."

•••

Around four, Will met with Green and two other men, Cook and Sanders. He told Green and Cook to watch the caterers coming in and out. Sanders was assigned to the patio and kitchen entrance. Will told them he'd float around and watch everything.

When that was done, he strolled around the outside of the ranch house. He spotted two of Grayson's bodyguards watching the patio door to his second-story bedroom.

Will went inside and found two more bodyguards protecting Grayson's office. Brace had a man in the kitchen and another at the stairway to the second floor. As Will left through the front entrance, he saw two more men. It was a minefield of problems for Sadie to make it to the SUV. Will gave them a 50 percent chance of making it out alive.

He ended the tour in his apartment. It was 4:30. Will sat on the edge of his bed and fell back. He needed five minutes to clear his mind and search for any holes in his plan. Even though he looked forward to getting back to the Bureau, he wasn't thrilled with leaving either. The ranch was like home to him now.

Slapping himself several times in the face, he re-centered his mind and focused on the mission. He and Sadie had to get clear of the ranch and Brace. If not, the boneyard awaited.

Sitting upright, Will took in several deep breaths. Then he grabbed his backpack and started putting everything he needed in it. The cash—and there was lots of it—went at the bottom. His beautiful watch stayed in the box, resting on top of the money. A spare gun went in next, along with extra magazines and a box of ammo. In case someone searched through the bag, socks and underwear topped it off.

The pack was fat and wouldn't fit under his bed. Instead, he put it in his closet and shut the door. He would come back later, grab it, and run.

It wasn't time for dinner, but Will went to the kitchen anyway. He didn't want to engage in conversation with anyone, so he fixed himself a sandwich and sat at a table in the corner. The only one there was Mrs. White. She came over.

"Mind if I sit down?" she asked.

"Go ahead," Will replied. "I was just trying to shove in a sandwich before things got hectic around here."

"Are you skipping dinner?"

"I am. You're just feeding the men, right?"

"That's right. The caterers will handle the party tonight. Are you enjoying your new promotion?"

"I am," Will replied, "but it's a load more responsibility. Sometimes, it's easier to follow instructions."

"I'm sure you'll do fine." Mrs. White patted his hand. "Got any big plans for tonight? Are you allowed to watch the fireworks?"

"No. I'll be handling the security for the ranch house. Do you have any plans?"

"Yes. Grayson lets me off New Year's Eve. I'll be out back watching them. I'll bring you a sparkler."

I hope you don't come looking for me at the wrong moment, he thought to himself. *That would be a disaster.*

"Any New Year's resolutions?" he asked her.

"Oh, I want to start the morning by reading the Bible. Hear what God has to say about my day. And you?"

Will thought for a moment. "I'd like to be a better leader. Learn more about managing people."

"There's a lot of leadership information in the Bible," Mrs. White said.

"And a lot of killing. I spent time reading it when I was in prison."

Mrs. White smiled and said nothing.

Will picked up his plate. "I've got to run and get back to work. Have fun tonight."

"I will," she replied. "See you around."

I hope not.

Will walked around the ranch house again, checking on his men. Everything was zipped up tight.

Glancing at his watch, it was 5:30. He had plenty of time to kill.

With the light fading, he made his way to the mechanics' shop and found Hector playing cards with some of the men. A portable heater was on one side and Waylon on the other.

"Has he exercised?" Will asked.

"Yes, but he's always ready for more," Hector replied, drawing a card from the deck.

Will took Waylon and tossed a stick for him to fetch for twenty minutes. Then, he sat down and watched the men playing cards. As they talked, Sterry came in to work on her sniper rifle. She set it on a table and disassembled the components. Will got up and went over.

"Are you watching the fireworks?" he asked her.

"No," she replied coolly. "I'm on duty. I'll be making sure no one tries anything stupid."

"I might be checking the perimeter tonight."

"Don't bother," she said, putting her gun back together. "We have it under control."

Will nodded. "Are you on all night, or do you get off at any point?"

Sterry cocked her head and smirked. "If you're trying to buy me a drink, that's not going to happen."

Will's eyebrows raised as she turned her taut body to walk away. But she stopped and slowly swung her head back to Will. "Because the drinks are always free at the Thirsty Goat." She disappeared through a side door, the rifle strapped to her shoulder.

Will shook his head. *What just happened there?*

He started back toward the house, thinking about Sterry out in the woods somewhere with a rifle, waiting to shoot him and Sadie. Halfway to the house, Tori intercepted him. With the evening light mostly gone, she moved closer to see his face.

"I want to thank you again for saving my life," she said. "Santos's men would have caught up to me. They would've made sure I didn't escape a second time."

"Just doing my job," Will told her.

"I'm sure, but it made a big difference to me. I know you like it here on the ranch, but would you consider working for me in Houston, handling my security?"

"When are you going back to Houston?"

"Not for a few weeks, maybe several months," she replied.

Will grinned. "Then I guess I have some time to think about it."

"You do. In the meantime, here's a gift to show my appreciation." She handed him a package, kissed him on the cheek, and walked back to the house with him, her arm in his.

Sadie. Sterry. And now, Tori? I've got to get more of this cologne, Will said to himself.

• • •

The time was 8:30 p.m. His watch told him he had fifteen minutes to try and get Sadie off the ranch. This might be the riskiest stunt he'd ever pulled. And even if he got Sadie off, she might not cooperate. There were so many ways this could go bad, he didn't want to count them.

Outside, a slight breeze had brought the temperature down into the high thirties. Will zipped up his leather jacket and, once again, made a turn around the ranch house.

Two catering trucks had arrived and were unloading the food and equipment to the main dining room. Several workers came and went. Green and Cook were on duty, watching everything with powerful flashlights.

Green came over to Will. "How are we looking?"

"Good," Will replied. "Grayson's outside bodyguards will be taking a break soon. At 8:45, take Cook and man a post outside his upper balcony. The men might still be there. If they don't take a break, oh well. I'll cover this area."

"How long do we stay there?"

"Nine o'clock," Will replied. "I'm going to check the ranch perimeter at that time and need you back here."

"Are you sure you're not going to see the fireworks?" Green teased.

"Pretty sure, unless some idiot starts firing at me," Will joked.

"It won't be us."

"I'm counting on it."

Will walked around the ranch house one last time, stopping at the patio. He told Sanders to take a break at 8:45 sharp and come back on duty at nine. Then, he hustled to his apartment and cleared his mind.

Will double-checked his backpack. Everything was still there. He put the gift from Tori—an expensive burlwood cigar humidor engraved with F Bar A on the lid—next to the watch box and zipped it up.

He pulled the gun from its holster and checked the action. It was fine. He removed the magazine and inspected it. All fourteen rounds were there.

The time was 8:47. *Sadie should be in the SUV by now. This wait is killing me.*

Will sat on the edge of the bed, watching the seconds tick off. Suddenly, he remembered his cell phone in his jacket pocket. That had to stay behind. He had almost made a critical error.

His watch finally read 8:54. Will put his backpack on his shoulder, surprised at how much it weighed. Grabbing a water bottle from the table, he flicked on his flashlight and closed his door for the last time.

Will moved smoothly toward the SUV, the same one he'd prepped an hour earlier. As he walked, he spotted the parking lot attendant and went over to him.

"I'm going to take that Range Rover and check out the perimeter," Will said. "Tell the men to let me through."

"Yes, sir," the attendant said, unclipping his radio.

Will moved back to the SUV, hearing the attendant giving instructions on the radio.

This is going to work. I'm almost there.

Will opened the driver's door and tossed his bag onto the passenger's seat. Seeing the lump under the covers, he knew Sadie was there.

"Will!" a man cried out. "Will!"

Will looked over the roof of the SUV and spotted a man running toward him. This was the disaster he feared.

"Hang tight," he whispered to the back of the SUV. "A man is coming."

Will stood up and moved to the man, meeting him ten feet from the rear of the SUV.

"What is it?" Will's tone was abrupt.

"Cole wants to see you right now," the man said. He was one of Brace's top bodyguards.

"I'm on my way to check out the perimeter," Will told him. "I'll see him when I get back."

The man stepped in closer. "He said it was an emergency. He needs you now. In fact, he's standing at the entrance."

Will stared toward the ranch house and saw Cole waving at him.

"Alright, I'm coming," Will said. "Let me secure my backpack and close the door."

Will went the SUV and leaned over the driver's seat to grab his backpack. As he pretended to mess with it, he whispered to Sadie, "Cole has an emergency. If I'm not back in ten minutes, see if you can get out and slip back to the house. We'll have to call it off for now."

"Oh no," Sadie cried from under the blanket. "I left a note for the twins on my bathroom sink. And one for Cole, too."

"What?!" Will said as loud as he dared. "I think you just killed us."

"Get those notes, Will!" she said as he tossed his backpack to the passenger's seat and closed the door.

I can't believe this. He set his jaw, trying not to grind his teeth. *Dr. Z always said the weak chain in the link causes the entire operation to fail. I'm going to die because of it.*

Will walked with the man to a waiting Cole. Instantly, he saw the distress on Cole's face. When they made it to Brace's office, Cole closed the door, trapping him there with the two men. Brace was on the phone, listening to a voice on the other end. His face was a deep red.

They've seen Sadie in the SUV. I can kill these two and try to shoot my way out.

Will exercised his right arm, but it was only an excuse to ease his hand to his gun. As he coughed, he undid a snap on his holster, making the pistol easier to pull out.

"What's going on?" Will asked the men.

"It's bad," Cole said. "Real bad."

"What is?" Will said. "Tell me!"

Brace slammed his cell phone down on the desk. "There's been a mass shooting in Vegas. Declan's wounded. Lots of people dead. I'm sure it's Santos. We need to get into the war room right now!"

Will processed the information, forcing his hand to leave his holster. He silently sighed and followed the two to the war room. But he remembered his other problem.

I've got to get upstairs and find those notes. I'm not out of this mess yet.

Chapter Twenty-Three

Will leaned against the wall of Brace's office, silently tapping the wood paneling with his fingers. He needed to find a way to get up to Cole's room before Cole did.

"What are you going to tell Dad?" Cole said.

Brace looked up from his desk. "The truth, as soon as we know what it is."

Explosions roared through the walls. Will drew his gun as Brace pulled one from his desk drawer. Cole searched desperately for a weapon until Brace set his down on the desk.

"Oh hell!" Brace said, shaking his head. "It's just fireworks. Dad is there watching them with the twins. Remember?"

Everyone relaxed.

"Still, I need to check on my men," Will said, "and make sure this house is secure. Do you need me right now?"

"Go," Brace ordered, putting his gun back in the drawer and retaking his chair.

Will eased out of the office and closed the door. He hurried through the ground floor, checking the bodyguards and the windows. He wanted to make a good show.

After a few minutes of that, he went to the stairs. A bodyguard blocked his path. "No one allowed upstairs," he said.

Will put his hands on his hips. "Grayson Sterling has put me in charge of the house security. I need to check upstairs."

"I know that, but I have my orders."

"From who?" Will asked, knowing the answer.

"Brace."

"I just left Brace," Will said. "I told him I was checking upstairs. Oh, there he is." The man glanced to his right, giving Will a chance to slip past him.

"Stop, or I'll shoot," the man said.

Will stopped and slowly turned around, spotting the gun pointed at him. "I'm going upstairs. If you want to come with me, fine. If not, shoot me now and prepare yourself for the consequences."

Will turned around and kept walking, waiting to be shot. When he made it to the upstairs landing, he knew he was safe.

He moved fast to Cole and Sadie's room. The door was ajar, so he pushed it wide open. A window on the far wall was exposed, its curtains pulled back. He went to the window, checking to make sure it was locked. Outside, fireworks continued to burst. Muffled explosions came through the glass panes. He closed the blinds. As he turned around, Cole appeared at the entrance.

"The bodyguard told us you had come up here," Cole said.

Will's heart raced. "I wanted to check out the security, make sure no one had gotten in."

"Is it safe?" Cole asked, moving toward the bathroom a few feet away.

"Let me check the bathroom for you," Will said, trying to cover the distance before Cole could enter it.

"That's why I came up here," Cole said, unzipping his jeans. "To use it."

Cole beat Will to the bathroom. Will thought of heading down the stairs, but he knew he'd never make it.

"What is this?" Cole asked.

I'm done for, Will thought through the roar of adrenaline in his ears. He pulled out his gun and aimed it at Cole's back, seeing him stopped at the counter.

"It's a hot water bottle," Sadie said, coming out of her side of the bathroom. "It's used for sick people."

Will lowered the gun, exhaling silently.

Cole held the water bottle up. "Why won't you let me call for the doctor?"

"I will," Sadie replied, "if I still feel bad tomorrow."

"Can I check your closets?" Will asked.

"Sure," Cole replied.

Will spotted his backpack on the floor, barely sticking out behind Sadie's dresses.

"Are we safe?" Sadie asked sarcastically.

"Yes," Will said, discreetly putting his gun back into his holster. "Let me check the other rooms."

Will left Cole and Sadie behind, making a cursory check of the other rooms. Then he hustled out down the stairs, receiving an elbow from the angry bodyguard, and went outside to check on his men.

In the sky, fireworks exploded. Will found Green and Cook at their posts. He told them the news from Vegas.

"I'll grab you each an M4 and extra magazines from the bunkhouse and be back," Will said.

He stopped first at his apartment to fetch his phone. Several missed calls flashed on the screen. He pressed the call-back button.

"Where the hell have you been?" Brace demanded.

"Checking out the house," Will replied softly. "I missed your call."

"All three of them?!"

"I had it on silent by accident. Sorry."

"That can't happen again," Brace said.

"I understand."

"Get rifles for yourself and your men. We're going to need them. Then, come back to my office. We'll need to tell Grayson what's happened."

Will put the phone down and hung his head. That had been way too close. He'd almost been dead.

He fell back on his bed and stared at the ceiling. He couldn't believe he was back in his room. He'd thought he'd never see it again. And now, Sadie had his backpack. Leaving this family would not be easy.

• • •

Three exhausting days later, Will sat in Grayson's office. Two long tables had been brought in so Cole and Brace could pore over the reports and data they'd been compiling. Grayson had the speakerphone on, waiting for a nurse to get Declan on the line. Finally, a groggy voice spoke.

"Hey, Dad," Declan wheezed, his words barely audible. "My throat's sore from the tubes."

"That's okay, son. You listen, and I'll talk. Cole and Brace and Will are here. We're hoping you recover fast. Here's Brace." Grayson pointed to his oldest son.

"Declan. I want you to know I have plenty of security in place there at the hospital for you. As soon as the doctor says we can move you, I'll have a plane pick you up and bring you back to the ranch. We are setting up a room here with nurses to tend to you. We'll get you back on that stage in no time."

"I doubt that," Declan croaked. The phone line crackled a little as he fell silent.

Cole spoke up. "Hey, baby brother. It's me, Cole. I just looked online, and your record sales are off the charts. I guess we'll have to go through a personal assistant to talk to you from now on."

Silence.

Cole pointed to Will. He took a breath before speaking. "Declan, we can't wait for you to come back to the ranch. Your dad and Brace may send me to pick you up. I'm looking forward to seeing you again."

Grayson chimed in. "We're sending Will so he can eventually save every member of this family. Besides, none of us want to miss any of Mrs. White's cooking."

"Oh, the chicken fried steak," Declan moaned.

"I know you've been on an IV drip," Grayson said, "so hopefully, you can get back to solid foods soon. You didn't need to lose weight, but at least we'll be able to build your health back up."

Declan coughed and said nothing.

"Okay, son, we all love you. You get better. We'll check in tomorrow." Grayson put the handset back in the cradle. "That went okay," he said, his tone neutral. His voice rose as he picked up the tabloid sitting on a nearby table. "Until I had to read *this*!"

Will looked at the tabloid with a picture of Declan on stage just as the gunfire erupted. The headline read, "Shooting Star."

"At least we won't have to endure Russell Simmons anymore," Brace said quietly, but loud enough to hear over the crackling fire.

"What happened to his body?" Grayson asked.

"I had it shipped to a funeral home in San Francisco near his mother," Brace replied. "His dad is dead."

Grayson turned the tabloid over. "Are we paying for the funeral?"

"Absolutely, since we'll pay for it anyway once his mother files a lawsuit against us. She'll also sue the property owners, the stage company, the security firm, the city of Vegas, the gun manufacturers, the weatherman…"

"Okay, I get it," Grayson said, cutting off Brace. "That's what lawyers are for. At least we have Declan alive."

Cole changed the subject. "I think we should talk strategy. The man we captured was able to give us some information. I just received it."

"About time," Grayson said, rubbing his hands together. "What did he say?"

"That he was told to head to our ranch from Vegas and join an assault that's coming in a few weeks."

"Anything else?" Grayson asked.

"No. He ran out of juice shortly after that."

Will imagined the suffering the man had endured. He also pictured an acid bath followed by a desert barrel burial. A chill ran down his spine.

Grayson pointed to Brace. "Opinions?"

"There is no way Santos would tell a man on a hit job about the next hit," Brace said, balling his fist. "Too much information. Santos planted that for us to find."

"So, he knew we'd capture him?" Will asked, shaking his head.

Brace faced Will. "Maybe he had people there to make sure we captured him alive. Maybe he told all the shooters the same information, figuring one would survive and tell us that story. It's basic psyops in the military. Fake your enemy out."

"I'm not so sure," Will said. "Santos's organization has been downgraded."

"You mean degraded?" Cole asked.

"Yes, degraded," Will replied. "He's running low on men. He must attack before he runs out of men. He needs to push his poker chips into the pot for one big final blowout. Santos can't outlast us, and he knows it. While he still matches up, he needs to strike—or he'll be running until he's dead."

"That's what he wants us to think," Brace said. "He's not ready to die in a hail of gunfire here. He'll hit our tanker and oil fields and maybe our European friends. If he loses some men, he doesn't care. He'll grab money from these hits and start degrading us fast."

They paused, giving Will a chance to think. He needed to find a way to convince them they were wrong.

Grayson leaned forward, swirling the scotch in his glass. He rubbed his clean-shaven and tan face before clearing his throat. "It seems I remember Napoleon matching up nicely with Wellington, maybe even had 4,000 more men. Yet Wellington presented himself for battle and dared the Emperor to fight. Napoleon knew Wellington was heavily dug in, but he needed to attack Wellington while he still could. Napoleon's hold on France was tenuous. And the Prussians, with 74-year-old Blücher at the head, were out looking for him. If they showed up, Napoleon would be in trouble. So, he attacked Wellington, confident his Grande Armée could outfight him. That's what Will is saying. Santos must attack because he's Napoleon and we're Wellington."

Will sat upright, his face brightening. "That's right! That's what I'm saying."

"I thought so," Grayson said. "The problem is that Napoleon was a military genius. His battles are still studied today. I know Santos. I was his business partner for many years. I was his best friend. And believe me, Santos is no Napoleon."

Will's shoulders sagged. Grayson was making a huge mistake.

"Brace, pull whatever men you need from the ranch to protect our assets here and overseas. We'll make sure the ranch is secure even if I have to take a watch."

The three men got up and started to leave. Will turned back to Grayson. "What happened in the battle? Who won?"

Cole and Brace stopped at the door to listen. "It had rained so hard the night before that the ground was a mess. It was hard to fight on, much less march over. With the sun out, Napoleon waited until noon to attack Wellington. His canon barrage, to soften up the British, landed mostly in the mud and failed to explode. But the French fought hard. They eventually busted through the lines and were about to roll up Wellington's men when a miracle occurred. Blücher showed up with his army. They attacked Napoleon's right flank, sucking much-needed men from his reserves. Wellington's army, seeing this, was revived. Soon, the French morale sagged. Because Napoleon had waited, he gave time for Blücher to arrive. Thus, the small town where this battle was fought became famous. They call it Waterloo. And that was the end of Napoleon."

Will wasn't done. "So, in the end, Napoleon attacked Wellington but lost because Wellington had plenty of extra men provided by Blücher. And we're pulling men off to fight somewhere else."

"That's correct," Grayson said. "And I'm betting you're wrong."

Will went with Brace and Cole to continue the meeting. They discussed the defenses for the ranch. With so many men being pulled off, they agreed to draw the perimeter in tight. Instead of having men in the forest, they would put them in the barns and other structures. This would give them clear lines of fire. Plus, their night vision gave them the advantage of seeing anyone in the forest at night.

One change they made was to move Cole from the office next to Grayson to Brace's larger office. With Brace about to leave, Cole wanted the extra room without having the security monitors continually staring at him.

Will was assigned Cole's office, the original war room. He would be responsible for watching the monitors and organizing the defenses, with Cole's and Grayson's help.

Will spent the next day walking and driving the ranch, getting to know it like never before. He wrote down the name of every man and solicited their ideas.

Late in the afternoon of January 4, he found himself at the horse barn, studying its defenses. Sterry showed up.

"What, not cleaning your weapons?" Will said.

"They're meticulously cleaned and loaded," she said.

He noticed that she wore a well-worn black leather biker jacket zipped up tightly. "Come to check on the horses?"

"No, I've come to talk to you," she said, moving closer with a blue folder in her hand.

"Alright," Will said, growing interested. "Let's talk."

"Brace told me what you said. I completely agree with you and your assessment. I think this ranch is in total danger. I told Brace you were right."

"I guess he didn't listen to you or me."

"No. I'm going with him to protect an oil tanker. But I have some advice for you. Do you mind if I share it?"

"Of course not. Let me see it."

Sterry laid out a map on a table and went over the weak points in the defenses. Will asked a few questions but mostly absorbed the information. When she finished, she passed the folder over.

"Keep this. It may help."

"May?" Will said with a smile. "It *will* help. I can't thank you enough."

Sterry smiled in return, but she said nothing and didn't move to leave. Will decided to go for broke. "And while we're on speaking terms, what does Sterry mean?"

"You've never heard of that name?" she asked, the corner of her mouth turned up.

"No," Will replied.

"Neither have I. My given name—my *Persian* name—is Shahzad."

"I'm guessing that means beautiful flower or expert with a sniper rifle," Will said, his mouth turning into a full grin.

She laughed. "No, it means prince, son of a king."

"Okay. That makes no sense."

"I agree. My father had one last chance for a son. Then I was born. Because he and his tribe had fled from Persia to another country, his standing as head of the tribe was precarious. It was important that he produce an heir. So he told everyone I was a boy. For the first seven years, I was raised as a male."

"Your family history is as messed up as mine," Will said. "Why are you called Sterry?"

"If I answer this question, will you answer one of mine?"

Will agreed.

"When I started working here, I didn't want to be called a boy's name. So, I took the name Terri. But the men called me Sterry, which they told me is short for sterilize."

"Sterilize..." Will said, leaning his head back and drawing out the word. "You clean up messes."

She nodded. "Now for my question. You've been here seven months, and you now run the ranch security. You're very smart. Who are you, really?"

The question rocked Will to his core. It broke through his undercover persona and reached his authentic soul. He wanted badly to tell her he was a special agent with the FBI, had several college degrees, and had been specially educated by a top government trainer. He couldn't keep telling her he was some hayseed from a doublewide who'd been to prison. It was obvious she wasn't buying that cover. His mind crunched through the problem. Then he came upon an answer.

"I'm a friend of Cole's. That's all I can tell you."

She nodded. "I thought so."

They said nothing for a few minutes. She stared at him, and he returned her gaze. She looked around the barn as she processed this information.

Will finally broke the silence. "Why do I feel you're too good for me?"

She started to leave. "Because, Will Roberts, you don't know me."

"Will I ever get to?" he asked when she was at the door.

"Protect this ranch when the attack comes, and I'll see what I can do." Will thought she was done, but she added, "If Sadie doesn't get there first."

She disappeared, and Will felt the panic rise up in his chest. *I've been exposed. She's seen everything that's going on.*

He thought back to his failed attempt to leave. *Why am I still here? I'm going to get killed if I stay.*

He remained at the barn until he was fully composed and back in character. Satisfied, he went to the mechanics' shop and talked with Hector.

"The Thirsty Goat is closed, eh?"

"Yes," Will confirmed. "Until this blows over. We need sober lookouts, not dead drunks."

"What can I do?" Hector asked.

"Exercise Waylon. He has great hearing. And bring several ATVs to the ranch house and bunkhouse. Leave the keys in them in case we need to ride."

"I can wire them, so you don't need keys."

"Do it," Will said, patting Hector's shoulder. "And put them up against the building so the attackers can't use them as shields to hide behind."

"Will do. And after this is over, you're buying drinks."

"Just keep a lookout and do your job. When we survive this, drinks are definitely on me."

Will left Hector. He walked outside to find Sadie playing with the twins.

"You're feeling better," he said.

Sadie gave a half-smile. "After I grabbed those notes, I felt wonderful."

"Me, too," Will said. "I need to get my backpack back."

"I know you do," she said, her half-smile disappearing. "But that backpack is my security. You'll get it when we leave this place. With Brace gone along with his men, we can slip out anytime."

"Sadie, you know I can't leave these people behind. They'll be killed." Will bit his cheek. He shouldn't be having these feelings. It went against his training.

"What do you care?" she asked, stepping a few feet away from him.

"They've been good to me. And I know Santos is coming here. Everyone could die, including the twins." Before she could respond, he said forcefully, "Listen, I want that backpack."

Sadie folded her arms. "You're not getting it. And don't come looking for it."

"Or what?"

"Don't come looking for it," she repeated, her expression hardened.

Will was completely pissed. He left her behind, ignoring the calls from the twins to come and play.

All that cash and she's holding it. It could do so much good. I've got to find a way to sneak up there and get it.

•••

Dinner was a subdued affair. Will didn't want the men lingering over a massive steak, so he'd told Mrs. White to make food that was packed with energy instead of leading them to naps. She delivered.

He had just finished his chicken salad sandwich when Mrs. White removed her apron and sat down. "How are you holding up?" she asked.

"Fine. The men are still getting used to me running things."

"It takes time. They'll trust a strong leader."

"I'm trying to be that," Will admitted.

"I hear they're mostly happy."

"Mostly?" Will grunted as he pushed his plate away.

"Are you getting your sleep?" Mrs. White asked.

"No. I need to watch the security monitors."

"Don't neglect your sleep, Will. You'll make bad decisions otherwise."

"Don't I know that," Will said, mostly to himself. "Listen, it might get rough around here. I want you to keep an eye out and be prepared to duck."

Mrs. White's eyes flashed dangerously. "You don't worry about me, Will. I'm tough."

"I'm sure, but a plate won't block a forty-five-caliber round."

"That's true," she said, her nostrils flaring. "I'm only a cook. But they say revenge is a dish best served with a 9 mm round."

Will leaned back and grinned. "Okay, I'm worrying less about you."

She hugged him as he stood up. "We all know you can protect us. Just let me know if there's anything you need."

Will felt good. He hoped his next meeting would go as well.

•••

"Please, sit down," Grayson said. "Scotch?"

"Yes," Will replied. "Just one."

"I understand." Grayson poured the 100-year-old spirit for both of them. As the men sipped on it, Grayson raised a glass. "I saw Brace and his crew off. It's just us now. But I'm confident this ranch is in good hands."

Will raised his glass. "I'll do my best."

"So far, your best has been stellar," Grayson said, leaning back in his high back chair.

"If it comes to shooting, do you have a weapon?"

Grayson pulled out his drawer and lifted a gold-plated pistol. "It's a replica from the James Bond movie, *The Man with the Golden Gun*. It's based on the German Luger."

"If I recall, that golden gun held only one round," Will said.

"This one holds eight." Grayson chuckled, removing the magazine. "These Germans make great equipment."

"Let's hope it stays in your desk."

They sipped on their scotch until it was gone.

"Is there any other advice you can give me?" Will asked.

"Yes. I have a hidden door that goes down to a tunnel. In the tunnel are rockets and explosives. Let me show you." He touched a stone on the fireplace and a door clicked open.

"This place is full of secrets," Will said.

"You only know the half of it."

• • •

The steady stream of fluorescent light and endless monitor feeds lulled Will to sleep. He was in the war room, leaning back in a chair and snoring. He needed deep sleep. A soft tapping pricked at the edges of his mind and grew louder until he awoke.

"Uh... come in," Will said groggily as he wiped dribble from his cheek.

"It's breakfast time," Mrs. White said. "Want to take a break?"

"Sure," Will replied. "Just let me go to the restroom, and I'll be right there."

Will relieved himself and splashed water on his face. It had been a long night. He needed to clear the cobwebs.

In the kitchen, Mrs. White had his place set. A steaming cup of black coffee and a plate of eggs, toast, yogurt, and figs awaited him. Will wasted no time diving in.

No sooner had he finished the meal did popping sounds come from outside. Mrs. White looked through the window as Will jumped up and grabbed his weapon. "What is it?!"

Mrs. White turned her head, her expression cold. "Gunfire. They're here."

Chapter Twenty-Four

Will rushed to the stairs to find Sadie bounding down the steps. "What's happening?" she asked, panting.

"We're being attacked by Santos. Where are the twins?"

"Upstairs in their room."

"Get them now and come to the war room," Will commanded. "I'll be there."

Will ran to the war room and quickly studied the monitors. He picked up his radio and pressed transmit. "All team members, we're under attack. Sitrep, please."

"Gun range reporting," a voice said. "Four shooters have us pinned down. No injuries... yet."

"Do you have the fifty-cal set up?" Will asked.

"Roger that. We are engaging but targets not always clear. Need to conserve ammo."

"Hold them back. I'll see if we can get you more ammo and support. Parking lot. Report in."

"One man down, two of us left," he said with gunfire in the background. "Five to ten enemies, hard to tell strength. We are protected by vehicles but need support."

"I understand," Will said. "Hold on. Horse barn. Sitrep."

Silence.

"Horse barn," he said again.

"Mechanics' shop here," a man whispered. "This is Hector. Two men down. I'm in a hidden closet. Waylon took one man down and saved me. I killed one shooter. Too many men. They're headed to the house."

"Understood. Stay safe."

Will studied the monitors, specifically the upper floor of the house, from the exterior camera angles. Four rifles protruded from several bedroom windows on the south elevation, firing intermittently. It appeared Cole, Tori, and two other men were firing toward the barns and gun range.

Another monitor showed men creeping up from the north side. They had circled the parking area. One rifle from the second floor checked their advance.

Will rubbed his face and scanned the office. Papers and folders covered every surface. A bottle of water sat unopened next to the phone. A hand-carved wooden trashcan overflowed with crumpled paper.

Will collected himself and checked the automatic rifle leaning against the wall. It was operational. He pulled out his handgun and checked it. Suddenly, the door burst open. It was Sadie and the twins.

Will helped the three in, locking the door behind them. "Are you okay?" he asked.

"Yes, but terrified," Sadie replied. "What's going to happen to us?"

"Nothing," he said. "Just calm down." He saw Kodi's lips quivering. "And calm them down. Sit on the other side of this desk and let me do my job."

Gunfire in Grayson's office brought his focus back.

"Dammit!" he said, pounding on his desk. "They breached the house." Brooke had crawled under the desk and was pushing on the wall under the credenza behind Will.

"Sadie, can you keep Brooke over…" He stopped talking and watched as the child tried to slide the wall. Kneeling down, he pulled her arm away and studied the outlines of a panel. "Is this a way into Grandpa's office?" he whispered.

She nodded.

Sadie collected Brooke as Will gave her instructions. "I'm going in there. Once I'm in, slide this closed behind me. And turn off all the lights until you close it. I don't want them giving me away."

Sadie bent down and kissed him on the lips. "I'm counting on you to come back to me." Then, she hit the wall switches as Will pulled out his Glock. After taking a deep breath, he slid the panel aside and crawled through the narrow opening.

A chair partially blocked the lights of Grayson's office. He crawled very slowly forward on the hardwood floor, carefully pushing the chair back. Between the backrest and the seat, he took in the scene.

Grayson's bodyguard was near the entrance to the office, flat on his stomach. Blood oozed from his body. Grayson was in his leather high back chair, his head bent over on the desk. A man dressed in combat gear held down the back of his head while he worked the radio.

"I have the old man," he said in a thick Spanish accent. "I'm in his office." There was a crackled response that Will couldn't understand.

The man presented a large target. Will quietly shifted his Glock to the chair's seat pan, using his arm to steady his aim. A click behind him sounded. It was Sadie putting the panel back in place.

Will glanced at the panel, then back to Grayson. The man now pointed his gun at Will.

"Drop your weapon!" he ordered Will. "Or he gets it." He jerked Grayson up as a shield, putting the muzzle of the gun to his head. "If you shoot, I'll shoot the El Jefe."

"But at least you'll be dead," Will said, remaining perfectly still.

The man squinted his eyes. "You'll miss me and hit him."

"Maybe," Will replied. "But you'll lose your shield. Then, I'll shoot you. Either way, you're headed to hell."

The man rammed the gun into Grayson's gray hair. "Does he agree with your strategy?"

Blam!

The gunman wilted, crumpling to the floor behind Grayson. Will pushed the chair away and went to Grayson.

"I can't believe you took that shot!" Grayson yelled.

Will stuttered. "Uh... I-I'm sorry. I felt I had to. He was going to kill all of us."

Grayson patted Will on the side of the head. "No, I mean I can't believe you *made* that shot. That was incredible. Let me get my gun and let's rid this place of these rats."

Grayson pulled out his golden gun, jammed in the magazine, and pulled back the slide.

"The rats are all together," Santos said, walking into the office and pointing his gun at Grayson. A man at his side aimed an automatic rifle at Will. "Guns down. Hands up. Step away from him," Santos ordered Will.

Grayson and Will set their weapons on the desk.

"Santos, we can work this out," Grayson pleaded.

"Of course we can," Santos said, pushing his hat up with the muzzle of his pistol. "Just like you did with all my dead men. And just like you did with the Vanderilla property. You remember that—when you took it for yourself? I've had enough of your deals."

"So, what happens now?" Grayson asked.

"This has been a heavyweight fight. It's the fifteenth round and we're tied. It's time for one of us to go down."

"Please leave my children alone," Grayson begged, his voice cracking. "I'll pay you to leave all of us alone."

Santos leaned his head back and laughed. "Oh, you'll pay me alright. The debt has come due. It's time for me to collect."

Santos raised his handgun at Grayson.

Blam! Blam!

Grayson leaned forward, checking for entry wounds. There was no blood anywhere on his clothes. Santos reached out a hand toward the desk and missed, falling forward to his knees. The man next to him was face-forward on the floor next to Grayson's dead bodyguard. In a split second, Will picked up his gun and aimed it at Santos's head.

Blam!

Will shook his head. He hadn't pulled the trigger. He turned to his right and saw Grayson's gun smoking. Santos fell forward, banging his head on the desk.

Back at the entrance, Mrs. White moved into the office. She had a Sig Sauer 9mm in her hand, still smoking.

Will grinned. "You have more than cooking utensils in that kitchen."

"You're damn right!" she said. "I told you how I like to serve my dish of revenge."

Gunfire continued from the second floor, bringing them back to the present.

Cole and Tori came running into the office. Cole had two men with him. "There are fifteen more outside. We have two men upstairs holding them off. They're almost out of ammo."

"Grab Santos's radio," Grayson ordered Will as he pressed the button to his secret tunnel. "Let's get the explosives and rockets and clean this place up. Time to put these fuckers on an expressway to hell."

Epilogue

A dented and scratched microphone faced Will, its long black cord twisting away to a digital recorder. Three assistant U.S. attorneys sat opposite of him, their ties loosened. In front of each were Apple laptops and electronic tablets. Will grabbed a bottle of Fiji water and unscrewed the cap, taking a swig.

"What about Declan?" Will asked.

"One of our sources checked, and he's scheduled to be released from the hospital on January 31," the lead prosecutor said. "He should be back at the ranch shortly after that."

"I mean, what about any criminal charges?"

"Your report doesn't link him to anything other than the family dinners. We've got nothing on him, so he'll be back singing country songs."

"Maybe his next hit will be, 'My Daddy's in Prison,'" the second-chair prosecutor said.

The three prosecutors chuckled.

"How could you be confident enough to shoot the bad guy and miss Grayson?" the lead prosecutor asked.

"The truth is, I fired at the gunman and didn't think about it." Will took another swig from the water. "Either way, I'd win because a criminal would be dead."

"That's still a hell of a trick shot."

"Maybe if I take that shot ten times, I hit Grayson five. Like I said, it was a win-win situation."

The second-chair prosecutor scrolled through his electronic tablet. "Your report said there were another twelve guys you and your team had to take out after that shootout. Those bodies must have been a hell of a load to transport to the boneyard."

"I didn't see that," Will said. "Sterry and her crew loaded up trucks and took off within eight hours of the last shot being fired."

"That's damn fast."

"She would've been faster if she hadn't been at a port in Panama watching the family's oil tanker."

The lead prosecutor chimed back in. "A jury's going to love hearing about that tanker. After all, doesn't every family have one?"

"What about the dog?" the rookie prosecutor asked. "Is he still at the compound? What was his name?"

"Waylon. And yeah, he took out one of the turds. He can tie Brace back to the bodybuilder, L.E. Gaetti."

"Did Brace ever find out you brought that dog back?"

"If he did, he never said anything to me."

"Are those bunkers easy to find?" the lead prosecutor asked. "The ATF wants a crack at them."

Will tapped a yellow piece of legal paper in front of him. "This is my detailed drawing. It shows where to enter the bunker from Grayson's office. If they can't find it, well... there's no hope for them."

"Don't forget the IRS is drooling, too," the second-chair prosecutor added. "So is ICE. They're ready to corral some illegals. Time to bring the Sterling family down."

Will nodded as if in agreement.

"What reason did you give them for being here?" the lead prosecutor asked.

"I told them I had some family in Virginia. When I stayed with Cole and Sadie before Key West, I used that excuse to slip away and phone in my reports."

"Well, Mr. Rockton, this is the case of a lifetime. We will have one hell of a prosecution if it goes to trial. The press on this will be tremendous."

"What about me?" Will asked.

The lead prosecutor looked to the prosecutor on his left and the one on his right, then back to Will. "Get ready for your choice of assignments. You will most certainly get your choice of legat assignments anywhere in the world, baby! Boy, are the Sterlings going to be shocked when they find out who you really are."

Will leaned back in his chair. "Any negatives to this case?"

"Yeah, it's like a fiction novel. The jury will think we made it all up. I mean, the little girls show you a secret way into Grayson's office. The Black cook shoots the two bad guys in the back, saving everyone. You and the head honcho get M72 LAW rockets and fragmentation grenades from a hidden secret tunnel and kill the rest of the attackers without losing another man. If we didn't have the explosions on satellite to match your story, I'd swear you made it all up."

Will closed his eyes. *Sometimes I wish it was all made up.*

The debriefings went on for several more hours before finally ending at 5 p.m. And why not? That was quitting time for all government employees.

Will left the Robert F. Kennedy, Main Justice Department Building and walked along Constitution Avenue, trying to clear his head. It was too early for dinner. Besides, he wasn't hungry.

Three blocks away was the Capital Grille. With nothing else to do, he decided to go there. Maybe a good stiff drink would calm his spinning mind.

The long wooden bar and the luxurious interior said one word: success. Will planted himself at the bend in the bar so he could see anyone coming in and be out of the way. Chris Brown's "With You" played in the background.

"What'll it be?" a burly bartender asked.

Will looked around. "Where is everyone? I know it's only Tuesday, but shouldn't it be more crowded?"

"The Capitals have a big game tonight," the bartender replied. "And Kobe is playing LeBron on national TV. We're not a sports bar, so a lot of folks are at those events or home, watching it on TV. Around eight or nine, the lobbyists will be here with their politicians. It'll fill up then."

Will slapped the smooth bar with his palms. "Their loss is my gain."

"For sure. I'll take care of you all night long. Your face tells me you might be here a while."

"Very perceptive," Will said. "I've had a long, hard day. I'll have a Balvenie."

"Excellent choice. You're getting on my good side." The bartender left to prepare the drink.

As Will watched him walk away, he reminded Will of someone from his past.

In seconds, the bartender placed the drink in front of him. "Want to run a tab?"

"Here's my credit card," Will said, handing it over.

He took a sip of his scotch and searched his mind for the bartender lookalike. A few minutes into his search, he found it. Stevie Ranson, a meth ringleader. What a case that had been.

Will, or John Starnes, had infiltrated a white suprema-cist gang from the bottom, doing grunt-work and earning his reputation. Once the FBI busted the gang, they arrested Will, too, hoping to keep up the charade until they questioned each member. Sure enough, the interviewing agents extracted reli-able information from several members, but not Stevie. He was the one holdout.

At Stevie's trial, Will took the stand and testified that he worked criminal enterprises in an undercover capacity for the FBI. Will detailed his training and experience. Stevie listened to this for an hour before jumping up and yelling to the judge, "I don't know what you did to him, but he's one of us! He's not an FBI agent. Never was. You've brainwashed him!" That's how deep Will had gotten into their world.

Will's phone rang. "Hello?"

"This is your long-lost mentor."

"Dr. Z?"

"The one and only. Do you have time to talk?"

"For you, anytime," Will replied. "I'm at the Capital Grille. Want to meet me here for a drink?"

"No," Dr. Z said. "Why don't you come to me. I'm at GX-19. You remember how to get there, right?"

"Of course, I do."

"Great. Then put that scotch down… or finish it quickly and come over to see me."

Will stared at his caramel-colored drink and silently laughed. Dr. Z always knew way too much about his pupils. "On my way."

With his left hand, Will signaled the bartender. "Could I have my tab, please?"

"That was quick."

"Don't worry, I'll be back. I have a lot of thinking to do and need a lot of time to do it."

"I'll be here for you."

Will stepped lively down the rain-soaked sidewalks of the city. It was freezing out, but the phone call had warmed him up. Seeing his mentor would be a special treat to take his mind off things for a while.

He found the covert government location and knocked twice on the metal door. Dr. Z opened it, and the two men embraced.

"Come on back to my office, Will. It's so good to see you again."

"You, too," Will said, following him down a sparsely lit hallway. "I have some things I need to discuss with you, that's for sure."

"Wonderful. But first, let's step into this room. I want to introduce you to someone."

Will entered a small conference room next to Dr. Z's office, where a tall Black man wearing a dark wool suit stood.

"Will, this is Xavier Lewis. He's the attorney general for the United States."

Will shook his hand. "I know who he is."

"Pleased to meet you, Will," the attorney general said. "I want to say you've done the most unbelievable work I have ever read. The Justice Department and the FBI are so very grateful for your dedication to this country. It's special agents like you that the American people depend on to protect and serve this country."

"Thank you, sir," Will said.

"Would you like to have a photo taken with me to place on your wall?"

"Of course," Will replied.

The attorney general picked up a Nikon camera. "Dr. Z, would you do the honors of taking our photo together?"

Will and the attorney general both smiled and shook hands while staring into the lens. After two quick clicks, the attorney general turned to Will. "I hate to run, but I'll let you talk with Dr. Z."

Will nodded and stepped aside, allowing the attorney general to leave.

When the two had moved to Dr. Z's office, and the sound-proof door was closed, Will said, "What was that all about?"

"Please, Will," Dr. Z said, "take a seat."

Will plopped down in one of the gray fabric guest chairs and looked around the office. There were no windows—typical of all secret locations. Photos of Dr. Z standing next to various politicians covered the walls. One wall held dozens of plaques and accolades. It was very impressive. He said nothing and waited for his mentor to take a seat so the conversation could begin.

"First of all," Dr. Z said, picking up a fresh green stub to chew on, "let me echo the attorney general's thoughts on the job you've done. It was completely masterful. Likely the best that's ever been performed here at the Bureau or the Agency."

Will smiled. "Thank you, but why do I feel like a steam-roller's headed my way?"

"You're so very perceptive," Dr. Z said, pointing at him. "I always admired you for that. You know the part where you thought I had outed you to Cole?"

"Yes. I want to talk to you about that."

Dr. Z removed his wire-framed bifocal glasses. "I'm sure you do. The truth is, Will, you were played. Cole made an intelligent guess and got lucky."

"Oh, come on," Will said. "He knew all about me."

"No, he didn't. When I was a kid, my sister and I broke a lamp playing in the living room. We swore to each other we would keep our mouths shut and not tell Dad. When Dad saw it, he called my sister into his study. They were in there for quite a while. Once he was done, he left her in there, came out, and pulled me into the kitchen where my sister couldn't hear. He told me to tell him the truth because my sister had finally spilled all the beans. I was angry because she had promised me. I confirmed what she said was true. Turns out, my dad had conned me. She had held the line. It was me who had blown the entire operation. That was a valuable lesson I learned as the paddle hit my backside. Cole tricked you, my friend."

"So, you didn't give me up?"

"Of course not. That would be in total contravention of everything I stand for. You know that."

Will hung his head. "I couldn't believe you'd give me up."

"But according to your report, you didn't give yourself up, did you?"

"No. I left some wiggle room."

"That's good," Dr. Z said, pointing his glasses at Will, "because that's going to be advantageous for the next revelation I have for you."

Will tensed up, ready for the unexpected.

"As you know, the Sterlings have operations in Europe, Asia, and the Mideast. Prostitution. Brothels. Gambling. Loansharking. Narcotics. Even hitmen for hire. Because of this, their operations bring in a great deal of raw and defined intelligence, not to mention compromised diplomats and politicians. The Sterlings do things the United States government cannot and would not do. Thankfully, they share that intel with us."

"Okay, so? Where is this going?"

"Will, when America has a mistake that needs to be corrected, many times, international law prevents us from fixing it. The Sterlings haven't signed any international treaties. They don't belong to the G-7, the United Nations, or the World Bank. They're free agents. Their erasers are unencumbered. You see, the Sterlings can correct mistakes we, the government, can't. Do you understand what I am trying to tell you?"

"So, they're invaluable to the U.S. government," Will said with a frown, heat rising in his chest. "What happens when they all go to prison?"

"Right now, we need them more than ever. The world is a very dangerous place. It's possible that in a few years, we won't need them anymore. At that point, your work will be invaluable to us."

Will stood up and pounded the wooden desk. "Are you telling me there aren't going to be any prosecutions?! I risked my life for nothing?"

Dr. Z held his hands up. "You didn't risk your life for nothing. The information you provided allows us to keep tabs on them. It's invaluable. The attorney general wanted me to tell you that."

"That's why he left so quickly. He couldn't be part of this conversation. Right? To keep his hands clean," an agitated Will retorted.

"I don't know," Dr. Z replied. "Regardless, we'd still like you to consider going back to the family. Feed us information so we know everything they're doing. This will allow us to squeeze them later if we need to."

"You mean to correct another mistake somewhere. Or pull the right trigger next time. Or explode the right bomb at the right place."

Dr. Z said nothing.

Will folded his arms in disgust. "The meetings I had with the U.S. Attorney's Office—that was all for my enjoyment?"

"Don't get angry. Those attorneys didn't know. They'll be told in the morning. As for you, the government greatly appreciates your commitment. They've approved a raise outside of your pay scale. You'll make an extra $5,200 a year until you're promoted into another paygrade."

Will's blood boiled. "Really! $5,200?! Are you kidding me? One hundred dollars more a week for what I've been put through?!?"

"That's all they could manage with budget deficits and all. But they did approve a one-time performance bonus of $5,000. That will buy you a nice vacation somewhere. Yes?"

Will's body sagged. "That won't even cover *one* of my divorce attorney's bills. What a complete waste of time. I want to tell the world about how I've been used and abused here. And for what?"

"Look," Dr. Z said, pulling out a document, his tone changing. "Here's the NDA you executed when you signed on to tradecraft training. Remember, you can't tell anyone about this operation or any of your work assignments. You also can't talk to any reporters, either."

"You're fucking unbelievable!" Will yelled, turning away.

Dr. Z's voice grew firm. "I know everyone's writing a book about everything these days. But don't even think about it, Will."

"Man, I'm done with this undercover work. It's all take and no give. I've wasted my life, my marriage, and destroyed a lot of good relationships."

"Listen, Will, take a few days and think about it. Don't do anything rash. The government needs you there, someone on the inside, letting us know if the train is going off the tracks."

"No way," Will spat back. "I want to move on with my life. I've given everything I had to the government. My tank is empty, with no way to refill it. I'm done."

Dr. Z's voice changed to one of persuasion. "Don't forget the adrenaline rush you experience each time you step on the set. You get to be someone you're not. There aren't many people in the world who can say that."

"Other than professional actors who make $20 million a movie." Will turned to go.

"Hey," Dr. Z said with controlled anger, rising to his feet, "don't forget which side you're on. And don't become a mistake we need to correct."

• • •

The entire world had just caved in on him. The arctic cold air of D.C. felt twenty degrees colder as a sullen Will made his way back to the Capital Grille. There, he discovered that his previous chair was still vacant.

"You're back," the bartender said as Will sat down. "But it looks like you've lost that good mood. Maybe you've seen a ghost."

"It happens," Will said dryly, avoiding the bartender's gaze. "That's what alcohol's for."

"Another Balvenie?"

"Definitely."

Will placed the backpack on the empty chair next to him. He had picked it up from his hotel room after leaving Dr. Z.

The bartender set the drink in front of Will. "Run up a tab again on your credit card?"

"Sure." Will reached for his wallet, then stopped. "Uh, no. Let me run up a tab with this." He dug into his backpack with both hands and produced a brand-new one-hundred-dollar bill, handing it to the bartender. "See how far this gets me."

"That'll work," the bartender said, placing it in the cash drawer and typing in notes on the point-of-sale screen.

With the pack open, Will dug around and pulled out the wooden box from Grayson. Carefully, he opened it, removed the Rolex, and strapped it on his wrist. The gold band was a little loose, but the watch stayed in place.

"Wow!" the bartender said. "That's unbelievable. A gift?"

"Yeah," Will said, holding his arm out as he studied the timepiece. "For a job well done."

"I'd say. Sounds like someone knows how to take care of their people."

Will's phone rang. He stared at it, letting seconds pass. Finally, he answered it.

"Will, it's me," Sadie said. "Are you missing us?"

He hesitated. "Maybe."

"We're missing you. The twins ask about you all the time. We're outside and they're playing in the bounce house Grayson set up again."

"Sounds like fun," Will said, his mood improving slightly.

"It is. And there are plenty of fun things here," Sadie said, lowering her voice. "Come home and enjoy some of them."

Will took a sip of his scotch.

"Are you in a bar?" she asked.

"Yes."

"We have a bar here, and it doesn't charge for drinks."

"I know."

"Come on home to the ranch," Sadie urged. "The gang wants you to join them in the Thirsty Goat."

"I'll think about it. Kiss the twins for me." He hung up before Sadie could speak. Then he glanced at his watch and sighed.

"Family calling?" the bartender asked.

Will nodded as he lifted his Balvenie, breathing in the smooth release. He tipped it back and set the empty glass on the bar.

"Would you like another?"

"Nah. You keep the change." Will put his phone away and zipped up the heavy black kevlar backpack.

"Thanks a lot," the bartender said. "Safe travels."

Will smiled.

•••

It was a bright, sunny day, warmer than D.C. The F150 slowed, turned right onto an asphalt entrance, and stopped. Massive stone walls on each side displayed a large F Bar A Ranch. A small sign on the right side read, *The Sterlings Welcome You.*

Will rubbed the inside of his upper arm. The black tattoo still hurt.

Pulling his backpack close, he unzipped it and removed the Glock. He jerked the slide back and chambered a round. Then he looked inside the backpack at all the money. Chuckling to himself, he zipped up the pack and tossed it behind him.

Sitting at the entrance, he took a few more seconds. He wanted to be sure.

Jaw clenched, Will gripped the wheel with both hands and moved his foot from the brake pedal to the accelerator. Then, with a loud exhale, he gunned it. There was no turning back now.

I hope you enjoyed Family Above All. *This is the first in a series of Will Rockton novels. Keep an eye out for the next one. You will not be disappointed.*

Liam Stone

About the Author

Liam Stone was an undercover FBI agent for more than 18 years. While serving a federal arrest warrant, he encountered gunfire when entering a residence. This resulted in numerous injuries to law enforcement personnel and, ultimately, the death of the shooter. Liam's exceptional performance during this dangerous situation ensured the safety of his team members. As a result, Liam received one of the FBI's highest awards: The FBI Shield of Bravery.

During his long FBI career, Liam led highly successful investigations into various criminal enterprises in both the United States and internationally. He also worked on numerous task forces such as Violent Street Gangs Task Force; Joint Terrorism Task Forces; Safe Trails Task Force, which concentrated on Indian Reservations; and Project Safe Neighborhoods.

Liam received the Texas Department of Public Safety's Director's award for outstanding service to law enforcement. He also received a State of Texas Senate Resolution for his tenacity on one of the first human trafficking investigations in the United States. As a result of this investigation, Liam helped make human trafficking a felony in the State of Texas.

Near the end of his career, Liam was an FBI instructor and mentor. After more than 26 years of faithful service, he retired from the FBI as a Supervisory Special Agent.

Before joining the FBI, Stone was a police officer with the City of Irving. There, he earned two lifesaving awards, as well as numerous other awards and commendations.

Liam is a veteran of the United States Marine Corps, where he received an honorable discharge.

In his free time, he enjoys exercising, playing golf, and almost anything outdoors.

Liam is currently the CEO of Stonewater Investigative Group, LLC. He can be reached at FamilyAboveAllTheBook@gmail.com.

Made in the USA
Middletown, DE
27 April 2021